"The hotel is touchy about suicides," said Rutledge. "They've had two here. We'll talk to everybody we can. As quickly as we can. How about hanging around? I want to know who saw him fall."

Morris looked again at the air over the balcony. The little man must have been desperate.

"You're surprised," said Rutledge.

"Well, I knew him."

"Nobody knows a man climbing over a balcony two hundred feet high."

Follow the Leader

"AN ENTHRALLING, INGENIOUS, AND GRIPPING BOOK. IT IS THE ULTIMATE MYSTERY NOVEL ABOUT AN OBSESSIVE SPORT."
James Dickey
Author of DELIVERANCE

FOLLOW THE LEADER

John Logue

BALLANTINE BOOKS • NEW YORK

This book is fiction.
The characters are invented,
with the exception
of the few historical persons who are named.

To Helen
And to Jesse Hill Ford

We were born lucky. . . . But it is good that we do not have to try to kill the sun or the moon or the stars. It is enough to live on the sea and kill our true brothers.

ERNEST HEMINGWAY, *The Old Man and the Sea*

MORRIS HOARDED HIS LAST BOLT OF COFFEE, CIRCLING IT IN his cup, a centrifuge of warmth in his hand. He watched the colors grow in the rain, swelling open with umbrellas. People in the gloom of the street moved as swatches of pigment in a watercolor wash. The floor-length glass of the restaurant was cold. Morris felt it with his palm. He shivered at the damp and the strangers who turned into the hotel, heads tilting to marvel at the twenty-one-story height of the lobby. Glass elevators climbed the outside of the walls like time capsules. A single thread of steel spun two hundred feet down to flower in midair, a mothlike canopy fixed in space over the tangle of glad sounds in the raised cocktail lounge.

The Peachtree Towers was not a hotel; it was a school of geometry, thought Morris. No Atlantan had ever grown up in such a space. There was no refuge here, even in a cup of coffee. He took the last swallow and looked at his watch. Still thirty minutes to kill. Julia Sullivan was many things, but never early.

Morris braced himself upright with his cane, his stiff left knee giving his thick bulk a certain formality. The low divider between the restaurant and the lobby shrank under him like a toy fence. He moved easily, the slightest pressure on his cane keeping his balance. The woman took his money without speaking.

It was a deliberate effort not to look up at the height of the lobby. He walked through two glass doors into the night's rare dampness after three days of June heat. He had not lived in Atlanta in twenty-five years. The city seemed to have been invented in the air, yet was strangely familiar. Across Peachtree Street a massive sculpture gathered its iron wings against the mist. The old Capital City Club receded under the avenue of hotels, its great elm tree long absent in the wet air. The impatient traffic probed in both directions. Morris knew that miles to the north, after the street became Peachtree Road, a neon sign counted in the night each new anonymous face among the city's one million, four hundred thousand people. The Atlanta of his youth was like a country whose borders had been redrawn after a great war, and the colors reversed on all the maps; only the names of the streets had not changed.

Morris turned back inside. He moved toward the front desk through faces mesmerized by the lobby. Perhaps New York had left a message. There was a crowd waiting for keys and information. In the middle was a caddy, Old Thompson. The coat he wore was misshapen, its right shoulder hanging two inches below the left, the threads at the collar broken like the veins in his face as though some life force had escaped from inside them both.

"Mr. Rossi. Mr. Jim Rossi. What room's he in?" Thompson asked, his voice as whiskey ravaged as his face.

"I'm sorry. We don't give out room numbers of our guests." The clerk looked past him as if he had been swallowed alive by the crowd.

"Rossi's here okay," said Morris. "Call him on the house phone." An angry woman pushed against him, complaining that it was eight o'clock and her room still hadn't been made up. Morris was pinned to the desk. He could see there was no message in 1624. He angled his heavy shoulders into the confusion of people. Old Thompson had gone. If he needed money Rossi would help him.

Morris still had twenty minutes to kill. He balanced himself on the escalator leading to the restaurant under the lobby. Two women in long dresses rode behind him, their faces eager at being transported into some lower, more interesting life. Morris waited at the bottom. The President of the United States Golf Association glided down as his family in Virginia must have done even before the electricity of escalators. He was tall and pale and thin and seemingly without emotion. Frank LeBaron was behind him, already smiling at Morris. LeBaron was as tall and as spare as the Virginian, but there was nothing in his face the sun had not burned, including his gray eyes. He was Tournament Director of the PGA and too aware of the random turns of weather and fate to be at ease. He walked down the last few steps, not trusting the momentum of the stairs.

2

"Morris, the only man who walks with a two-iron," said LeBaron.

Morris dipped the cane that Monty Sullivan had once made him.

"You fit? Tomorrow's our twenty-second Open," said LeBaron. "Morris, you know Jim Colburn."

The Virginian bowed slightly, but did not speak.

No one in golf called him John. It was always Morris. He could not remember how it had begun. He was the one reporter in America who covered twenty-five PGA tournaments in a year. He had done it for twenty-one years. Home was the Associated Press and the sound of bargain typewriters in an improvised tent.

"The course will stand up," said LeBaron, as if it were the only possible subject of discussion, as if he and Morris were responsible that it not falter.

Morris thought, no course can start out great. It can't be done. Time alone can nurture greatness in a golf course, and only over the marvelous debris of the men it discards. "Yes," said Morris, "I think it will." It was a young course. Yet he meant it.

"Meeting Julia?" said LeBaron. Morris nodded. "Tell her she's in bad company." LeBaron moved ahead, waving a salute.

Morris rode the escalator back up into the lobby.

Four players, all standing unnaturally in their jackets, waited for an elevator. Their faces were burned around their eyes as if they had come from the tropics; only the tops of their foreheads, protected by their caps, were strangely white as though their hairlines were dying of a rare disease.

"Hey Morris, don't you want to join the Central Airlines Cap Banquet?" Al Morgan took an obscene stance above an imaginary golf ball. The airline paid them fifty dollars a week to wear its caps and to attend certain functions.

"Oh no," said Morris, "that's a rowdy group." He ran his heavy fingers through his dark hair, ragged with gray. "But I'll ride up with you. I haven't seen the restaurant on top. And I've got fifteen minutes until Julia gets here." They all knew each other too well to feel a need to speak.

Lee Washburn stood apart, as if his current British Open title might be somehow tarnished by the three older golfers. His blond, curly hair, just receding from his high forehead, gave him a look of athletic intelligence. The petulance in his mouth was only visible from very near. His temper could be as sudden as the speed of his clubhead. The players called him "Nasty," but only to each other and to reporters. Never to his face. He hated the name. But every newspaper used it. He was six feet three inches and, at thirty-one, possessed the most powerful swing in golf. It was only June and he had already won $63,000.

Ted Dolan, dark and compact, was the oldest of the four at forty-six. He had won the Open ten years ago. His return to the tour this winter had been a serial disaster. Dolan had missed the cut in the first four tournaments, and was fighting a lethal hook off the tee. He looked unnatural without a cut of tobacco distorting his right cheek. Morris suspected him of dyeing his hair India black.

Morgan was a shorter, sloppier version of Ted Dolan, down to the crash hook that was destroying his own game. He wore steel-rimmed glasses and moved without grace. His straight dark hair was running suddenly to gray. Half the tour despised him for his columns in *Golfing World*, all the more because they were accurate. The other half he owed money. Morris could still see him two years ago, disintegrating, squandering a five-stroke lead in the Open on the last round. The title would have paid his gambling debts for the rest of his life. Morgan was forty.

The fourth man waiting for the elevator was also forty and had the same birthday as Morgan. They had nothing else in common. His name was Art Howard. His arms were abnormally short, emphasizing the abrupt roundness of his stomach. He was bald and wore dark glasses over his light-sensitive eyes, giving him the look of a congenial tortoise. The pros called him "Doctor Zero." They loved to be paired with him. He never spoke, and they could club themselves off his tediously consistent shots. Except they could not bear to watch the loop in his swing. Even old friends turned away to keep their own image of a correct backswing embedded in their minds.

The elevator door opened and the five of them pushed inside, Morris leading the way with his cane.

"Who got us under these crummy caps?" asked Dolan.

"Not me," said Morgan. "It was Art. He talked us into it. He didn't say they looked like dead buzzards."

"We oughta make him ride up on the outside," said Dolan.

"Yeah, these elevators are just big enough to hold either Art or his backswing."

Art smiled a half-circle in his round face, his eyes hidden behind his tinted glasses.

Morgan said, much louder, "They're gonna put Art's body in one of those deep freezers, and bring it back to life in the year thirty-five hundred, and see if it can still swing like it was driving holes with a corkscrew."

Art Howard's mouth smiled nearly a full circle. "I don't see anybody giving back the fifty bucks a week."

"Who's got fifty bucks?" said Morgan. "Dolan's gotta hock that ten-year-old Open trophy and try for a job on a Japanese driving range."

Dolan's face darkened as though the sun had gone behind the elevator shaft. His big hands made two knots at the ends of his coat sleeves. Morris was ready to hold him, if necessary. Dolan had walked out on a seventy-five-thousand-dollar club job in the desert without leaving a forwarding address. He'd made six thousand dollars on the tour since January. Everything he hit hooked the dimples off the ball.

"Washburn, you're too quiet. You need that Central cap. Covers up that bald spot," said Morgan.

"Why don't you crawl back in your bottle?" said Washburn.

Morris was sure that Al Morgan owed every player in the elevator at least a thousand dollars. He owed Morris five hundred dollars. No use to grow old and die waiting for it, he thought. All of them stood away from the elevator's glass walls as the lobby floor receded far beneath them.

"Hey, look," said Morgan, "there's the Great Rossi."

Jim Rossi was standing on a balcony to their right, his closely cropped hair entirely undressed without the white Hogan cap placed squarely on his head.

"FEEL that clubhead." Morgan imitated Rossi's television voice. "I think the guy's queer for the golf swing." The four golfers were laughing as Rossi sank below them on the balcony of the eighteenth floor.

From this height Rossi stood powerfully balanced. But against Morris's bulk he became a miniature, a toy of a man, five feet six inches, and one hundred twenty-five pounds. Morris knew it was an exercise of will for Rossi, standing on

5

the balcony, not touching the fragile iron railing that came only to his waist. He was afraid of heights, and seemed pleased with the perfect balance of his slight weight between his two feet. The impossible distance to the lobby fell away below him. Now he cast his eyes, testing every plane for the perfect swing, tracing an imaginary clubhead up and down as if he could draw the answer in the air.

Rossi had grown up in New England and had given forty thousand golf lessons. His fee was fifty dollars a half hour. He taught six days a week, and didn't have enough hours in the year to accommodate the golfers. The professionals he helped free, for the advertising. He only made them pay by publicly discussing their swings like awkward secrets out of their lives. He had won the first big-money tournament in golf, twenty years ago in Chicago. He took the fifty-thousand-dollar first prize and retired to teaching. And to the TV tower. He had done the color for the Open for twelve years. Morris wondered if he were waiting for Old Thompson. Rossi was always an easy touch.

The elevator shaft closed around them, and they emerged, the door opening into the revolving restaurant, turning like a blue bubble above the city.

"Okay, everybody. Look solvent," said Morgan, leading the way to the banquet.

Morris stood at the bar. There was no place to sit. He started the night with a vodka and bitter lemon.

"Some weather," said the bartender, drying his hands on a towel.

"Glad I'm standing here, and not flying somewhere," said Morris.

"You here for the golf?"

Morris nodded.

"Never tried it," said the bartender. "If they ever move it inside, they might have something. Who needs all that sunshine? What'da you think of the city?"

Morris did not say he had grown up here. "There's only one thing wrong with Atlanta," he said. "It's entirely surrounded by Georgia."

The bartender laughed. He had an order of drinks to fill. Morris had forgotten the chill of the rain in the street he no longer knew. He looked at his watch. Sullivan would punch him out if he were late.

Morris stood alone in the elevator as it started down. ˙ ̣ held without shame to the metal rail inside the glass walls that left him vulnerable to the empty air. A movement, a noise: he looked to his right, coming *out* of the balcony, arms windmilling, in the air without sound, a man pitched, then he was *falling* screaming, unbelievably *down*, wheeling obscenely over into nothing. Morris twisted the thin metal rail loose from the screws, shocked to find himself alive, his own scream gone inside the glass walls. The express elevator sank to the floor of the lobby. Both of Morris's hands were bleeding. He recovered his cane as the door opened to mass shock. The falling scream had ended. No one had moved. A few in the crowd stood as if they had seen the tumbling body, covering their ears from his screams as though it could block out the sight of his descent. Now dozens were pointing as though to re-create the fact of him in midair. The cries in the lobby competed with the trapped terror in the lounge where he had fallen. Morris was across the lobby, wheeling his stiff leg with his cane, while men forgot their wives, ran one way and then the other, uncertain where they were safest. Women held onto chairs and planters as though the floor of the lobby were two hundred feet high.

Morris poled himself up the circular metal stairs into t̥ ɛ raised lounge. Plexiglas shrapnel had exploded into nois⸗ stabbing into tabletops, into flesh so instantly that its clear edges only now ran bloody; the fairy-tale wings the Plexiglas had made above the room were shattered into sounds of parrots screaming inhumanly in their beaks, their wings tearing the exploded air of their bamboo cage, more terrifying in the room than the still painless fragments lodged in flesh. Chairs and tables and glasses had fallen over and under bodies, the terror seemingly as real in the flying objects as in the people. Only the shock in the air had saved the packed lounge from crushing its life out at the one winding steel staircase where Morris stood in amazement. The bartender, huge in his coat and shirt, created a pool of strength in the panic. The parrots, now mute with flying unnaturally over the room, sank exhausted, clutching the low round rim of the elevated lounge.

"Anybody a doctor?" asked the bartender. Three doctors

identified themselves. Two had medical bags in their rooms and gave their room numbers. Wives, crying, were reassuring their husbands. One man was seriously impaled in the back. Two of the doctors lowered him face down on their own jackets.

"One at a time," said the other doctor, his words repeated by the bartender as if they needed his voice for authenticity. "Let's clear the lounge. Anyone who is hurt, even slightly, please keep your seat."

None of the men or women dared look up into the shattered, irregular hole in the roof, or down into the splintered bamboo cage, as if their sight could repeat the horror of what had happened.

The man lying between the two doctors was conscious. They did not attempt to remove the long Plexiglas splinter from his back. He asked something weakly. A cop ran past Morris and was leaning over the low rim of the lounge, looking down into what had been the huge parrot cage; it was shattered as though a great beast had broken out. Morris jumped, startled by the raw squawk of a parrot beside him; they were perched around the room like evil aliens. The cop turned away from the cage. The lounge was emptying now except for the injured. "Who are you?" the cop asked.

"John Morris. Associated Press."

"Give us a hand," the cop said. He was short but thick through the chest.

Between them, Morris and the cop lowered the third doctor into the bamboo debris to reach the sacklike object below the main level of the lounge.

Morris looked down into the splintered interior of the cage. The cop handed a flashlight to the youngish man. "Don't move anything," he said.

"Some mess," said the doctor under them. Morris was not prepared for the careful way he probed into the heap of clothes and angles at his feet.

"A him," he said, kneeling, his face almost on the floor. "Jesus, he must have jumped out of an airplane." The flashlight bore directly down into the side of what had been a face. The coat. The cropped hair. The rest of him even from this height made Morris queasy.

"Was he a small man?" Morris's own voice sounded unreal to him.

"He's smaller than he was." The doctor under them actually chuckled.

Morris was too amazed at what he said to be shocked. There must be a convention of doctors in the lounge, he thought; only doctors stood over open wounds and walked around shattered bones like they were curiosities.

"Anatomy's not my line," said the man up to him. "I'm in pediatrics. But he was not a large man. Tiny feet. One of them, anyway. Give me a hand up."

"I think I know him," said Morris. For the first time he needed to lean against the circular rim of the room. When you were in a different city every week for twenty years, you held onto so few friends; though you might speak to them four times in a season, still they came walking out of the trees or into the press tent or the clubhouse; some part of you was intact when the spoke; the years were saved in some way.

"I'm sorry," said the doctor, who was now standing absurdly in the remains of the cage.

"Is it all right to look in his wallet?" asked Morris.

"Sure," the cop said, "but don't move him until the photographer comes."

The doctor cursed, trying to hold the light and carefully fumble in the ripped trousers. Finally the wallet came free. It was remarkably intact. "James Rossi?" he said, his voice making a question.

"Yes," said Morris. He did not feel any weaker. "He was a golf professional. He was the finest teaching professional in America. He was a good man." Morris said it dispassionately; he did not trust any other tone in his voice. Rossi lived to teach golf, thought Morris; he had been so alive this morning. Morris had to get to a telephone, to use an old friend one last time. The story would make every major newspaper. Morris and the cop were gripping the hands of the doctor. Morris could see how young he was. He came out of the cage with ease.

"What happened to your hands?" asked the doctor.

"Nothing. Just a scrape." For the first time Morris looked overhead. The jagged hole in the flimsy canopy was a cry for help. "God," he said, not realizing he had spoken. "I have to tell his wife, Margaret. She's in the hotel. She's not well. Perhaps you could go with me," he said to the young doctor.

9

"Sure," the doctor said. "My name is Wilson. Aubrey Wilson. Let me find my wife. She's somewhere in the lobby."

"My name's Morris. John Morris."

"Sorry about your friend. I've read his books. And seen him on television. He had a good mind."

"He did that," said Morris. "I've got to call New York. I'll meet you back here in a few minutes."

The doctor looked downward. "Thank God he fell where he did. We could have had a massacre."

Morris walked back through the lounge. Two women had flesh cuts on their shoulders and arms. The man on the floor was barely conscious.

2

MORRIS STARTED FOR A TELEPHONE. THERE WAS A GREAT restlessness in the lobby. "It was a woman," someone said; "she was nude." Morris walked between their words: "A couple. They jumped together." He kept moving for the row of telephones against the far wall. All the time he was looking for Sullivan. People were waiting in line to use the phones. Morris turned to the reservations desk.

"I'm sorry," a clerk was telling a very angry man, who slapped his open palm on the counter. "The police want to speak with everyone in the lobby." Morris caught the clerk's attention; he was relieved to turn his back on the man, who was demanding to see the manager.

"Associated Press," said Morris, opening his billfold. "Can I use your phone?"

The clerk handed it to him, keeping his back to the man, who was now arguing with a policeman.

"The wrong guy jumped," said the clerk. He looked quickly at Morris, afraid of what he had said. Morris smiled in spite of himself.

Whitfield answered the phone in New York. Who else now

could improvise dictation. They only know how to read a computer screen. "Mike. A bulletin. Jim Rossi fell to his death from a balcony in the Peachtree Towers Hotel, tonight, eight-twenty-five. You knew Jim."

"How old was he?" asked Whitfield.

"Forty-seven. I don't know if he jumped. Looks like it. Stay with *fell*, for now. Until we know more. He fell into a crowded lounge. One man was seriously injured. He may not make it. Rossi won the first fifty-thousand-dollar purse in golf. In Chicago. In 1957. The World Open they called it."

"Is it bull he gave forty thousand lessons?"

"No. He was also teaching half the girls on the pro tour who make a living at it. Not so many of the men pros took from him anymore. Two of his golf books were best sellers. He was here to do the color for the Open telecast. He's done it for at least twelve years. He lived on St. Simons Island, off the coast of Georgia. There's an up-to-date biography there in my files. I've got to tell Margaret, his wife."

Whitfield never stopped typing.

"I saw him fall. I was going down in the elevator from the roof. It's a glass elevator. He was already out from the balcony. He seemed to be diving out. The elevator was going down. I felt I was in the air. His arms were windmilling, and then he was gone, two hundred feet down, through the roof of the lounge. It's a hell of a mess."

Whitfield finished the bulletin while they talked. Morris knew he was already feeding a smooth text into the computer.

"Yeah," said Whitfield, ringing off.

Morris dialed the Atlanta office. The bulletin was already on the wire. They would send a reporter immediately. They would get a quote from the network's anchorman for the Open, Don Murray. Morris hung up.

The police were letting no one into the lobby. Morris looked out the glass doors onto Peachtree Street. Julia Sullivan was standing against one of them. She breathed on the glass and wrote in the vapor: W h a t s —she ran out of vapor and breathed again— u p ?

Morris raised a finger toward the top of the hotel, then plunged it toward the floor. She understood. Morris showed his identification to the cop on the door. "Can I speak to the lady outside?"

"Sure," he said. "Who jumped?"

"Fell," said Morris. "A golf pro. A teaching pro. His name was Rossi." Morris heard himself say the name as if the third person had never truly existed, or ever held a golf club in his hand, or remembered Travis Walker's baggy trousers of 1954. The cop cracked the door.

Sullivan stuck her hand through for him to hold. "We can't get in trouble this way," she said, her voice as ironic as ever.

"Bad news," said Morris. "Jim Rossi."

"Oh." Sullivan let her hand fall out of his large one. "Jumped?" she asked, her eyes gathered.

"Maybe." How could you explain it, thought Morris. "I have to tell Margaret. And talk to the police. I'll meet you at the Peachtree-Forsyth on the sixth-floor terrace. Have a drink. Have one for me."

She spread her palm on the glass of the door, her fingers long and slender; through the glass she looked young. She would never be anything but a handsome woman.

The doctor was waiting at the foot of the lounge. A man was with him, an older man, obviously in charge.

"Lieutenant Jack Rutledge, of Homicide." He offered his thick hand into Morris's strong grip.

"Morris. John Morris. Associated Press."

The detective was probably in his fifties. He seemed older. His hair was as thick as Morris's and shot through with gray. Age had come on him in lumps. He stood powerfully, but his thick body had lost all definition. Morris looked down on him. He was taller than he seemed. Maybe six feet. He popped the button of a ballpoint pen in and out with a stubby left hand.

"Did you say homicide?" asked Morris, spreading his own wide hand over the top of his cane, balancing his heavy frame about the detective.

"Killing yourself is a crime," said Rutledge. "Rarely prosecuted." He allowed himself a near smile.

"Is that what happened?" asked Morris.

"I understand you knew him?" The detective's dark eyes ignored his question.

"For twenty years," said Morris. "Twenty-one to be exact." The two large men stood apart as if there were a terrible secret between them. "Rossi was once a tour player, a very fine one. He became the best-known teacher in the country. Be ready for a lot of attention. There are three hundred

12

reporters in town. And Rossi was the regular color man on the Open telecast.''

''Oh yes,'' said Rutledge, who suddenly seemed to place him. ''Then you know his wife. She's in room eighteen-o-four. It's where he went off, okay. There's a vine on the balcony. He's still holding a piece of it in his hand.''

Lord, suppose he changed his mind, tried to hold himself back, thought Morris. No, he couldn't have known what he was doing. Unless he was . . . thrown over. But that was ridiculous.

''How did you know it was Rossi?'' asked the detective. Now he was not snapping his pen.

''I recognized the jacket. Some of the face.'' Morris winced at the memory. ''I saw him fall, but I didn't know it was him.''

Rutledge's dark eyes were fixed on his own. ''Where were you?''

''Coming down in the elevator.'' Morris felt a need to take a breath. ''I was just even with his balcony. I could almost reach out . . . and he was gone. Before I knew who he was.''

''Who was with you?''

''No one. I'd been in the bar on the roof. Five of us saw him on the balcony going up. About ten minutes before. He was waiting. Standing alone. That's how I remembered the jacket. He rarely wore the same outfit twice in a month.''

''Who were the other four?''

''Golfers. Lee Washburn. Al Morgan. Art Howard. Ted Dolan.''

Rutledge had not taken a note. ''I have to interview his wife,'' he said.

''She's not strong . . . emotionally. She'll break into pieces.''

Rutledge led the way across the lobby. The manager was holding an elevator. Going up, Morris felt sick. He could not look down at the lobby. Two cops were standing outside room 1804. The hanging philodendron was broken, and some of it twisted back against itself. He must have dived through it. An image of him reaching *out* was burned into Morris's mind. He forced himself to look down at the small, visible hole in the roof of the lounge directly under him. It shone there, an exit from time.

13

Lieutenant Rutledge was already knocking on the door. He had to knock with his fists before there was any sound of life.

Margaret Rossi, a once-flower, folded in her robe, opened the door. Her eyes did not adjust to the light. She saw Morris. She raised one hand. When she saw a police uniform she screamed. She never stopped crying. Morris held her. She was so light the robe could have been empty. "Where are we?" she begged hysterically. The young doctor looked at Rutledge, who shrugged. He prepared a syringe. Morris let her down easily on the bed. He had been unable to tell her anything. He felt as if he had failed her for twenty years.

Morris and Rutledge walked onto the balcony, leaving the doctor in the room.

"She has a sister somewhere in the East," said Morris.

"We'll find her," Rutledge seemed preoccupied. "We can't question a thousand people in the damn hotel," he said. He was talking almost to himself. "With twenty-one stories of open space, and five glass elevators, someone had to see him jump."

Morris looked up and down.

"The hotel is touchy about suicides," said Rutledge. "They've had two here. We'll talk to everybody we can. As quickly as we can. How about hanging around? Get a cup of coffee. I want to know who else saw him fall. Then we'll wrap it up."

"I'd like to go over to the Peachtree-Forsyth, and have a drink. Someone's waiting for me."

"Sure. Take your time. We have a lot of people to talk to."

Morris looked again at the air over the balcony. The little man must have been desperate.

"You're surprised," said Rutledge.

"Well, I knew him."

"Nobody knows a man climbing over a balcony two hundred feet high."

3 ✣

THE PEACHTREE-FORSYTH HOTEL WAS IN A GEOMETRIC COMPE-
tition against the Peachtree Towers. Water flowed artificially under concrete lily pads. The ceiling was an elaborate
series of high, interlocking circles. Julia Sullivan was holding
a table alone on the crowded terrace without effort.

She put both hands up into Morris's one.

"What happened?"

"He fell," said Morris, "from the eighteenth floor."

Her hands tightened.

"He hit the lounge. One man's badly hurt. It could have
been murder in there."

"All the years we worried about Margaret," said Sullivan.
Her pale hair was more brown than blonde; her thin bones
belied the strength in her hands and arms; she looked as
young as she did when Monty was killed eighteen years ago.

"Why?" she asked.

"That's the question." Morris ordered a double vodka and
tonic. He balanced the end of his cane on the toe of his shoe.
"I saw him falling, Sullivan. He was reaching *out*. I didn't
know who he was."

His drink came.

"It's crazy. I can't imagine him climbing over the iron
railing. I heard him scream, Sullivan."

"Rossi, damn you!" She hit the table with her small fist.

Morris understood. They all went back so far together. It
hurt that Jim could regret all those years. Morris was full of
energy from what had happened, from being there, and from
the terror of it. Fatigue would hit him later, and he would be
empty.

"Do you believe in another life?" asked Sullivan.

"I don't believe in this one."

She was amazed at the size of his hands. "How could you

15

be a writer with hands like that? You sure you're not a carpenter?''

"Monty loved him," said Morris. Monty Sullivan, who should have won the U.S. Open twice, but who could beat Hogan? Monty, who, with the only money he ever hung onto, bought a block of Denver before anybody discovered Colorado, and died a rich man. Morris had grieved as much as Julia. But Monty would be pleased they had found each other. Morris was sure of that. If only he could talk Sullivan down out of the mountains of Colorado to join him on the tour more than five or six times a year.

"I wish you could miss me like you miss my husband," she said.

Morris held her hand like ~ ~~~ ~~~ ~~~ own.

ratigue shone in the face of Lieutenant Rutledge, made a liquid gloss of perspiration, aged him around his dark eyes. Morris could see he was not prepared for the network camera crews in the lobby, the correspondents for the news magazines, the reporters from thirty states here for the Open. Rutledge motioned for Morris to join him in the manager's office.

"How can a thousand people in a hotel with a two-hundred-foot-high lobby not see a man climb over a four-foot balcony and jump on top of them? Tell me that.'' Rutledge did not wait for an answer. "Of course, two thousand people saw him in midair, or heard him. Until you ask them to swear to it under oath. Then how many saw him? Three. Three! And you, Morris.'' Rutledge looked at him as if there were a conspiracy.

"You should have heard me explaining it on television. I sounded like the village idiot. The mayor, in case you haven't met him, he called twice. He said, 'Why couldn't this Rossi jump off somethin' down there on St. Simons Island?' Good question. We've got every reporter in North America here, and he has to pick Atlanta to land in. Sorry. I forgot he was a friend of yours.''

"You have three witnesses who saw him fall?'' Morris asked.

"Three that I believe. We've screened the hotel as best we can. I'm asking the three to go over it again. How about sitting in? See if they ring true. You saw it better than anybody we know."

"Sure," said Morris.

"Sergeant!" A thin, awkward man opened the door. "Sergeant Bolton, John Morris." They nodded. "Bring in the old lady." He turned to Morris. "Her name is Blankenship. Old. Widow. Lives in New Orleans."

Bolton opened the door again. She would not let him help her. He struggled along beside her, not sure where to put his hands, awkward, as if he were somehow defective for having arms.

"Thank you for coming back," said Rutledge, leaning with his arms on his heavy knees. "Could you tell us exactly what you saw?"

"Yes," she said, settling herself in the chair. Morris almost smiled. She sat erectly, like a witness out of the *Times-Picayune* that thrived on accidents and murders. She might have been having her morning coffee in the Vieux Carré.

"I was waiting for my son on the balcony on the eighth floor. He's an engineer with the Lockheed Company. I can't imagine why. He's an engineer, I mean. I never could thread a needle. His father was in the antiques business. We have these awful new hotels in New Orleans also. Sometimes you have to meet someone in them. My son's divorced. It's the scandal of our time, divorce. He puts me up in the hotel, but never before in this one; it's like the Hanging Gardens of Babylon. But you will look up, you know. I was waiting for my son and I was looking up and this figure was falling. My eyes are rather good at a distance, and I'm still able to do my crossword puzzles, with bifocals. I hate them. He seemed to be falling *out*, if you know what I mean, as if he were trying to reach something. I don't know why I knew it was a man. Oh, he was tumbling at the end. It just never entered my mind that it might be a woman. I don't hear so terribly well, but I heard him. It was awful."

Rutledge tried to obscure himself behind his own voice. "When you first saw him, he was in the air?"

"He was *out*," she said. "He was reaching. When I first saw him. I couldn't see anything else but him. I can't get the sight of him out of my mind."

"Thank you, Mrs. Blankenship. Sergeant Bolton will help you to your room."

17

"Did the man, Mr. Rossi, leave a note?"

Morris almost smiled again. The *Times-Picayune* would never overlook such a detail.

"No, not that we've found," said Rutledge, standing as she walked to the door. "Send in Martin," he said to Bolton. He turned to Morris. "A businessman from Memphis. Staying over Thursday for the first day of the tournament."

Martin came into the room at once, talking almost before he stopped. "I was walking to the lounge to have a drink, before dinner. I'm by myself. I've been here on business all day. I'm staying for the tournament tomorrow. I looked up. It's impossible not to look up in this lobby, and he was coming down on me. I thought he was going to hit me. Then he started screaming. I never moved. He went through the roof of the lounge. I couldn't move my feet. Or even think. You wouldn't believe a man falling in so large a space could scream so loud."

Martin sat down. He seemed surprised that he needed to.

Rutledge, with no inflection in his voice, asked, "Did he seem to fall straight down?"

"He was diving," said Martin. "Head first. And then I started to tumble. At the end he was falling like a bomb."

"Did you see him jump?"

"He must have dived," insisted Martin. "I didn't see him, but it must have been from the top of the hotel. He didn't seem to be moving, and then my God he was falling. You could hear him in Memphis. I read his instruction articles in *Golf World*. He was on television. Why would a man like that kill himself the day before the U.S. Open?"

Morris wanted to ask the question again, aloud.

Rutledge excused him. "The next one's Jamison. A construction man," he said.

Jamison walked easily into the room. He was almost as large as Morris. Rutledge did not introduce them.

"I've never been afraid of heights," said Jamison. "I didn't start out owning my construction business. I've looked down from higher places than the twenty-first floor of this hotel with a lot less under me. I was looking at the space. It's gimmicky, okay, but you got to hand it to 'em. It works. He came right out under me. He couldn't have been more than four or five floors below me. He came right out head first. He was wheeling his arms in front of him. He must have dived out. Then he fell fast, If you have ever seen a man fall off a project, they go down the size of a dime. In seconds. He wasn't screaming at first. I couldn't hear him so well, falling away from me, but I heard him."

"Do you think you would have seen him if he had climbed outside the railing before he jumped?" asked Rutledge.

"No, I don't think so. The ledge sticks out a good two, two and a half feet on every floor. It blocks the view under you. I did look across the space after he was gone."

Rutledge moved in his chair just slightly. He seemed to curse himself for not sitting still.

"I saw four girls. They looked like four young girls with long blonde hair. They were running toward the elevator, to the left of where I was standing, away from where he jumped. I don't know for sure they were on the same floor. One of them was screaming. I didn't see what happened to them. I took the elevator for the lobby. I was sure there would be an investigation."

"They were running?" said Rutledge, sitting up now. "Was anyone with them, or after them?"

"I didn't see anybody. I think they must have been frightened by seeing him, or by his screaming."

Rutledge went to the door. "Bolton," he called. He came inside. "Have we interviewed any four girls together?" Bolton shook his head. "They could be in their rooms. Four girls with long blonde hair. Or they could have taken the elevator to the basement floor. We didn't get them stopped for several minutes. We haven't talked with everybody in the hotel. We never will." Again Rutledge seemed to be talking to himself. "See if there are four girls sharing a room," he said. "Check the eighteenth floor first. Ask if anyone remembers them. You say they were young?" he asked Jamison.

"They had long blonde hair. Typical of kids today. I don't know why they were running, or if it means anything."

"You didn't mention it before."

"I started to. We were interrupted. I figured they would show up."

"Could you identify them if you saw them?"

"I don't know. I doubt it. They were just there and running."

"You'll be here this weekend?" asked Rutledge.

"I'll be at the tournament. I'm flying home Sunday night. To Louisville. You have my business card. My wife's waiting

19

for me. She hasn't left the room. She's not crazy about heights.''

Rutledge stood up when the door closed. ''The television people want something for the eleven-thirty newscast. They'll have to live with 'fell.' For the time being. Let's get a cup of coffee. There's a door here into the restaurant.

''First, let me be sure I have the players straight in my mind who were in the elevator with you,'' said Rutledge, looking at his notebook.

Morris could not remember when the detective had begun to take notes.

''The big guy, with curly hair. That's Lee Washburn,'' said Rutledge. ''The one the others call 'Nasty.' ''

''Not to his face they don't,'' said Morris. ''He might answer to it.''

''He's also big on the tour?''

''Yes,'' said Morris. ''He's the British Open champion. He has the talent to be champion of everything.''

''Why do they call him Nasty?''

''If you had ever interviewed him after he'd triple-bogeyed the last hole, you'd know. It's all noise. He stays mad at himself, mostly.''

''The older player, with the dyed black hair and the tough jaw. That's Ted Dolan.''

''Yes,'' said Morris. ''He won the Open ten years ago.''

''He must have known Rossi. They were about the same age. He didn't show any emotion over his death.'' Rutledge looked up from his notes, his dark eyes giving away nothing.

''That's Dolan,'' said Morris. ''Master of the one-word answer. He knew Rossi. They were never close. Dolan is a loner. Many of them are. Golf out here is not a team sport.''

''The bald guy with the dark glasses?'' Rutledge turned a page in his notebook.

''Art Howard.''

''He seemed the most upset.''

''Art hides behind those dark glasses. Everybody likes him. Everybody kids him. You're right. He seemed more upset than the others.'' Morris could not remember anything specific Art had said, but his hands kept moving nervously to adjust his glasses.

''Why do they call him 'Doctor Zero'?'' asked Rutledge.

''Because he won so much money, and nobody knew who

he was. Until the nickname, he was just a round little man with a funny swing. But he's mentally tough. You don't survive on the tour if you aren't. And he can putt.''

"Morgan is the wise guy," said Rutledge. "With the steel-rimmed glasses.''

"That's Al. The tour intellectual.''

Rutledge looked up. "You're serious.''

"Oh yes. He's a writer. A good one. He better be. His game is not what it was. All of them, except Washburn, are having their troubles.'' Morris set down his cup. "Why do you want to know so much about them? They all saw the same thing in the elevator.''

"You said Rossi was *waiting*," said Rutledge, not taking his eyes off Morris. "He had to be waiting for somebody.''

Morris tried to see Rossi exactly as he had been standing. Looking over the balcony. Lifting an imaginary clubhead. Looking *toward* the elevator as they rose over him. "He *was* waiting," said Morris. "Rossi was all energy. He couldn't bear to stand in one place unless he was watching the golf swing. Then he could stand for hours. He had to be up-and-down and get where he was going. He looked once toward the elevator. I doubt he could see us inside. He was standing, waiting. I'm sure of it.''

Both of them drew great swallows of their coffee. Morris sat forward, nearly tipping his cup. "Old Thompson! I forgot Old Thompson!''

"Who's that?''

"A caddy. The last of the alcoholics. A savvy caddy when he's sober. He was fired only this morning on the practice range. He was in the lobby tonight at eight o'clock. He asked the desk clerk for Rossi's room number, but the clerk wouldn't give it out. I told Thompson to call him on the house phone. He disappeared. Rossi was always an easy touch for the caddies, and golfers, too. Maybe he was waiting for Old Thompson.''

Rutledge was making notes, carefully, not rushing. "Where can I find this Thompson?''

"God knows," said Morris. "In some dump. He'll be at the course tomorrow; you can count on it. He's looking for a bag to carry next week in Chicago.''

Rutledge led the way into the restaurant.

Morris recognized a few reporters at a distance, but none of them looked into the restaurant. The hotel lobby was back to normal, except for the barrier in front of the steps to the lounge. Rutledge took a corner table by the front window. Weariness increased the stiffness in Morris's leg. He balanced the head of his cane on his thigh.

Rutledge turned a fresh page in his notebook. "John Whitlow. *Old Thompson*. Travis Walker. Well, I know Travis Walker. I mean I know who he is. Look, Morris. We have the makings of a simple suicide." Rutledge sipped his coffee. "If Rossi had been John Doe, we wouldn't be here. But start from the first time you saw him today. Tell me everything that happened, and we'll wrap this thing up."

"The first time I saw Rossi was this morning," said Morris. He looked out. The mist had blown into a rain. It was hitting and running against the window. Morris drank his coffee. He remembered.

4

THE WALL-SIZED GLASS OF THE CLUBHOUSE HAD BEEN COLD. Morris had touched it with his palm. The colors were curiously alive in the rain, traveling always ahead of him to other tournaments to wait in the trees.

He stepped toward the door, ready to judge the wetness by the rhythm on his umbrella.

It was a trick to hold the cane and not drop the umbrella. He felt the weather with his whole body. His left knee ached with it. The early morning rain, suddenly drifting into a mist, only dampened the June heat rising out of the earth. The final practice round was in no danger. A deep rain would favor the long hitters, he thought. So would a drought, or a slippage in the San Andreas fault line. Only the wives are on the side of those who hit it short. The clubhouse was behind him.

"Morris." Jim Rossi spoke his name without turning his head. He was tailored from London in shades of brown with a furled and matching umbrella. Only the white Hogan cap, set directly on his sculpted head, was a gesture to America. They shook hands formally, Rossi never taking his eyes off the players on the practice tee. Morris was surprised as always at the delicacy of Rossi's palm and fingers, which could still deliver a ball two hundred and fifty yards with no effort.

No rain was actually falling, but the players were wearing their rainsuits; they made great blocks of colors moving through the air as if their bones were inflated. Their enormous bags were pitched under umbrellas. Each of them stood over a white puddle of balls, drawing one out with an iron, pausing over it against the dark air, and turning suddenly, flying downward, detonating the wet earth, sending the ball as small in the sky as an olive, watching it fall downward as of its own volition into the easy reach of a caddy under it, who willed it there with his eyes, catching it on the bounce into a bag. The players rose and fell over the balls, the air always silently full of them in great arcs like barren comets.

"Do you think anyone can stand up to him?" Rossi did not bother to identify Kirkland, the greatest player in the game, whose swing the other half of his mind was obviously memorizing.

"He won't win it," said Morris with a curious finality.

Rossi turned as if to see Kirkland's fate written in the air. "What did Hogan say, you can only lose the Open."

Morris did not answer, but he had come to *feel* when Kirkland would win. Somehow this year he was distracted. Perhaps it was starting his own tournament; perhaps it was the first ransom of age—he was thirty-seven; perhaps he would win anyway. Morris marvelled at the controlled violence of Kirkland's swing, torturing his layered blond hair around his forehead, his powerful torso threatening to rupture his tailored open-throated shirt, and shatter his rain jacket. His square features never lost their resolution.

Morris recalled the sight of him at twenty-one, winning his first U.S. Open in his rookie season as a pro; his Prussian crew cut, trimmed to the scalp; his stomach billowing in a formless T-shirt; his greatness apparent only in the power and discipline of his swing, and in his vast concentration. The crowds who now sought him out hated him then for unseating Travis Walker as the greatest player in golf. Even the immortal Bobby Jones bowed in his grave to his fifteen national championships. The people behind the practice tee caught their breaths at the velocity of his downswing.

Kirkland leaned his five-iron on his bag. Turning, he caught Morris's eyes with his own. "Morris," he said, walking over to shake hands. "Is this your ghost writer?"

"You wouldn't want to rent your swing?" said Rossi.

Kirkland shook his hand. "I'd be willing to lease my putting stroke. Cheap. Who's going to win this thing, Morris?"

"Whoever finishes ahead of P. Kirkland will have a helluva chance."

"I can get it in the air. I can't get it in the ground."

All of them laughed. Kirkland went back to his five-iron.

Each spring the sun burned Kirkland's face in uneven raw patches that showed up in photographs. He compressed his scorched lips in concentration.

"Sets up open to square," said Rossi, as if Morris had never seen Kirkland swing. "Plays the ball inside the left foot for every club. The club's waist high and he hasn't broken his wrists. Opens the clubface ever so slightly for the fade. The extension the man gets! Even the strange, interlocking grip helps; the small hands don't take over the clubhead. But you cannot teach legs like pistons. God, look at the height he gets on the ball!"

Morris thought, you cannot teach the way he *plays* with great intelligence. He had never heard Rossi speak of playing, only of the act of swinging.

A noise of voices and of hurrying feet spilled onto the practice tee. Morris turned to see Travis Walker coming toward him just ahead of his caddy. The power of his stride denied his age. Behind him was a moving line of people all the way to the clubhouse. The fans had forgiven Kirkland for replacing Walker as the greatest player in golf, much as they forgave Mantle for succeeding DiMaggio. But they did not abandon Travis Walker. They ran ahead of him and behind him and walked with him when they could, urging his ball into the air, cursing it out of bunkers, as if they could share in the pain of his diminishing skills.

"Hell, even I keep up with Travis Walker," said Lieutenant Rutledge. "Or I did. He doesn't seem to win so much anymore."

Morris looked at him as if he had never seen Rutledge

24

before. "No. He may never win again. Age has no sentiment." Morris was back inside his own image of Travis, only this morning: his squarely cut dark trousers and gray sweater did not quite adjust to his powerful torso. His features were rounded and not truly handsome, his hairline was graying and receding and yet even when he stopped he was not still; the animation never went out of his eyes. He was forty-six.

"Mr. One-Putt," said Kirkland.

"Save some earth, Pete," said Walker, watching Kirkland tear a giant divot effortlessly into the air. Reaching for a new glove, Walker opened it and worked it over his powerful hand. He stood, watching Pete's great divots fly off his club. Morris knew Walker no longer slept well, but standing with his spikes in the wet ground and his sweater tight over his shoulders, he looked as strong as at any time in his life. Morris also knew of the slight trembling in the backs of his hands. His caddy, who was nearly as famous as himself, placed his bag on a towel and fanned the clubs out against it, careful to keep the handles off the wet grass.

Walker twisted, loosening his steel-muscled upper body, careful not to pressure his left hip. Morris remembered how the hip had almost ended Walker's golf. His swing had suffered from the adjustments the pain had necessitated. He was looking around him, seemingly without thinking, only seeing the people, in a long line, single faces, a young girl, a man as huge as a Port-o-let who Morris knew followed him on courses all over America. His caddy was ready. Walker put down his driver and picked up his wedge.

Morris could feel his own fingers on the grip.

"His hands," Rossi said. "The secret we all missed. We saw him with his britches baggy, like 1938, the clubface shut, all the way up, then *never* releasing it, blocking it all the way through the ball. Teach that action to the PGA tour and it couldn't break eighty at Brackenridge Park. Nobody thought to look at his grip," said Rossi, as if it had been a national oversight of dangerous importance. "With that grip, with those arms, he can return the club to the ball from any position. Who could believe it would take Kirkland to beat him after seeing him swing?"

Rossi was giving him a hundred dollars in lessons, but Morris was only pleased that he remembered Walker's baggy pants of 1954. They had been pleated, he was sure, and drawn up around his waist like a laundry sack.

Morris did not let Rossi's words interfere with the sight of Walker, in his element like a child in a sandbox, flexing the grips on his clubs, searching out the bothersome action of a swing with the ball still in the air, saying to Kirkland now deep into his own fairway woods, with a blow like an artillery shot: "Pete, don't spare the furniture. If you can't keep it in Georgia, it won't hurt anything in Tennessee."

The crowd laughed, pressed around the tee, asking, "What did he say?"

Kirkland smiled, pleased with the enormity of his shot. "Catch it, One-Putt."

Morris looked up. Someone had called his name. It was the kid, John Whitlow. Writers along the tour called him the "Young Lion." He liked the name. He even let his blond hair grow longer, like a mane. The older players rode him about it. But Morris knew that on the course they feared him. They had better. The quality of mercy was not in him. He attacked every hole as if to reduce it to anonymity, no matter how famous the course, or how steeped in tradition the tournament. Whitlow was from Arizona. He was compactly built, like Travis, but without the gift of animation. He was one of the unending stream of graduates of the University of Houston, in his second year on the PGA tour. He won a record two hundred thousand dollars as a rookie.

His daddy had been a greenskeeper and a drunk. Morris remembered that Whitlow had told him, "Only time he wasn't drunk was when he was dead." Whitlow had laughed. It was after the funeral. He was twenty-one.

Whitlow called to Morris again. "Your buddy there, Rossi. What's he, lost? Is he lookin' for the ladies' tour?" There was no fun in his voice.

Morris did not answer him.

Rossi kept his eyes directly on Travis Walker, ignoring Whitlow.

"I can't get the club back with that zombie Rossi watching," Whitlow said, pausing over his practice balls.

Morris was certain that Rossi could hear him.

"I'd be back eatin' chicken-fried steak if I'd listened to him."

"Yeah, you're liable to get a double hernia haulin' paper

26

checks to the bank," said Art Howard, next to Whitlow on the tee.

Art Howard himself seemed to avoid looking back at Rossi, as if he were trying to block out the mental sight of his own curiosity of a swing, long familiar on the tour. His right arm folded into a flying elbow, then worked down under, finally, into a classic hitting position. The clubhead did a figure eight in the air, but it was a swing that had won three-quarters of a million dollars. Morris had written that he had perfected the swing in his four years in the Navy, hitting old range balls into the Indian Ocean.

The players and their swings were inseparable. Their lives rode their hands on the grips of their clubs, their fortunes turned with their shoulders. An immeasurable shift in tempo could slide their names into obscurity.

Whitlow burned another drive deliberately over the head of his aging and alcoholic caddy who ignored it, the third ball he had let go by him. Whitlow waved him after it. "Ever see a human hangover running?" He laughed at the sight of Old Thompson, dragging his shag bag behind him.

Other pros were laughing. Thompson was not really that old. Bad whiskey had aged him. No other drunks were left among the caddies. Now they had college degrees, thought Morris. Thompson had carried Travis during his big years, until finally he couldn't be trusted.

Old Thompson stumbled after another drive Whitlow had hooked deliberatey away from him.

Morris watched Art Howard block everything out of his mind but his own bizarre swing. He caught the five-iron cleanly but the shot fell ten yards short of where his caddy, Sam, was standing. Sam looked puzzled, as if Art had skipped a club in his warmup. Already the sweat was breaking out under Art's dark glasses. Five-irons like that, thought Morris, will put him back in Bossier City, Louisiana.

Whitlow punched his driver, the ball stopped fifty yards in front of Thompson, who hesitated to make the long run for it. Thompson began to shuffle forward, and fell over. He held his throat as if he were gagging. A ball tore into the rubber heel of his sockless tennis shoe; he jumped, the pain more astonishing for his not having seen it coming. None of the dozen players on the practice tee were swinging now, except

27

Whitlow, who slashed a shot off the ground with his driver, not bothering to tee the ball up.

Travis Walker started down the practice range, not hurrying, not looking back, walking crisply as he always did after a particularly strong drive.

Morris could sense the people on their feet in the stands behind him. The air was ugly with what someone near the practice tee was shouting at Whitlow. Travis stepped directly in front of him, not looking back. Whitlow gripped the shaft of his club, seemingly fighting an urge to drive one into Walker's soul.

"Be right back," said Morris to Rossi. He was pivoting on his left leg, digging his iron-and-wooden cane into the soft earth, broad as a poled barge in his raincoat. Old Thompson didn't look good. The drinking was bad enough without the high blood pressure. Travis bent over him; the two of them had walked home the greatest titles in golf, Morris remembered.

"Looking for last night?" said Travis. Thompson was too sick to lift his head. "Wish I'd been out with you. I couldn't sleep. We're both too damn old. Can you get up?" He had one of his iron hands under Thompson's left arm. The caddy got to his feet in a spasm of legs. He was dizzy but he could stand. He looked down at the long bag of shag balls. They might as well have been in another country.

"Forget 'em!" said Walker. He kicked the bag and the Titleist balls rolled their black numbers like round dice on the wet ground.

"That'll be it for me," said Thompson, despair seeming to rise up in his throat like the taste of cheap whiskey.

Travis looked up, surprised to see Morris. "Let's get some coffee in this man," he said. "I don't know what's worse, old golfers or old caddies." Travis laughed. Morris could see the slight tremors in the backs of his hands.

"What's with Whitlow?" asked Morris.

"Terminal stupidity," said Walker. "Maybe he'll grow up the day before he dies."

Morris walked back to John Whitlow. The same man in the stands was giving the "Young Lion" crude directions of how to get to the Grant Park Zoo. It sounded strange across the clipped grass.

"What's the problem?" asked Morris, not resting on his

cane, letting his strength lean down on Whitlow, who showed no remorse.

"Who can win the Open with a drunk caddy?" Whitlow said, now turning toward the clubhouse. "Not me. Must be somebody sober who can carry fourteen clubs."

Whitlow had gone a step when Rossi said quietly, "You're still moving off the ball," as if they were discussing his swing alone on the privacy of St. Simons Island.

Whitlow put all of his hate into his next step. He did not look back.

Morris cursed himself for not being a columnist. The sight of Travis casually walking down the lethal practice range without looking back would be something to write about. He filed it away to use when Walker would truly retire; or die, he thought, as we all must. The two of them were the same age. Writing about death gives you a feeling of imperviousness to it. Time will fix that, too, he thought.

He had to file a midday lead. His story would not please John Whitlow. Well, only forty or fifty million people would read it, or hear it.

5 ✠

THE MIST WAS BLOWING AGAIN, BUT IT WAS NOT YET A RAIN. Morris heard him the second time he asked the question. Headlights probed in the dark through the glass. "That was the last time you saw Rossi until you saw him on the balcony?" Rutledge was asking.

"Yes," said Morris. "He was waiting there. I'm sure of it."

Morris wanted to stand up and catch the lights in the street in his hands. It was too late. Jim Rossi had fallen beyond time.

"This John Whitlow was taking instructions from Rossi?" said Rutledge.

"He had been. He gave them up. Went back to his old sway on the backswing. He won two of the next four tournaments."

The lieutenant dropped change on the table and got to his feet. "We'll talk to this Old Thompson. What's his real name?"

"George," said Morris. "It won't help you. No one will know whom you mean if you use it."

"I'll send somebody to see him. Frankly, I doubt we'll learn anything we don't know. I think your friend Rossi jumped into the next world."

Rutledge walked toward the lobby where a crowd of reporters was still waiting. He stopped. "Morris."

"Yes."

"Who'll win the Open?"

"You can't bet against Kirkland." He paused. "I don't think he'll win it. I think one of the young guys. Whitlow. Maybe Tommy Fryer."

Morris looked at his watch. It was already eleven. He was empty with fatigue. Sullivan would be asleep. He would call her for breakfast.

Morris was almost asleep. His mind was dragging him along the fairway of the par-three seventeenth hole, the four girls . . . four girls, or was it three? moved in a jiggle of halters without bras, and stretch pants that knifed between their legs and clung around them as tightly as colors without fabrics. They were a composition of leans and bends and whispers, flashes of already tanned angles of themselves. One of their voices was suddenly high in the air and then smothered in a spasm of giggles. They ignored the bleachers behind them. Binoculars in the stands drilled into them without effect.

Morris heard the youngest one say, "Him!" followed by a round of laughter, muted with slim fingers of hands. Lee Washburn, his shadow behind him emphasizing his height, advanced in long, ruthless steps toward the finger of lake fronting the seventeenth green. His ball, a blip of white, lay within ten feet of the hole. He passed with his chin leading his long arms, his putter swinging in his left hand. The girls could not miss the petulance in his mouth.

Al Morgan in his steel-rimmed glasses walked mechanically behind him. He lifted his own putter at them with both hands, sending the girls on their knees with their faces in their slim hands.

Morris kneaded his fists into his eyes. Were there three girls or four? He couldn't separate their numbers from their colors.

Washburn made the putt for a meaningless five-under-par for the last practice round. Morgan missed his. It probably cost him a hundred dollars that Washburn would never see. God alone could have made the putts Morgan sank three years ago, when he won and spent two hundred thousand dollars. If only he could have cast that touch in iron and fixed it to the handle of his putter.

"How'd you like to go back to the hotel with that?" said one of the girls.

"We couldn't handle all of THAT."

"We could choose sides and take turns."

They were all hands and laughter, scrambling off thei knees in a flurry of colors to follow Washburn and Morgan to the eighteenth tee.

Morris switched on the table lamp. How could he remember what they said, and not be able to count them? It could have been any three girls, or four. Wednesday's practice round drew a gallery of twelve thousand in the rain. If he saw Rutledge again, he would describe them. He switched off the light.

Sleeping now was impossible. He was too exhausted. Sleep was too much like dropping in an elevator. He fell.

Julia Sullivan folded the newspaper and dropped it in an empty chair at the table. Her eyes were still puffy with sleep. "And that's it?" she asked.

Morris set his cup down.

"What about Margaret?"

"Her sister from New Jersey is coming for her. They should release the body in a day or two."

"Release it?" said Sullivan.

"Just routine. They're doing an autopsy."

"Routine," said Sullivan. She held onto the sleeve of his sweater.

Tommy Fryer, at the table next to them, was looking

directly over their heads. Morris turned to see the players' agent, Everette Holland, bearing down on Tommy.

Even this early, Holland sweated in the fatty lines of his throat. He stopped, groping for what he would say. "Tommy."

Morris was embarrassed for the fear in his voice. He was losing Tommy's contract. Morris had already written it. Only Kirkland had a greater record than Tommy's over the last five years. He was after his second Open title.

"Ev," Tommy raised his hand, "have a cup of coffee." Sullivan opened her newspaper as if it would give them more privacy.

Holland's legs seemed to give way under him as he sat in the chair.

"Tommy . . ."

Fryer stopped him. "Ev, we had five good years. You never lied to me, or cheated me. You made your share. But you were right about me. I'm a great player . . ." Morris listened deliberately. He lost what Tommy was saying until he said, "You've got *partners*." The word *partners* carried the slightest inflection. "I told you a year ago. We agreed to part friends."

"I had the kid then," said Holland. "You know a contract's no good if his word is no good. Whitlow told me yesterday, 'Sue me!' I'll starve in court. What player's gonna come close to me. I won't be an agent. I'll be a disease. Tommy, I knew what you had."

Morris felt sick at the sound of his voice.

"I shot the sixty-threes, Ev." Fryer stood up, without effort, the way he swung. He was six feet two inches and one hundred seventy, always upright, tremendously upright with his arc, but never stiff, FREE, thought Morris. God, how Everette had sold him: the Golden Boy, the California Look, Mr. Liquid, making a fifty-dollar suit walk in ads like Hart, Schaffner and Marx. He was twenty-seven.

Tommy Fryer did not look back as he walked toward the elevator. Everette sat unashamed of the self-pity that bled out of him with the tears. It had been forty years since Ev came out of Arkansas. Old-timers said he could hit the ball then, but he couldn't putt his name. He could never raise enough money on his own to sustain him, to pay his own expenses, to make it as a players' agent. He had had to take on partners, and then, too late, he had signed Tommy. Morris had never met his partners. Holland turned his chair toward their table.

"Here, Ev," Julia gave him her handkerchief. They had all been friends, from the time Monty Sullivan was a rookie.

"First time I saw him, he was seventeen," said Holland. "Had the weakest grip that was ever gonna win the Open, his damn thumb perpendicular on the club. I told him, 'Bud, never change nothin'.' Hit irons like they had eyes. Hagan never hit 'em nearer the hole and I seen Hagan."

Everette drank a glass of water. "Tommy's a good boy. The best. God knows he didn' need me, or any agent."

Fryer had won three hundred thousand dollars in the last year. That was petty cash compared to what he would make in the selling of his physical self.

"Tommy don't like my partners," said Ev. "I don't like my partners. Nobody can make enough money for five greedy partners." Everette stood up. He had his composure about him. "Losin' Tommy's bad enough. Losin' Rossi makes it impossible. God help him."

"Have some breakfast, Ev," said Morris.

Holland shook his head. "I'll give you a story," he said. "Before the sun goes down I'm callin' my lawyers. I'm filin' suit against John Whitlow for one point five million dollars. For breach of contract. If Whitlow wins the Open, I'll attach his purse. He'll have to borrow a dime to go to a pay toilet."

"Ev. You sure you want me to write that? I'll have to talk to Whitlow, too."

"Damn sure." Holland turned, his short legs moving him between the tables toward the front entry to the hotel.

"What did he mean, 'losing Rossi makes it impossible'?" asked Sullivan.

"I don't know. I wondered myself. Did we ever have such a happy tournament? Do you want to ride with me, or come later?"

"Later. I'm going back to bed." She punched him on the shoulder with her fist.

No golfers, no writers were yet on the club grounds. Only the caddies were lost in the trees, stepping off the pin placements, double-checking their fairway yardages. Morris turned stiffly under his umbrella. He looked back at the length of rock and glass and wooden shingles of the Atlanta Golf Club

33

that seemed to take on power in the mist. He waited to feel something of Jones come rising up around him, but it did not happen. The room inside in his name was somehow entombed in the clubhouse stone: replicas of his trophies from the Grand Slam year of 1930; a copy of his idiosyncratic putter, Calamity Jane; an insignificant cup, the first he ever won, at age nine. Many objects could be seen in that room, but Bobby Jones was not in this place.

The Atlanta Golf Club had moved north from the city to the Chattahoochee River. But Jones himself was only real in time-warped photographs of the old East Lake course. The United States Open was being played here in his honor. Still, Morris could not forgive the Golf Club its move from East Lake. It was as if they had taken down the Fox Theatre and routed Peachtree Street one way out of the city.

Morris shivered again in the strange dampness after three days of June heat. He did not know if he shivered at the mist, or at this unknown place in the trees.

He pushed open the door to the air-conditioned gymnasium that had been converted into the press room. The guard nodded him inside. The room was nearly empty at this hour of the morning.

"Morris, you moving Thursday's pairings?"

He did not know the young man who asked. All of the reporters used his name as freely as his wire service. Morris did not resent it. It pleased him, as if he were somehow the keeper of information more essential to their lives than the aggregate scores of the games men played.

"I'll move it in an hour," said Morris seriously, as if he had never moved it on Wednesday morning in twenty-one years. He was careful to answer any questions from the small-city journalists. Most of them were afraid of what they would write, of talking to the players, of being so far from home on expense account. He wondered which of them would ever huddle with the handful of famous columnists in the room; almost surely none of them. The old columnists never died and their numbers never increased; Morris ignored them as often as he could. There were perhaps ten gifted golf writers here, old friends, from large daily newspapers; they prepared for the Open as though it were an inauguration of the President. This strange game of chance and will seemed to belong only to those few who knew it and what iron malice it could ring down on men's souls.

His mail hadn't caught up with him. Such mail as he could expect.

It was too early for the golfers to be on the practice tee. Writers were not yet straggling into the press room with their hangovers. It was the hour Morris always managed to observe alone, when the tournaments seemed to belong to him.

Bobby Watson came toward him, wet grass clippings across the toes of his shoes.

"Mr. Morris," he said.

"I believe you've promoted me."

"Mr. Associated Press," corrected Watson with a grin. His hand was strong, even in Morris's grip.

"I read your story on Mr. Rossi." His face was serious. "It was frightening, just to read it."

Morris nodded.

"The caddies are sick about it. He was the only Social Security they had. He always seemed to know who was broke. I don't know how, on St. Simons Island."

"I wish you could have seen him play," said Morris.

"Alfred was telling me. Said he couldn't putt, and didn't need to."

"Is your man ready?" asked Morris, interested to know, wanting to put thoughts of death and autopsies behind him.

"Tommy could send his clubs out on a coyote and win it." Watson unfolded two scorecards. Both were coded with distances he had stepped off. "I always make two cards since Tommy lost the damn thing at Doral, and we were guessing all the way around. It cost us the tournament. I'll give you a tip."

"What's that?" Morris had no better source of information than the caddies. But it was important to know whom to believe.

"The fairways. Somebody made a mistake. They cut the grass too high. Every lie will be a fluffy one. We'll be hitting flyers all the way to North Georgia. It'll take a magician to stop the ball on these slick greens."

"You're not exaggerating."

"Oh no. Either the tournament committee doesn't know what it's doing, or the greenskeeper blew it."

Morris looked at his watch. "It's too late now. I can already hear the bitching and moaning."

"I'm lucky," said Watson. "I've got the only magician here."

Watson had caddied for Tommy Fryer for six years, since they graduated from Stanford. It started out as a lark, with Watson taking a vacation from five years of mathematics. He had seen the world and Tommy had made more than a million dollars. Tommy was generous. Not many twenty-seven-year-old math teachers were paid fifty thousand dollars a year.

"There's Alfred. You can ask him about the grass."

Alfred and the other caddies were drinking coffee out of the machines under the clubhouse. A two-million-dollar clubhouse and all a caddy could get was a cup of lousy machine coffee. The caddies gathered in a ritual of protocol. Those on hot bags rehearsed every mannerism of previous weeks. Ate the same food. Wore the same socks. Their opposites grieved over the failure of nerve of *their man* and of the lapses of an indifferent fate to the simple mathematics that determined their lives. Morris loved their feats of mysticism. They fought gravity's rainbow with superstitions and pitiful weapons not even in their own hands. Only the youngest caddies put all belief in pin placements and distances and wind directions.

Alfred was sitting off by himself. The other, younger black caddies ignored him; Alfred couldn't understand it; his rich language was as natural to him as his loping walk.

"He knows all there is to know about reading a green," said Watson. "He taught me plenty."

"Enough they had to change the rules," said Morris. No longer could a caddy squat behind the club, lining up the putt during the stroke. Watson had lined up a million dollars worth of putts until they changed the rule.

"Alfred, tell Morris about the grass," said Watson.

Alfred didn't look up from his coffee. "We be lucky goin' off early. If she rains. 'At grass grows so fast by afternoon we be losin' the last threesome."

"How about Al," asked Morris. "Is he getting it back?" Morgan had been struggling with his wild hook, and suddenly couldn't putt, which was the one thing he could hit straight.

"My dude so tight he can't keep his *swing* in the tee box. Let alone the ball up in the fairway," said Alfred, at the good luck of having someone to talk to.

"Maybe he'll make a putt and settle down."

"Lord, I hope not."

Morris looked up. Alfred always had the ability to startle him.

"Anyhow, he's puttin' crossways of the ball. 'Bout to cut it into his britches leg. Don't win me no Open! The money ain't no better'n plain Dallas. Put our pictures up in the papers. They run 'em all the way around the world on TV. Don't look to get paid for that! Now my man thinks he's s'posed to win whatever the PGA dabs on the ground and calls a tournament. Even out there in California on them crazy Crosby courses, him up all night and us shootin' sixes like we was at that Caesar's Hotel in Vegas. Why don't they put this Open business there where them sixes count for somethin'?

" 'Fore long we are 'Mr. Former Champeen!' Can't find a country we ain't 'Mr. Former' in, even in that Japan with them women caddies. We tryin' to fly it out over James Dent and we need a mountain to hit down off of to do that. We up in them U-ca-lyptus trees. In that San Francisco. You try gettin' down outa there in two. You might lose yo' automobile up in there. We got the Xemptions. But it don't help kill a rat when we shoots eighty-three on Thursday. We teein' off so early we got dew on our drawers 'fo' leaving the motel bed.

"We go'ne take us-a easy two-ninty-fo' and get on up to Chicago with sebenty-seben hundred dollars. We leave all that *former* stuff to these Crackers in Georgia. Why don't they will this United States Open business to Mr. Pete Kirkland until one of these boys grows up enough to win it from him. I expect he be 'bout sebenty-five when that happens."

Watson hugged his knees, drinking his coffee. Morris steadied himself with his cane to keep from falling over. He loved to get Alfred started. Of course, it was a hurricane of fantasy. He would give his soul to win the Open, or hock it to make the cut. He was the only chance Al Morgan had. Morris wondered how old Alfred was. He had caddied for Hagan. He never put any man up there with Hagan. "Did you hear about Jim Rossi?" asked Morris. He could not help it, interrupting the fun of listening to Alfred.

"Lord, on the radio," said Alfred. There was no glide of youth in his voice. "Never carried Mr. Rossi. Had a swing

37

you'd love to carry. Wadn't no real live putter, but always stoppin' eight feet from the cup. I remembers him playin' and me carryin' Mr. Monty. Oh, Mr. Monty could play, laughin' on his backswing. Fo'-foot putts never got in the way of his sleeping. Since Mr. Monty gone, whenever I be on hard times, missin' the cut, ridin' on the bus, be gettin' a check from Mr. Rossi. Be two hundred dollars, maybe three. Get me on down the road.''

Alfred reached into his long-sleeved shirt pocket and brought out a check. ''It was waitin' this morning at the clubhouse.'' He handed the check to Morris on his open palm as if it were too fragile to grasp.

Jim Rossi signed his name as precisely as he spoke. The check was to Alfred Mancha for three hundred dollars. Morris handed it back on his own palm.

Alfred folded the check away as if each crease had a meaning. ''You think they take it with him gone?'' he asked.

''Sure,'' said Morris. ''Whatever troubled Jim didn't have anything to do with his money.''

''Take lots of trouble to throw a man down off a hotel,'' said Alfred. ''Only thing, Mr. Monty be glad to see him.''

Morris looked carefully at the old man, his arms thinly powerful in his long sleeves. Damn Morgan's hook, he thought, and his booze. But Alfred could always get another bag, until he was as old as Old Thompson, whom whiskey had aged. Who would send the checks then, Morris wondered.

LeBaron was not in the dining room. He could be chasing his Tournament Director duties anywhere. It was too late for Morris to escape the hand motion of Players Commissioner Edward Horton. He would have to sit down. Morris was completely out of luck. Announcer Joe Goodner was also at the table.

''Terrible about Jim Rossi,'' said Horton. His voice was serious, but his eyes flicked toward the door to see who had come in.

Horton was up for re-election as Commissioner of the Tournament Players Division of the PGA. He weighed every face that had a vote. He looked around the large room as if he could hold onto it with his eyes. He had come to the tour late, after playing his best years as an amateur. The purses became too big to resist. And the insurance business never got easier,

38

no matter how many Walker Cup teams he made. Morris gave him credit. He did better than his age and size would have predicted. He won Greensboro and four hundred thousand dollars in his career. He was a dandy of a little man. You had to look closely at his handsome face to see that his mouth was too small and drawn too tightly. The Commissioner did not have to stand over four-foot, side-hill putts, or carefully steer the conversation back to life insurance. If he could be re-elected once, he had the job for life. Morris was sure he wanted it worse than life.

"The funeral isn't scheduled," said Goodner. "It will probably be Sunday. The network is sending a representative." The way he said it indicated a decision he had personally recommended.

Goodner had the permanently pained expression of a man whose golf career had been cut down at the moment of greatness by an injury. The Open he won, fighting the pain in his arm, could never compensate for the years he had lost. Nor could his job as a TV commentator. Two failed comeback attempts further embittered him at forty-seven. The players did not trust him. Safe on his tower, Goodner second-guessed all their judgments. Tension dominated his post-tournament interviews. Morris knew that Rossi had grown to hate working with him.

"I was just saying," said Horton, "how lucky golf is to have Joe, having lost so knowledgeable a man as Jim Rossi."

Morris accepted a cup of coffee without comment.

"It means a lot to have a color man who has won the Open, and can understand the pressures it brings to bear on the players," said Horton, looking again toward the dining-room door.

"Why do you suppose he jumped?" asked Goodner, drinking his coffee deliberately. He said it as if Rossi's suicide had been inevitable.

"What does Art Howard think?" Goodner asked, looking at Morris. "I saw him talking in the hotel lobby with Rossi about two hours before he died. Wonder what they were talking about?"

Morris did not answer. He would remember to ask Art what Rossi had said. He could not imagine why Rossi had jumped.

It was the question all golf was asking. Horton hesitated to speak. Morris did not help him, letting the silence build.

"Perhaps it was his health. It's a tragedy," said Horton, ill at ease with the subject.

Rossi had publicly criticized several of his actions as Commissioner. Especially his efforts to cancel the Tournament of Champions, and to change the dates of the—to Rossi—sacred British Open. Morris had written both of the stories. Yet, for all of Horton's career, Rossi had singled out his swing, in articles and in books, as a pure example to imitate. Horton was lucky, thought Morris. Who would remember Rossi's criticism, but his books would be in print for years.

"I think he was bored to death teaching old ladies how to tell the difference between a driver and a putter," said Goodner with unexpected viciousness.

Morris set down his cup. Think what you want to, little man. Nobody ever confused your opinion with reality. Morris was pleased that he didn't say it. That Goodner couldn't get that far under his skin. Morris stood up without looking at either of them. "About that time," he said, moving for the door.

Morris stood behind the first green. The sun was up over Duluth, Georgia, but the ground was still cool. Shadows reached across the fairways and into the greens. From such a distance the discreet little ceremony opening the tournament achieved a certain timelessness, a reel in a silent movie classic you could believe in. Jones would have approved the brevity of it. The first ball was in the air, a round flight of energy escaped from the earth, but then it was down, unmoving, pitifully wounded in the captive rough. Despite all of Morris's concentration, his mind flipped to Rossi. He wondered what the broadcast anchorman Don Murray would say to the television audience Saturday: I'm sorry Jim Rossi can't be with us today. He jumped two hundred feet down into a hotel lobby and killed a druggist from Mobile, Alabama. And himself, of course. The man in the lounge had not lived to reach the hospital. All the careful poise of the two doctors kneeling over him could not help the Plexiglas driven into his lungs. That would take the viewers' minds off the day's double bogeys.

Rossi could be an abrupt man, thought Morris; but to die

killing a simple druggist? To live so precisely and die so clumsily. Morris caught himself talking aloud; none of the already gathering crowd around the first green seemed to hear him. The autopsy. It would show something, a tumor, maybe, to account for the unaccountable. Morris, with an act of will, began to follow the flight of the second drive, which found the fairway.

Morris moved through the trees, his notebook in his pocket. It was his game now as much as theirs. The trick was to be always at the point of attack. To find the eye of the hurricane of pressure that settled over the course.

A hawk rode the air without effort, hunting the length of the river, sweeping over the rocks, banking on the heat rising under him into panic. His head jerked from the movement in the trees, the migration of unequaled colors threatening him even in midair. Morris watched him drop his wings and raise them in terror, unable to turn in his fear, passing down the length of the corridor of eyes watching him labor.

"Be damn," said Fryer. "Look at him go. The USGA must've grown the grass right over his nest." Watson balanced his bag rigidly on the fourth tee. Three pars and Tommy was bored. The shortest of the par-four holes had played four hundred fifty yards. Fryer's hands had been instruments of delicacy, flying irons two hundred yards out of grassy lies, the balls dying in the air of their own weight to balance their roundness on the slippery greens.

The hawk was gone over the trees. Fryer unsheathed the three-iron with one motion. Watson did not move in his Adidas, which Morris knew had made five trips between the green and tee and tee and green in the first light of day. Watson knew Fryer had selected too little club to reach the green, and could see the opening round going in the lake, and did not quiver. Fryer measured his club to the ball. Then slid the three-iron back into the bag, and flashed away the two-iron as if it had just been invented for the purpose. No practice swing. And the ball was arcing, drifting left to right over the lake, spinning itself to exhaustion into the green ten feet from the flag.

"Yeah," said Fryer, dropping the iron into the anonymity of the bag. Bobby Watson did not risk a flicker of a smile.

The roar for the birdie putt ripped through the trees before Fryer's ball disappeared into the cup. Morris turned on his cane toward the clubhouse. He stopped and focused his binoculars on the nearest scoreboard. The three gave Fryer the lead. But it was only the beginning. Morris started forward again between the trees. He did not want to miss a familiar locker room ritual. How many more would there be like it?

Travis Walker was sitting, his legs under him, strangely relaxed. The subdued tones of the locker room did not seem to be closing in around him. He did not have to invent noises with his spikes under the long bench. Fryer was out there with a game big enough to shrink the course. And Kirkland. Yet there was no panic in his hands to pick up his clubs.

"Morris, you got a cigarette?"

"You know I gave it up. Same as you."

Walker laughed. It was remarkable to see him so still, with no necessity for motion. He was at peace sitting on the long bench, the other pros changing shoes in a quiet clatter of sounds.

"I read your story," said Travis.

Morris shook his head in regret.

"We'll miss that bird."

"Knock all the pins down," said Morris. "Nobody would have been happier to see it than Jim."

Travis stood up in his strength. "Twenty-two years of Opens," he said, moving for the door.

Morris followed. Yellow ropes cut into the knees of the people straining to see Travis pass to the first tee. Only the noise of the words they shouted reached him. He smiled at the sight of his caddy, posing alongside his bag, mastering it as if it were a once living trophy he had taken at great risk. The scoreboard was a sea of black. Par or worse, thought Morris; the course is crushing the field. Morris squinted to catch bare fragments of red, the scores of those desperate few under par. No wind over the pines. Travis looked into the heat of late morning. It was his honor. His ball was away, burning a slow hook in the sky, curving softly for the fairway. Strange, Travis stood there, watching, as if he were seeing himself play. The noise of the crowd seemed to reach him from a great distance.

Lee Washburn's drive carried beyond Travis's. The amateur in the threesome hooked it into the rough. The three of them broke from the tee without speaking. The long grass rose up over the sides of their shoes. The only lies they would

42

get would be flyers. There was no way to put backspin on the ball. Good, thought Morris, Travis has seen every lie in twenty-two years of Opens. Travis smiled as if he could hear his thoughts.

Morris filed a quick running on Fryer's start. He was still two under after the turn. The muscles in Morris's legs tightened with eagerness at being back on the course. Even the left knee suffered without swelling. Al Morgan stood in the eighteenth fairway, seven over par. Morris only paused to see the iron resolution in Alfred. Morgan did not even look at his bag. He took the club Alfred handed him. Steam clouded his glasses. He did not bother to wipe them. His swing was quick and flat. At impact he was shouting, "Where are you, hook, you mother!" Alfred's dark and white eyes were fixed in a permanent squint, fighting the hook in the air with sight alone. Every inch of his skin shone with sweat. The hook began to come, and the crowd put up a storm of noise. They had not seen a ball that close to the number eighteen flag all day. Sink it and he had a fighting chance to make the cut tomorrow. Alfred had not spoken. Morris knew the words were building up in him, waterfalls of words, to pour over the caddy yard and drench the air above whatever bed he found for the night. It wouldn't matter if there was nobody to hear them.

Morris only moved to lift his binoculars. Pete Kirkland stood over his ball with great deliberation. He was waiting to feel exactly balanced. He had seemed uncomfortable on every green. His backswing was low enough, but his putter pulled the ball to the left of the hole a bare eighteen inches away. The crowd groaned at the sight of it. Word of the miss fled back through the trees. Kirkland carefully tapped in the third putt. He moved with no sense of panic, or of the field retreating irrevocably from him. Morris could not remember the last Open round Kirkland had played without a birdie. There were four holes left. It he could settle in his spikes on the greens.

Morris looked at the scoreboard. Fryer had dropped two shots. The kid, Mike Hall, the amateur, was the only player under par, by a stroke. Tomorrow he would need an iron lung. He would be unable to breathe on the first tee.

Kirkland walked solidly toward the fifteenth tee. The tournament was within easy reach of his game.

Whitlow was not a pretty player to watch. He slashed at the earth as if to scar it. Even when he was standing, he was the aggressor, challenging the course and every player on it. But somehow without the boyishness of the early Travis Walker.

Whitlow stepped off the distance again from his ball to a V-trunk oak. He did not seem to trust his young caddy. You'd like to call on Old Thompson now, thought Morris. He counted twenty-seven steps. Morris looked at his own card. The pin was two hundred eighteen yards away. Old Thompson would have known within a yard, drunk or sober.

Whitlow reached for the three-wood. He seemed to know it was home when he hit it, putting his head down, walking with quick, jerky steps. The lake fronting the green lay helplessly under the flight of the ball. It stopped twenty feet from the hole. Whitlow was already removing his glove to feel the putter in his bare hand.

If he swings this corner, thought Morris, he may overtake the golf course.

Whitlow climbed the green into a riptide of applause. It was a popular shot. Nothing to the putt but distance. He circled it. All the time he might have been playing the hole alone. Ted Dolan smouldered in his own shadow, watching him address the putt, all briskness. He rapped it thoroughly, directly into the hole for an eagle three.

Whitlow turned his back while he waited for Dolan and an obscure club pro to putt.

Dolan clamped his teeth in self-hate. Morris figured the putt at twelve feet. He hadn't made one all day. It left his putter weakly. Dolan shut his eyes. He looked surprised to hear the shouts of the crowd. The ball was not on the green. It was a gift. He still had a run at making the cut, but the cheap birdie threw him deeper inside himself.

Whitlow was already halfway to the thirteenth tee. He was looking straight ahead. He did not see Everette Holland standing carefully deep in the crowd.

Morris stopped to shake hands. "He's a cold one," said Holland. "No mercy in him. Let him win all he can. It'll belong to me. I don't know why I keep pullin' his ball in the lake with my eyes.'' Morris squeezed his shoulder and doubled back, riding his cane in long strides, to the perilous seventeenth hole.

Lee Washburn buried his four-iron face deep in the tee, violence on his lips. He drew it out, spitting on the grass as if it had mutilated itself. He did not seem to know if his words were pouring into his mind or out of it. The torrent slowed to a gentle flood of condemnation. Three times he had been voted the greatest long-iron player in golf, and he could not carry a ball two hundred and five yards over a flat lake. Washburn shifted his weight from one foot to the other, neither leg able to bear the indignation. An even-par round was slipping through his hands.

Travis Walker moved away from his own ball for the second time. Muscles in his arms flexed involuntarily. All the cool sense of isolation was gone with the sweat down the insides of his arms. He seemed to be holding himself together with an act of will. Morris could remember shots, exact shots, he had hit on every major continent. But it did not help him. He seemed to be standing in raw nerves.

Travis started the two-iron back far too fast, compensated, his mind crashing adjustments, his arms blocking through the ball until it was in the air, seeming to draw the strength out of his hands as it flew into the heart of the green. He dropped his head, too exhausted to measure the putt he had left himself.

Washburn took his penalty shot and played a wedge enormously high in the air, the ball drawing back onto the left fringe of the green, leaving him a sure double-bogey five. He ripped the clubhead into the surface of the water, fracturing it permanently into the air.

The people around the seventeenth hole rose up in their seats in a standing round of applause as Travis stepped onto the green, both hands raised to catch the strength of their hope in the air.

Washburn chipped indifferently close. Walker did not circle his putt. He rolled it away cleanly into the hill, and could not keep his feet on the grass as the ball came back inside the cup, bouncing off the round air to stop on the far edge. The people stomped the planks under their feet in anguish. Morris was sure that Travis slumped with fatigue, and not despair.

Morris lost himself, swarming with the vast crowd, pegging the ground with his cane, toward the eighteenth green. He stopped at a rise in the edge of the trees, and raised his binoculars over the vast migration of fans. Both drives were safely in the fairway, Washburn's the longest he had seen of the day, easily three hundred yards from the tee.

Travis seemed unable to assume a stance over his ball. He changed clubs for the second time. His swing was faster than Morris had ever seen it, a lashing, a blur in the air. Morris was sure the ball was in the lake, but still it clung to the sky, hanging, dropping to the front of the green as with exhaustion.

Washburn was away with his shot, his movement of the club almost leisurely. The ball covered the flag, but ran without backspin to the rear of the green.

Morris watched only Travis Walker. It had taken three years for him to look natural in metal-rimmed glasses. His arms cracked the air by his side as he walked. The cheers seemed everlastingly in the air. Morris was shocked at the fatigue in his eyes as Travis passed him. Not until he marked his ball did the green fall into silence, as if gravity had pulled the sound into the earth.

Washburn's first putt ran seven feet beyond the cup. He was already stepping forward in disgust when it was no more than halfway to the hole.

Travis walked once to the hole. And back. Morris figured the distance at thirty-five feet. Travis did not dare step away from the putt. He struck the ball flush, rolling it stiff to the hole. A tap-in for the one-over seventy-one. He was in the tournament. He raised his arms like weapons for quiet.

Washburn made a flawed pass at his putt. He got it down in three and turned and rifled the ball into the lake. The sight of it smashing into the water gave him no release.

Four girls, identically blonde in Morris's binoculars, ran in angles of legs to circle Walker with their congratulations. He walked through them without seeing them. Morris started forward, helpless with the mass of people sweeping in front of him. His left knee had lost all its enthusiasm. Still Morris reached the raw bleachers and climbed, awkwardly balancing himself on the boards, into the reserved press seats. The girls were nowhere to be seen among the thousands around the

46

eighteenth green. The crowd was again standing and applauding John Whitlow's improbable chip from ten years off the green that dived into the hole for a birdie, and a sixty-seven, and the first-day lead of the Open.

Morris turned to see Ted Dolan leaving the green in the blare of noise that had nothing to do with the respectable seventy-six he had scored. Morris found it even more awkward climbing down, advancing his stiff left leg below him. He gained the Press Room while Whitlow and Dolan totaled their scores. Dolan was to be interviewed as a witness to Whitlow's sixty-seven, not as the 1966 Open champion.

Only a handful of reporters filed into the gymnasium, running with sweat. The great body of them already lounged in their chairs, watching the players on closed circuit television. Scores were posted on a board the instant each hole was completed.

Dolan's dark hair was crumpled against his head by the Central Airlines cap that he had removed. He was being interviewed only as a witness to Whitlow's round. Whitlow had not yet entered the room.

"Is the course playing more difficult than you expected?" asked the United Press, full knowing the anger in Dolan's face.

"It's the worst set up Open course I've ever played," said Dolan. "Of course, I've only been in seventeen Opens," he apologized, all the bitterness in him fixed in the deep lines of his face.

Morris was sorry to hear him say it. Dolan was never a contented man. Yet, he had played the great courses well and with a sense of history. He better be ready tomorrow, thought Morris, to hear what thirty thousand Georgians think about his opinion.

The USGA's Jim Colburn had explained lamely: "The course superintendent made an honest mistake. Set the mowers a quarter of an inch too high when he cut the fairways."

"I don't blame the superintendent," said Dolan. "I blame the USGA. As long as we have amateurs running the tournament, it'll be run into the ground."

Morris could see the columnists loved it. They did not have to understand what was happening on the first day of the United States Open. They could quote Ted Dolan: "If I ever enter another Open, I hope somebody hits me in the head

47

with a ball peen hammer.'' Quoting him took no effort. The columnists could finish their typing and get back to some serious gin rummy.

Dolan would play in the Open again, if he could qualify. Yet Morris was sure the venom in his face was real. Perhaps his nerves were gone. Perhaps he was finished this time for good. It was never pleasant to see, but it happened. Morris, without thinking, suddenly saw Jim Rossi lying crumpled at the bottom of a bamboo cage. He shook his head and put a sheet of paper in his typewriter. The bitching about the course was only a twenty-four-hour newspaper virus. It happened every Open. The bulletin quoting Dolan wrote itself.

As Morris was finishing, John Whitlow, speaking in a drone of fraudulent boredom, began describing to the room his round of sixty-seven that led the Open. Morris automatically took notes. For him, the first day of the tournament was now only words, and in three days another year would have passed into time.

6 ❖

THE WRECKAGE LAY UNMOVING IN THE LOCKER ROOM. A TOWEL in a wad. Shoes abandoned on the floor, spikes up. A once-used glove crumbled under a bench. There were no bandages but there were scars in the room that would not heal. Half of the field would never qualify again for the United States Open. One lapse of concentration and any seat was an empty locker.

"Superintendent of the moon!" yelled Morgan, throwing a golf shoe against the wall in a clatter of disgust. All of it manufactured. Morris was sure he could not have been happier with his seventy-six. Where he had hit it, he was lucky not to have shot ninety-six. Morgan led the tour in lamentations. Other players joined the chorus, blaming the rough, the heat, the pin placements. The long grass in the fairways took

48

on the burden of all the bogeys in the room, even those flown out of traps.

Tommy Fryer was drinking orange juice, reading his mail, with his long legs crossed in front of him, letting the golfers and random writers step over his feet.

"Fryer, if all I drank was orange juice, I be damned if I'd go to the trouble every year of winning three hundred thousand dollars." Morgan could rarely get a rise out of him.

"They'll cut the grass tomorrow," Fryer said, not looking up from his mail. "The only thing that wasn't boring about the course today was the long grass that gave you a chance to practice up on your flyers, and the municipal-park number eleven where you gotta lay up with two one-irons and two putts. We ought to play number eleven eighteen times and call it the Open. We could set an outdoor record hitting one-irons." He laughed. He did not warn Morgan not to write it in his golf column. Morris knew it would take Morgan two months to get it into print. Even the PGA might fine Fryer. Morris laughed at the thought of a five-hundred-dollar fine against him. Fryer had shot seventy today by accident. It could have been a sixty-five. Three more seventies would win it. He might not score that high again. One long putt and he could take the course apart.

"The second Scotch is not the magic one," said Morgan. "I think it's the third. Did old Art hit 'em an honest seventy-two times?" he asked Fryer.

The room knew Fryer had totaled Art Howard's score at seventy-three. Art had nearly signed it, and would have lost the stroke if he had. Tommy uncrossed his legs. He did not respond. He was never embarrassed.

"How can you keep a man's score when you shut your eyes to keep from seeing him swing?" said Morgan, banging on a locker with his fist, giving his laugh a maniacal resonance.

Old Art, thought Morris, with his crooked swing and dark glasses, shooting a classy seventy-two. Cursing Fryer in the scorer's tent for his negligence. Maybe there was life in him yet. Maybe his caddy, Sam, could carry him around on his back.

Art sat drinking a beer, looking contentedly over his stomach.

Fryer kept reading his mail, not looking up.

Washburn walked through the locker room without a sound. One word and "Nasty" would take the walls down. An Ohio

49

writer had asked in the press room "if the pressure was too much" for him. Morris thought Washburn had killed him with his eyes. Even with a shaky finish, Washburn had shot a contending seventy-three. He sat down in front of his locker without speaking.

"Mr. Long-Iron," said Morgan, pouring his third Scotch.

"Stay in your bottle," said Washburn, kicking off his shoes.

"It's the way to play seventeen," said Fryer, impishly and unexpectedly. "You lay up in the lake and wedge it to the green."

"I thought you Mormons carried God around in your hip pocket," said Washburn. "I didn't know it was the rules of golf." He changed his shoes and walked out of the room without speaking again.

"Glad 'Nasty' doesn't take the game seriously," said Morgan, delighted at the fracas. "The third Scotch is the magic one, all right," he said.

The huge room wasn't full until Travis Walker was standing in it. He reached over and took the glass out of Morgan's hand and drained the Scotch to the bottom.

"He can't shoot par and he thinks he won the tournament," said Morgan, holding up the empty glass, pleased to have had Travis drink from it.

He owed Travis at least five thousand dollars, and had written in his column two years ago that he was finished; that month, Travis won two straight tournaments and signed Morgan's name on a bar tab for seven hundred dollars.

Travis sat down in a lump. Morris was concerned. There was no color in his face. He seemed beyond exhaustion.

Travis raised his head. He began untying his shoes. He said in an unusually careful voice, "I'm going to win the golf tournament." The color was coming back into his face. Morgan held his empty glass without speaking.

Now the room was as full as it could get. Pete Kirkland stopped beside Travis. "Are you ashamed of us all together, or just individually?" he asked in his high, boyish tenor.

Travis, in his press interview, had burned Dolan and the other players who criticized the course. He told the writers he was embarrassed for them.

"I take it back," said Travis. "Any course Kirkland shoots seventy-four on has to be illegal."

"Nice round," said Kirkland genuinely. "It's not a bad course." He wrinkled his nose. He picked up the five-iron whose grip Travis was replacing. "What'd you do, skip the back side?" Travis's laugh, like his voice, was an octave lower with age.

"Presenting! America's boy golfer," pronounced Al Morgan. "The only people who aren't suing him don't have a letterhead." Whitlow walked into the locker room, ninety minutes behind the news of his eagle on the back side.

Whitlow kicked off his golf shoes without sitting down. He walked around the row of lockers with his glass out for a shot of Morgan's Scotch.

"No soda," complained Whitlow. "You tend bar like you play golf." Morgan poured a hefty drink.

"There's a saloon-sized bar in the front of the room, and two bow-tied bartenders. Of course, you have to tip them, and by the time you pay Ev's lawyers, you'll be broke the rest of your life. Salute." Morgan raised his own glass, obviously glad not to be ignored, even pleased to be insulted.

"Takes a dusthead from Arizona who never saw real grass to shoot sixty-seven in this hayfield," said Art Howard. He straightened up gradually. His back was stiff behind his deep stomach. Morris knew the only thing he disliked more than the army of blond young players were their limber backs. Art walked toward the bar at the front of the locker room, which was as huge as a small aircraft hanger. Morris frowned. He never knew Art to drink before. Morris followed him to the bar.

"I'll buy you a drink, Art." The bartender poured the vodka. "To your seventy-two," said Morris.

"Thanks." Art did not slur the word.

"I hate to bring it up here," said Morris, "but Goodner told me he saw you talking with Rossi. In the hotel lobby. A couple of hours before he died. What did he say?"

Howard moved away from him, leaning back against the bar. "What're you talkin' about?" His words ran together. "I never talked to him yesterday. I was gonna, later. About my swing. Don't need him now. Not after a seventy-two." He laughed curiously high in his throat. Morris turned back to the far end of the locker room. Why should Goodner invent a story like that? It didn't make sense. Or why would Art lie about it?

Whitlow stepped in front of Tommy Fryer. "Tell your friend to get his hand out of my pocket," he said. "All he'll get from me is a Polaroid snapshot of the trophy."

Fryer casually stood up over the powerful young Arizonan. "Ev Holland's a good friend. You're right about that. You better save what purse you win to pay the lawyers." Whitlow turned his back. He did not like looking up at the Californian.

"I wouldn't build a shelf for the trophy," said Fryer. "Not yet."

"Listen at the boy wonders," Morgan chortled, putting down his bottle, trying not to pour his fourth Scotch.

Morris made no notes. The dressing room was inviolate to him. He only quoted answers to questions he asked. The players trusted him, and did not edit what they said in front of him. He came inside to smell the sweat of the tournament, the fear that was in the air, not to write gossip.

Whitlow walked in his sock feet to the bar. He put down a handful of paper chits. "A civilized drink," he said. "Scotch and easy on the water." He waited for the black man to pick out the necessary chits, and stuffed the rest of them in his pocket. He discarded a five-dollar bill for the tip. "Twenty-seven putts," he said to the room. "Tap after that, boys."

Travis Walker did not look up as Whitlow passed with his drink. Whitlow did not miss the snub. He sat in front of his locker, which was open. "What am I supposed to do, keep all the drunk caddies on retainer?" He said it loud enough for Travis to hear. Travis did not look up. Whitlow suddenly began unstacking boxes of balls, and gloves, and extra pairs of shoes, and changes of clothes from his locker. He looked under the bench, then stood on it and looked on top of the locker. "My blade," he said, forgetting the drink in his hand. "Anybody see my putter?" Nobody laughed. Nobody kidded about a putter.

Whitlow started to drink, but concern seemed to rise up in the glass at his lips. He set the drink in his locker, not bothering to shut the door. Morris had already searched the room with his eyes. He could see three putters. None of them was Whitlow's.

"Hey," said Whitlow toward Dolan, sitting in the obscurity of his seventy-six. "Did I bring the putter in with me?"

Morris could see the "Hey" burning in Dolan's parched face. "I counted your strokes, Sonny, not your clubs." Dolan stood up and turned toward the door and the heavy crush of the crowd outside it.

Whitlow was one of a half-dozen players who could not sleep without their putters safely in their lockers. Morris could not remember if he had had it in the press room. Maybe he did. Usually he did. Whitlow was walking around in circles now, looking where he had looked twice already. Morris could see his mind leaving it in the scorer's tent, and on the course, and in the press room, and in his bag where it would be safe enough.

Whitlow slipped on his loafers. Morris started after him. It might be an interesting short subject. The Open leader in search of his ultimate weapon. Morris knew his father had given Whitlow the putter, the only one he had ever used in competition.

"I'll kill that kid if he lost my putter," said Whitlow.

"Are you going to run him to death?" asked Morris, following behind him. The irony of it bounced off Whitlow's anxiety. He had forgotten Old Thompson, whom he had abused. All he could see was his blade putter. He slowed down for Morris to propel himself through the jammed clubhouse. He needed the confidence of another pair of eyes in the search.

The caddy master took him to his bag. Morris followed, his cane ringing on the concrete floor. Whitlow's hands slid over his clubs like those of an anxious parent. The putter was not there. "I'll kill him," said Whitlow.

The press room was a fury of letters smashing into rubber rollers, carriages jangling in their metal tracks, voices on telephones. The guard in charge of the door was no help. The putter was not on the interview platform.

Whitlow paled. "I've holed three hundred thousand dollars with that putter. I hit it twenty-seven times today. Never missed it once." His career seemed to be escaping between the empty palms of his stubby hands. Morris felt some of his panic, tightening his grip on his own cane. The sun was gone, but there was enough light to distinguish the tree line along the fairways.

"Let's see, you holed out a chip on eighteen," said Morris.

"I two-putted seventeen," said Whitlow, his feet already in motion. It was the last time he knew he had held the putter in his hands. It took him a moment to get his directions. Then

he began to trot, awkwardly. Morris moved forward, but his
left knee was agony. It would be long dark by the time he
could get to the seventeenth green. Whitlow's stubby legs
jolted his powerful body. Golfers only walked. Breaking into
a trot was unnatural. Morris could imagine his breath coming
in spasms, like an old man out of shape, like Old Thompson.
The empty bleachers circled the eighteenth green with layers
of broken shadows. Whitlow's trot failed into a ragged walk
as his silhouette advanced the length of the practice range that
stretched to the seventeenth green. He was about at the
distance Old Thompson had fallen sick on his knees.

Morris lost sight of him as he dodged into the thin rim of
pines guarding the flank of the seventeenth green. In the dark,
the trunks of the trees seemed to have been driven into the
earth by an unnatural force.

Just then a voice called, "Morris." It was the guard on the
press room door. "Telephone."

It was the detective, Rutledge. "Did you ever cover an
autopsy report?" he asked.

"Oh yes," said Morris, "a helluva long time ago."

"It'll be the end of it, I'm sure," said Rutledge. "If you
want to be there. The morgue's not your average country
club."

"I'll be there," said Morris. Something about Rutledge's
voice, about his calling at all, bothered him.

7 〓

THE OLD CORONER GREW THINNER IN FRONT OF THEM, THE FLESH
wasting away on his hands and arms, outlining his bones.
Even his smile grew thinner.

"Morris? I read your stuff," he said. "Most of the time
they don't put a name on the wire stories. Sometimes they do.
I like the stories from Pebble Beach, especially when there's
weather there. You writers are probably drinking in the bar."

Morris liked him.

The old man looked at his own thin arms. "I know," he said, rolling down his shirtsleeves. "I grow to look more and more like my clients. Not this one." He tuned his head toward the lump behind him under the sheet on the table. "It would take an encyclopedia of anatomy to report all the bones that are broken. Our boy didn't do himself any good."

"Nothing out of the ordinary?" asked Rutledge.

"Nothing beyond the knees up where the arms are supposed to be," said Dr. William Moseley. "The Plexiglas roof and the bamboo lacerated him, and his clothes. The sudden stop killed him, all right. You see the time on his watch. Eight-twenty-five. I'd say there was no doubt about that. Best I can tell, a healthy man went off that balcony. Didn't smoke. Didn't fall off of there with a heart attack. Or any physiological disorder I can determine. Of course," said Moseley, "you can't dissect what might have been on his mind."

"Probable suicide," said Rutledge, as if he were quoting it in a newspaper.

The old man nodded. "Who's leading the Open?" he asked Morris, washing his thin hands intensely, water and motion giving them a strangely youthful shine, as if layers of age were being scrubbed away.

"John Whitlow. A kid from Arizona, by way of the University of Houston. Shot a sixty-seven. Do you play golf?"

"Oh yes. At Piedmont Park. Wonderful crazy little course."

"I know it," said Morris. "I used to caddy there."

The old man stopped drying his hands, as if he were looking back on his own youth. "Short," he said, "I just use irons. Never could hit a bloody wood shot. Those fellows of yours are something. They couldn't play the Park. They would made convertibles out of all the automobiles."

Morris smiled, remembering the way the cars wound through the course.

The old man hung up his towel, both the ends precisely even.

"The suicides always make you wonder," said Rutledge. "Half of them, you say, why didn't they do it years ago. Poor. Sick. Drunk. Hopeless. Half of them have everything. Youth. Money."

"I'd miss a beer too much." Moseley's lips thinned again. "It's too short a jump now for me to bother with."

"We'll get the body out tonight. To New Jersey," said Rutledge. "Have a beer for me."

Morris shook hands with the old man, the boney fingers lost in his own grip. "Keep those irons out of the traffic," he said.

Outside Rutledge said, "You can release it. Probable suicide."

Morris looked down at his wide shoes. "It'll get about six paragraphs, on page twenty-seven. The afternoon paper has already given over its street edition to the early first-round scores. You can't die in two editions of a newspaper. Not anymore."

"No," said Rutledge. He moved toward a squad car parked at the curb, then stopped. "I sent a man out to the course today. He couldn't find this Old Thompson. We'll try again. If you see him, call me. If he isn't already in Chicago."

"Did you ask me to come here to tell me that?"

"No. I wanted to see if you still believed in his suicide."

"What else can we believe?"

"Yeah," said Rutledge, opening the door of the car.

Morris arranged his spare shaving kit among the bottles in front of the mirror. "Is this a bathroom, or a chemistry lab?" he shouted through the closed door. No answer. He stuck his head into the bedroom. "Sullivan, you're drinking my drink."

"I earned it," she said. "I read the AP story all the way to the end. Tell me this. Who is last?"

"A three-way tie," said Morris, pouring himself another drink. "One of them is a fine player, Jerry Bell. Shot eighty-six. It's not as hard to do as you might think."

"I heard it on United Press International," she needled.

"You know what you've got in this hotel?" he asked.

"Yes, but they're too young to be legal."

"A swimming pool. You know what I've got in this sack? A bathing suit."

"Top or bottom?"

"No more drinks for you, Sullivan. Come join me. I want to swim a couple of laps."

"Great God. One man in my life was always *on* the golf course. The other one is always *at* the golf course. Now he wants to get in the swimming pool. Why don't you come to

Colorado for the skiing? I'll wait here," she said. "United Press International has a special on the U.S. Open."

"Know who used to swim with me in the old days? Jim Rossi. He used to make up golf swings underwater. Only time I ever saw him when he wasn't serious was in the water. We used to swim outside in those days. Cold as a bat on the winter tour out in California, or down in Florida. Wet, he wasn't much more than a kid." Morris hesitated. "Who else remembers Travis Walker's baggy pants?"

"What?" said Sullivan. She was watching the ten o'clock news. They were interviewing John Whitlow. He was cocky sexy. He wasn't impressed with his sixty-seven. Now they were talking to Tommy Fryer. He was California sexy. He wasn't unhappy with his seventy.

"Fryer's a Mormon, isn't he?" she asked. "I suppose soon you will have to have three wives to be a fashionable Open winner."

"Three mistresses, maybe," said Morris from the bathroom, his two hundred eighteen pounds compressing the scales. "No man with three wives is going to make the cut."

He pulled his trousers over his bathing suit. The swimming pool was on the tenth floor, in the health room. Putting on his bathing suit that was too stiff, trying to untangle the drawstring, looking down at what his body had become, a solid mass, Morris laughed. He took on the same kind of meaningless enthusiasm that used to come over Rossi twenty years ago: Morris could see him, jumping into the water over his head, holding his breath, pushing off the slippery tile, floundering around. Morris had never swum laps in his life; it was something you said. He couldn't think his way around the silly impulse to jump in with his trousers on and come back to the room stark naked.

The elevator dropped under him from the thirty-ninth floor. Riding the escalator back up to the tenth level, he felt undressed in his stiff bathing trunks as though he were not wearing any trousers. He found the door to the health room. Inside was the heavy medicinal smell of chlorine. The pool seemed to be empty. No, there were two heads above and then under the water in a corner of the deep end. He opened the door into the men's locker room. A young man was sitting in a chair, leaning against the wall; he did not take his eyes from a thick book in his lap. Morris walked close enough to see that it was a textbook in some advanced science. The boy looked up, startled.

"Heavy reading," said Morris.

"Quiz tomorrow." He held up a towel. "Your room number?" he asked.

"Thirty-nine-fourteen, Sullivan," said Morris. He did not attempt to explain that the room and the name weren't his. It was too complicated.

"The locker's to your left." The boy was back inside his book.

Morris found the locker. He was sure he saw Tommy Fryer disappearing into the steam room. He would join him after his swim, but he would be careful not to talk golf.

Morris stepped on the damp concrete surrounding the pool. The air was smoggy with water vapor and the smell of chlorine. There were no heads visible in the pool. His heavy body was suddenly in the air, his mind captive inside it, his thick legs not without some grace behind him. The warmth of the water made him open his eyes. He was still plunging, his weight driving him near the bottom under the open, startled eyes of a girl, young, passing over him, her short, dark hair parted with her own motion, her body entirely nude. Two hands from above were closing around her free breasts as Morris kicked under the length of the girl, her arms now windmilling frantically. The blank, unlighted wall of the opposite side of the pool came strangely hard against his open palms as though he had expected it to yield like flesh.

Morris looked back. The two heads appeared just above the water in the far corner of the pool. Morris thrust with his right leg, pushing himself back across the open water. Only when he lifted his arms in the air did he lose his sense of weightlessness. He raised himself out of the pool, his feet kicking him easily up despite his bulk. He limped on his scarred left knee into the locker room without looking back.

This time the boy saw him. "That was quick," he said, his eyes back in his book, seeing into the formulas and numbers printed like a lost language on the pages.

Morris took his time showering and drying off. His swim was aborted. He would skip the steam bath. He twisted the water out of his bathing suit and walked through the door, making no effort to look into the pool or away from it. There

58

was a noise and a swirl of water behind him, but he did not look back.

The leader of the United States Open might be interested to see his wife's own surprised reaction in the pool of the Peachtree-Forsyth Hotel. It would have made a startling cover for the sports magazines. The public only knew them as the perfect couple. He, burned blond. She, darkly beautiful. Morris had once quoted her. The thing she liked best about the tour, she said, was the travel. The underwater travel seemed particularly exciting, thought Morris. The man with her was Al Morgan. Morris could not say how he knew. Her head had blocked his face. But the chunky arrogance of his body was somehow unmistakable. He was seventeen years older than Whitlow, and nine shots behind him, but he was playing a different game in the hotel pool. The stimulation of seeing them there dissipated, leaving him tired. Morris suddenly wondered if Whitlow had found his putter.

8 ▦

THE EIGHT-THIRTY SUN CAME DOWN THROUGH ITS OWN HEAT reflected off the clipped grass of the deep Georgia hills. Even in the shade of the trees you could feel the gathering warmth in the still air. Morris stood well away from the players, who rose and fell in a prism of colors on the practice tee. He did not want to be asked for another explanation of "probable suicide." Even he himself had been unable to let it rest during breakfast with LeBaron. Squinting his eyes against the heat rising from his coffee, Morris had asked, "Why kill himself the day before the Open? He scheduled his life around it. He was already talking about next year's Open in Oklahoma."

"I'm no psychiatrist," said LeBaron. "I know there is a thing about special dates. Birthdays. Anniversaries. Christmas. For some reason depression can be worse at those times."

"Maybe so. But two mornings ago he was memorizing all the golf swings. Lecturing me on them. Digging Whitlow about his sway. He was as excited as a kid with a windup toy."

Morris squinted at the sun, now breaking full force through the thin covering of clouds. He wondered again what had happened to Whitlow's missing putter. Given a choice between his wife and his putter, it would be no contest. He was not on the practice tee. Morris looked at the morning's tee times. Whitlow was scheduled to tee off at nine-thirty. He tried to remember seeing him all morning. He couldn't. He must be on the practice putting green. Morris started toward the clubhouse. His left knee was slightly puffy, but without pain. At least for now. The putting green was a variation of languid and abrupt strokes. But no Whitlow. Morris turned himself into the surf of bodies outside the locker room. Whitlow's locker apparently had not been opened. Dolan, who was paired with him, was changing his shoes.

"You gonna reverse the seventy-six?" Morris asked.

Dolan gave him a rare smile. "I'll take three more of the same, and see you in Chicago."

"Have you seen the kid—Whitlow?"

Dolan looked around him as if he might have been sitting in an empty room. "No. I haven't. I haven't been looking for him."

"I was wondering if he found his putter."

"He could putt with a crowbar," said Dolan, the smile gone from his face. "I like one thing about Whitlow. On the course, he keeps his mouth shut." He finished tying his shoes.

"Hang tough," said Morris. Now he was concerned. Whitlow had no respect for golf, or its traditions, or for anybody who picked up a club against him for money. But he was not careless about his practicing. Morris advanced behind his shoulders into the jammed corridor outside the locker room. He looked again at his watch. Whitlow had fifty-nine minutes before his tee time. Maybe he had a showdown with his wife. Maybe he was already driving into the parking lot. Morris stepped outside. The sun had now begun a formal assault on Georgia.

The caddy master was prowling the long storage room under the clubhouse, watching the bags. "Where's John Whitlow's caddy?" asked Morris.

"I'm here," said a young man, overturning a bag behind him.

Morris introduced himself.

"I'm Jesse Harper," said the caddy, retrieving the bag. "I was supposed to meet Mr. Whitlow on the practice tee forty-five minutes ago. He hasn't shown up."

The caddy master looked across the golf bags as if they were responsible for their owners.

"You wait here," Morris said to the caddy. "I'll talk to the starter. He was probably held up in traffic." Harper didn't let the bag out of his grip.

Morris walked at a tilt toward the first tee, negotiating the streams of people coming from all directions. Two men were seated at a table outside the starter's tent. Official scorecards were carefully stacked in front of them. Morris spotted an angular older man whose USGA blazer hung from his wide, thin shoulders with all the precision that money could provide.

Even the blue and scarlet USGA band around his upper sleeve seemed to have been tailored for the purpose. Morris knew his name was Bryan.

"John Morris," he introduced himself, "Associated Press."

"Robert Bryan."

Bryan was preoccupied with keeping the players on schedule.

"Unless he just drove up, John Whitlow isn't here," said Morris.

"What do you mean?" Bryan looked at his schedule. Whitlow was to go off at nine-thirty. He looked at his watch. It was eight-forty-five.

"I've been looking for him," said Morris. "I wanted to know if he found his putter. He misplaced it yesterday. He was not in the clubhouse, or on the practice tee. He was supposed to meet his caddy there at eight."

"It's his responsibility to be here. Not ours," said Bryan.

"I think I know that," said Morris. "I also think the USGA would hate for the leader of the Open to lose the tournament by missing his tee-off time." Morris was walking away. He would find Colburn.

"Mr. Morris," said Bryan, the reality of Whitlow's absence suddenly etched in his face.

61

Morris stopped, but did not speak.

"I'll get on the walkie-talkie. If he's here, we'll find him."

Morris followed him into the starter's tent.

Bryan identified himself on his battery-powered mike. "Is John Whitlow in the locker room?" He was shaking his head, in answer to his own question.

"The security guard says he still hasn't shown up," said Bryan. Now he was talking to the practice tee. Then to the parking lot, and finally to USGA headquarters. He handed over the walkie-talkie, embarrassment on his face. "Jim Colburn wants to talk to you."

"Do you know where John's staying?" asked Colburn.

"At the Peachtree-Forsyth. You might also page his wife here at the course." Morris suggested it without thinking. Maybe they'd had a fight and John had split. It didn't sound like John.

"We've just call one answers. The switchboard says his room left a six A.M. wakeup call. It was made. They are sure, because it was circled. We're paging his wife." Morris handed the walkie-talkie to Bryan.

Three golfers were standing, swinging to stay loose, on the first tee. A threesome in the fairway waited for the green to clear.

"Will Mrs. John Whitlow please report to the starter's tent." The announcement went up again over the heads of thousands of fans, and throughout the clubhouse.

Morris moved into the crowd away from the tent. He watched for Jackie Whitlow. She was from New Orleans, he remembered that. They had been married two years. They had already been separated once. Whitlow was no ladies' man. He only slept with his golf game. Morgan said that, remembered Morris. Morgan should know. There she came, moving toward the starter's tent, her chin high, but her hands making tight fists as she walked. Morris angled in behind her, staying out of sight. He felt awkward, as if it had been himself, and not her, naked in the pool. She walked hesitantly to the starter's tent.

"Mrs. Whitlow?"

"Yes." The sound of her own voice seemed to give her confidence. She relaxed her hands.

"I'm the starter, Robert Bryan. We're concerned about John. Afraid he might be caught in the traffic."

"I didn't ride out with him," she said. "But he's not in the room."

"Yes. We called your hotel," said Bryan. He began to lose his sense of efficiency. He was moving his arms nervously under the tailored jacket. Had the first-round leader of the Open ever failed to show up for his tee time? Morris doubted it. All the responsibility seemed to be in the USGA band around Bryan's arm.

"Do you know whom he might have ridden with?"

"No," she said, a certain finality in her voice.

Bryan looked at his watch. "He still has thirty-five minutes. We have the police checking any stranded automobiles. We have a helicopter on alert." There was no confidence in his voice.

"I'll be in the clubhouse," said Jackie Whitlow. She turned, seeing Morris for the first time. Her hands were fists again. She did not speak. She disappeared into the crowd in the direction of the clubhouse.

Colburn joined them outside the tent. "Was that his wife?"

"That's her—Jackie," said Morris.

"She didn't know whom he was to ride with," said Bryan, glad to have someone to share the responsibility.

"That's strange," said Colburn. He looked at Morris. "What do you think?"

"It doesn't look good," said Morris. "Whitlow's not the type to skip practice."

Colburn dispatched two golf carts to the parking lot to rush Whitlow to the first tee. "We've opened his locker," he said to Morris. "We're holding a pair of shoes, balls, and a glove."

The caddy, Jesse Harper, stood now with his bag near the tent, counting off the minutes with his eyes.

LeBaron wheeled up in another cart. "Nothing yet?" He looked at Morris. "Want to check the parking lot?" Morris lifted himself into the cart.

"How did you know he wasn't here?" asked Frank.

"He lost his putter yesterday. I was curious to see if he found it."

Traffic outside the parking lot moved improbably forward, stopping every few yards to pant its exhaustion. Neither of them spoke. LeBaron looked at his watch. "He's got a couple of minutes. He'll never make it."

"Let's go back," said Morris.

A circle of officials had grown around the starter's tent. All of them were double-checking their watches.

"Defaulted," said Bryan quietly, in the middle of the circle. He had regained his composure.

A public address voice announced flatly, "John Whitlow is defaulted, having missed his tee time." The gallery fell away in bursts of reaction, spectators repeating to strangers what had been said, the news moving in relays the length of the fairway, so that a player on the first green was forced to back away from a short putt because of the noise.

"Now on the first tee," said the voice, "Ted Dolan, former Open champion." The announcer had to ask for quiet twice. Dolan ignored the noise and split the fairway with his drive, shifting his wad of tobacco to his left cheek.

"... costly absence—John Whitlow," said Jim Colburn. The President of the USGA might have been dictating his recollections of the tournament in the distant future.

No matter how Young a Lion he is, or how gifted, thought Morris, he may never win the Open. It's a championship that has eluded great players of every generation.

Colburn turned his electric golf cart toward the clubhouse.

The caddy was crying. Morris took him by the shoulder. "No fault of yours, Jesse. I'll see that you get paid."

LeBaron dropped Morris at the press room. The news was being announced as he stepped inside. A blizzard of words was suddenly being typed. There was no permanence in them, thought Morris, as he finished his own bulletin. It was like writing on a crowded blackboard to be erased for the next day's class. He finished and started for the locker room.

Even Pete Kirkland felt a necessity to look into Whitlow's open metal locker. He reached inside and lifted a dozen Titleist balls still in their box. He dropped them as if they had failed in their wrappings. Kirkland looked at the clock on the far end of the wall. He had ten minutes until his own tee time. Morris saw all the players uncomfortably checking the clock.

Travis Walker reached past Kirkland and closed the locker door with a force that startled the room. "God knows I've blown the title often enough," he said.

"You never left it in the locker room," said Kirkland,

impulsively slapping him on the arm as though to lift him over a personal disappointment.

"Maybe it'll be like old times," said Travis, "you and me. He wouldn't want to get squashed between us."

Kirkland laughed his tenor laugh. He obviously hoped it would happen. He started for the door, pulling on his glove.

Travis still had forty minutes. Morris had seen his caddy waiting at the practice green.

Morris sat down by Tommy Fryer, sliding his left leg out of the way against the wall. Tommy did not avoid his eyes.

"You saw them?" asked Fryer, tying his shoes.

"I dived in the pool with them," said Morris.

"Al went too far this time. He could have at least found a pool that wasn't in the middle of a seventy-story hotel."

"Do you think John knows?"

"He must, or he'd be here. He'd cut off an arm to win the Open."

"Or *your* leg," said Morris.

"Funny, I feel sorry for Jackie. I don't know why."

Al Morgan stepped into the room. There was no look of embarrassment about him. "It's official," he said to nobody in particular. "We don't have to worry about the kid winning it. The Young Lion has retired to his den. Hey, Rookie," he shouted over Fryer's disapproving quietness to his morning partner, "you gonna shoot zero on the front nine, or do I need to take a pencil?" Morris was sure it was the longest sentence Morgan had spoken to the boy in two days.

"Maybe your partner better take an adding machine," said Morris, now standing on his feet looking down on Morgan. "You might triple that seventy-six you shot yesterday." He dragged his stiff leg past Morgan, not waiting for his reaction.

Reporters and cameramen cornered Tournament Players Commissioner Edward Horton in the clubhouse.

"Has Whitlow been in an automobile accident?"

"Is he busted?"

"Why doesn't his wife know where he is?"

Horton fielded the questions without losing his patience. "We are concerned about John. We have no report of his being in an accident. State officials are alerted that he is missing. Jackie is understandably upset. She's in no condition to be interviewed."

"Do you think he just pulled out of the tournament?"

"Is the course that lousy?"

There was a round of laughter among the reporters.

"It's terribly unfortunate," said Horton. "I'm sure there is a simple explanation. John is a great young golfer. And a fine young man. We'll let you know when we have any further news." He began pushing through the ring of reporters.

"Whitlow is a nasty, greedy little man who wouldn't walk away from a million dollars unless he had an open wound in his head," a writer was saying to another.

He is right about the million dollars, thought Morris. An Open win would be worth that to John Whitlow. How could he think that much about a wife he paid so little attention to.

9

THE SUN SEEMED TO CLIMB DOWN, BRINGING THE HEAT AND THE middle of the day closer to the Georgia trees.

Morris waited to pick up Dolan and the rookie, Mike Hall, on the seventeenth tee. You could not look at the two of them without missing John Whitlow, who was scheduled to play with them. Whitlow's absence was felt by the gallery at every hole. Dolan was hanging tough at even par. He was putting out on sixteen.

Here on the seventeenth, Masters champion Harry Ward smoothed a four-iron into the unmoving air. The flight of the ball obviously pleased him. Morris followed it into the heart of the green.

An amateur from LSU, Marty Thomas addressed his ball. He could not seem to breathe in enough oxygen to clear his head. He had played an uneventful round of seventy-one Thursday to find himself near the lead. Now he was nine over par. He kept losing the club on his backswing. Morris could not see his ball on the seventeenth green.

"Better play a provisional ball," said Ward as gently as

possible. "It might have spun back into the water. It's awfully steep there."

Thomas played a provisional ball over the green. It was stopped safely by the crowd. Ironically, the third player in this threesome was also missing. The club pro paired with them had damaged his wrist against a root on the fourth hole.

Morris decided to wait for Dolan behind the seventeenth green, out of the direct angle of the ever swelling sun.

Ward left the tee with his quick, abbreviated steps. He was five over for two rounds. It was a respectable showing for the Masters champion, and the Georgians did not forget it. He waved his putter at the applause as he stepped onto the green. Even the people in the bleachers behind the green were standing and applauding. The kid was already looking for his first ball. Morris squeezed in under the shade of a tall pine tree.

Two marshals on the bank were indicating the ball had rolled back into the lake. Morris knew the bank dropped off very quickly. So did the water. Thomas was now searching in the edge of the grass on the steep incline. Ward felt obligated to help him.

The kid could hardly keep the two-iron steady in his hand as he pried with it into the taller grass near the water. No way his ball could have stopped, thought Morris. The kid was stubborn. He was nine over par, but you don't make the LSU team, and you don't qualify for the U.S. Open, if you are a quitter. He seemed to see something in the water. The lake was not clear. The bottom here was all mud. The two caddies were leaning over to lift out the ball should he bring it to the surface. "That's not a ball," said the closest caddy. "Looks like the end of a panty hose." The two marshals watched. Ward looked over the boy's shoulder. Morris was suddenly amused at the sight of them, and himself, and five thousand spectators, all stopped for a go at a $1.45 golf ball. Up out of the water, dripping, came the club, and then bending the shaft, stiff over the clubface, came a hand, frozen open in the air.

No word, only horror came out of the mouths of the caddies; the boy holding the club was unable to put it down or lift its burden higher; a marshal screamed, his foot slipping into the water, the wetness climbing over his leg as though the lake were claiming his body. The two caddies scarred the green on their hands and feet like human crabs. The marshal whimpered, pulling his wet leg under him. The boy, Thomas, let the hand down into the water. Only when it disappeared did he gag and throw up between his legs as he squatted helplessly on the slope.

The people standing near enough to see raised and lowered their feet in their screams, running in place in their horror. The people in the bleachers clutched one another, vulnerable in the air, hollering for help to stop the terror they could not imagine.

Morris was sure the security man was an old officer. One marshal called him Major. He stood in the middle of the green with both arms over his head. Not moving. Waiting for the crowd to focus on him. He did not try to shout over the noise. Two marshals behind the green cautioned people not to run. Now the Major had their attention. The crowd, after its panic, fell quiet. People talked in whispers, afraid words alone would raise the awful hand back above the water.

"Help is on the way," said the Major on the green. "Please leave the area. Don't run. It's not going to be a pretty sight." The marshals repeated it.

God knows there's no helping whoever's in the water, thought Morris. The lake curved innocently against the clipped grass, a toy, an elaborate game of water drawn on a board and set down for its symmetry.

The shock remained in the air. Morbid curiosity will come later, thought Morris. The people behind the green and in the stands began to file away toward the clubhouse.

Morris looked to the seventeenth tee. Dolan's twosome had been joined by a threesome. Morris was sure the air over the course was alive with radio signals to stop play.

"My God, what do we do?" asked Ward of the Major on the green, who was trying, over his walkie-talkie, to explain what had happened to officials at the clubhouse.

"Mark your ball," said the Major. He spoke again into his walkie-talkie. He couldn't seem to make the other officials understand him.

Ward marked his ball. The kid from LSU was on his feet. He left the two-iron lying in the grass, marking the spot where he had lifted up the hand. Ward put his arm around the boy's shoulders.

"You okay?" he asked.

"I think so," said Thomas.

"A marshal's protecting your provisional ball," said Ward. "We can't help whoever is in the lake. We'll just have to wait and do what the officials ask us to do."

Morris had moved onto the green, careful not to sink his cane into the putting surface. He could see three golf carts gathering speed from the clubhouse, turning silently around the now empty wooden bleachers.

Colburn was the first man out of the lead cart. He went directly to the Major. The marshal on the ground could not get his nerves under control.

"You're Major Murphy," said Colburn.

"Yes." Five other men surrounded the marshal, one of them a Fulton County Deputy Sheriff. "This young man's tee shot," Murphy indicated Marty Thomas, "rolled back into the lake." Thomas shook his head in disbelief. "He thought he saw the ball or something in the edge of the water. He reached in with his club." The Major indicated the two-iron on the grass. "What he lifted up was not a ball. It was a hand." The six men looked at the water as if they expected it to speak.

"Good Lord," said Colburn.

"We have a rescue unit coming from the clubhouse," said the short, balding deputy sheriff. "They aren't equipped with diving gear. How deep is it out there?"

"It falls off quickly," said the Major. He was wearing the blazer of a club member. "Unless the body has moved, they can reach it, all right."

"You couldn't tell who, or what age, the victim might be?" The deputy looked at Colburn each time he spoke, as if to clear his question with the USGA President.

"It was a man," said Morris carefully, causing them all to turn quickly around. "I'm sure," he said, feeling queasy again at the memory.

A fourth golf cart pulled noiselessly onto the apron of the green. It was Frank LeBaron of the PGA. Following him was a motor vehicle with a portable stretcher. Two young men bounced off the front seat and ran onto the green, ignoring the looks of disapproval at their running.

Major Murphy re-created the scene again for the three of them.

LeBaron spotted Morris. "Did you see it?"

"Yes. It was the damnedest thing I ever saw."

"Who is it?"

"God knows."

The security men were preventing the crowd from returning to the area. "It's not going to be a pretty sight," repeated the Major. Curious fans were now running toward the lake, but the marshals had established a perimeter out of sight of the water. A photographer from the Atlanta papers was allowed through the line. Two highway patrolmen came behind him in their boots.

Players will have to putt this green with a pitching wedge, thought Morris, despite the fear in his throat.

The deputy sheriff was not taking charge. He was waiting for instructions. It would take half an hour for the sheriff to get there. The two young paramedics broke off a conversation between themselves and moved toward the edge of the lake. One of them picked up the two-iron and began fishing into the muddy finger of water. The other held onto his belt from behind. Very quickly the hand and forearm were raised, bodyless, out of the water. Morris leaned forward to see the first medic step forcefully up to his knee in the lake, seize the hand and arm, and begin to retreat up the slope. The other medic now had both arms around his waist, helping him keep his balance and his momentum.

Out of the water, eyes and mouth sockets of mud, hair plastered alive over his dead face, came the undeniable form of John Whitlow. Officials staggered backward as if the green had tilted. The two paramedics lost their balance against the steepness of the bank, falling over backward, holding onto their terrible burden, heaving him on the grass up to his waist, his arm and hand pointing astonishingly toward the green.

Only the two patrolmen and Morris were left standing above him. Fear again was in the air like an element of matter. The others who had been on the green pushed into the trees before they stopped to look back.

"Better leave him as he is," said the deputy, walking back, embarrassed at his own flight.

"His name is John Whitlow," said Morris.

The deputy looked at Morris for the second time. He leaned forward as if to take him under arrest.

"Did you say Whitlow?" LeBaron ran onto the green. He almost doubled over at the sight. "Oh-my-God."

"Who is this Whitlow?" asked the deputy.

"He was missing. He was a golfer. He was leading this tournament," said Morris. His own skin felt cold and damp in the heat. "You had better call the police. Call Lieutenant Jack Rutledge. Tell him who the body is."

The medic who had dragged him onto the grass stepped carefully past Whitlow and washed his hands in the lake water.

"Don't touch him," warned the deputy again. "You're sure that's the golfer?" he asked Colburn.

Colburn did not approach the body. "Yes. LeBaron knows him. And Morris too. Morris is with the Associated Press." The deputy looked at him with greater suspicion.

"There don't seem to be any marks on him," said the second medic, examining him closely without touching him.

The photographer had recovered his nerve and was taking pictures, careful to avoid the fixed horror of the victim's face.

"You had better get more help down here," said Morris to Colburn. "You'll have thirty thousand people and three hundred reporters in your lap in about five minutes."

Colburn had stopped the tournament, but not until four threesomes had stacked up on the seventeenth tee. Actually, they made an "elevensome," thought Morris, looking through his glasses toward the tee; Ted Dolan and the rookie were playing without Whitlow, or knowledge of what had happened to him.

Four of the players walked around the edge of the lake. One of them was Dolan. He walked up to Morris, just in sight of the body. "Looks like the seventeenth is playing tough," he said. "Who is it?"

Morris touched his shoulder with his hand. "Whitlow," he said.

Dolan actually flinched. Then shut his mouth tight. "God, can't they get him all the way out of the water?" he said.

All four golfers looked again at the form in the front of the green. It seemed smaller and colder.

"Dry land won't help him now," said Dolan.

*　　*　　*

The tournament had been stopped for two hours. The huge crowd in the North Georgia trees was under control, but restless for play to resume. Curiosity over the bizarre death had been talked away. The players had grown stiff waiting on the tees. They had not been permitted to return to the clubhouse.

Colburn deliberately faced the green so that the others on the USGA Executive Committee could look away from the lake. He avoided the eyes of Frank LeBaron, whose advice he had carefully sought. Colburn motioned for the group of thirteen men to come closer together. His own Tournament Chairman, a heavyset man, seemed to lose confidence with every minute the investigation was delayed and play was suspended. Morris only knew the chairman by his last name, Hammond.

Morris stood carefully still in the trees.

"The sheriff and the deputy are obviously idiots," said Colburn as dispassionately as if making a simple interpretation of ground-under-repair.

Morris remembered the first question Sheriff Harvey "Hap" Goodwin had asked when he stepped up to the body an hour ago. "What, was he drunk?" He asked nobody in particular. He was still confused and thought Whitlow had fallen off the green during the morning's play.

"The city detective, Rutledge, seems to know his business," said Colburn. "He will be moving the body into town immediately. He doesn't want the area near the lake disturbed. In fact, he wants it roped off. He's finished with his photography. He's putting two divers into the lake. We've got one-third of the field on the course. We can delay another forty-five minutes and still get most of the round in today. That's what I suggest we do."

Heads in the group were nodding their assent. Morris knew that a Monday playoff would be unwelcome enough by the TV network. A scheduled Monday finish would be deadly. It would drag down ratings on Saturday and Sunday as well. "I suggest," said Colburn, "that we take a vote of this committee. We have a quorum here. I suggest we move the cup to the south front of the seventeenth green, rope off the rest of the green, allow a free drop for balls that land inside the rope, and continue the tournament. Depending on what they might

72

find, the investigation could go on for days. We could wind up having to cancel the Open."

Morris could see only two men shaking their heads in disagreement. The others stared ahead, seemingly afraid to even think of stopping the tournament.

"There is no precedent for moving the cup," warned Tournament Chairman Hammond, "even if a green is flooded, it isn't permitted."

"No," said Colburn," and there is no precedent for the Open leader drowning before the second round of play."

Hammond stood motionless to obscure his objections.

"Isn't anyone going to mention the loss of a human being?" asked William Gwen of Rochester, New York, not at all fearful of his own opinion. "This is a golf tournament, not a national emergency. It isn't essential that it be continued on schedule, or even that it be concluded at all. This group is responsible for protecting the human feelings of the contestants and their families. I think there is no question but that play should be discontinued today until more is known about what has happened." Gwen, an erect man with rimless glasses, stood with one foot against the root of a hickory tree.

"There is great precedent for continuing the Open," said a man Morris recognized as a committee member from Massachusetts. "USGA officials, golfers themselves, have been stricken, some of them mortally, during the course of past tournaments, all of which have been completed in due process. Lightning very nearly struck tragically during the tournament in Chicago last year, and yet we never considered cancellation." The way he looked over the heads of the committeemen he might have been delivering an annual lecture at Harvard.

A number of heads were nodding in agreement. Each man in the trees was aware of the four hundred thousand dollars the Atlanta Golf Club had spent to put the course in shape for the Open, of the millions of dollars at stake for the network, of the hundreds of thousands required to operate the USGA for the coming year. No one mentioned any of those sums or circumstances.

Colburn said, "I have talked with Frank LeBaron of the PGA. He assured me the pros would rather play. Moving the

73

cup creates problems. But only two threesomes have played through the green. We would have to permit the present twosome to putt out at the cup they shot for. Activity in the lake could be disturbing to some. But no one wants to threaten the tournament.

"Do I hear a motion to continue the tournament under the conditions just described?" Morris heard two seconds. Hands were raised. "So voted," said Colburn. Morris did not miss the four arms that were raised against him.

10 ⊞

R UTLEDGE STOOD WITH HIS SHORT, THICK ARMS FOLDED, LOOK- ing over the water. The direct sun aged the gray in his lumpy suit. Morris waited beyond the green until the detective saw him. The other reporters still had not been allowed inside the rope barrier. The body was being lifted onto a stretcher. Morris stood as Rutledge moved toward him.

"Any chance of a golfer living all week?" Morris asked.

Neither of them felt the need to shake hands.

"So that's Whitlow," said Rutledge. "We're still looking for his ex-caddy, Thompson. I think we'll find him now."

Morris watched them lift the body into the motor vehicle. "Did he drown?"

"As far as I can tell. There's not a mark on him. But he belongs to Doc Moseley now. You were here when the boy found him. Why?" The "why" was sharp enough to irritate Morris.

"I'm paid to be here for the golf. I'm not responsible for life and death in this county."

"I mean, why did you happen to be at this particular spot?" There was no sharpness in his voice. He might have made an effort to keep it out.

"I was waiting for Dolan and a rookie to play through, if you like irony. They were on the tee. Whitlow was originally paired with them. I wanted to describe how Whitlow seemed so physically absent to the gallery.''

Morris was irritated with himself for explaining so much. He plunged on. ''I may have been the last person to see him alive. Or the next to last,'' he added.

Rutledge turned and looked him directly in the face with his round dark eyes.

''Déjà vu,'' said Morris. ''It's happening all over again.''

''Where did you see him?''

Morris again was surprised that Rutledge did not take notes. ''At the clubhouse, late in the afternoon. Whitlow suddenly missed his putter. He put it in his locker after every round.''

''In his locker? Is that normal?'' said Rutledge.

''For Whitlow, and a couple of others. It's the only putter he's ever had. It wasn't anywhere in the locker room. I planned to file a brief sidebar if it was truly lost. He only took twenty-seven putts yesterday. We looked. It wasn't in his bag. The kid, Harper, his caddy, was gone. The putter also wasn't in the press room where he'd been interviewed. Whitlow thought maybe he left it on the course. He didn't use it on eighteen. He chipped in from off the green. That left seventeen. It was almost dark. He started jogging toward the lake.''

''What time?'' asked Rutledge, still not taking notes.

''It must have been seven-thirty.''

''You didn't follow him?'' There was nothing implied in his voice.

''My knee was swelling. And you called,'' said Morris. ''If I hadn't met you at the coroner's, I might have waited to see if he found it.''

''Has his putter turned up?'' Rutledge looked around the green.

''I don't know. You can ask the caddy master at the clubhouse.''

''The ground here is a problem,'' said Rutledge. ''I understand it's been mowed since last night.''

''Sure,'' said Morris. ''And the caddies stepped off the pin placement at daylight. I think the whole city has stomped over the green. If there was a struggle I don't see how you'd know it.''

''He's been in the water all night, okay.''

Morris was surprised the lieutenant offered the information.

"Was he drinking?" asked Rutledge.

"He had a couple," said Morris. "At least one of them was a stiff one. Straight Scotch. But he wasn't drunk."

"Three ounces on an empty stomach? The jogging. Maybe he's woozy. Loses his balance on the incline. Loafers slip out from under him in the dark. Panic. It could happen."

"He also could have been pushed," said Morris.

"Pushed or not. Drunk or not, why couldn't he swim six feet?" asked Rutledge.

"He couldn't swim at all." For the second time, the detective looked him in the face with his dark eyes. "He was terrified of the water. I wrote about it. *Sports Illustrated* picked it up. He had to get medical permission to graduate from Houston. Some of the guys tried to throw him in a motel pool after his first win in Philadelphia. He went berserk. He put knots on several of their heads."

The sheriff, Goodwin, followed the body to his own vehicle. He had been careful not to claim jurisdiction for the investigation. Not with thirty thousand anxious people on the grounds, and two days of national television coming up. Let the cops worry about it. Golf's a game for city slickers, thought Morris. He heard the sheriff say again, "Betcha ten dollars he was fallin'-in drunk."

"Here comes your golf president," said Rutledge, ignoring the sheriff.

Colburn stopped between them. He seemed relieved to have Morris there. "With your permission, we voted to continue the tournament," he said to Rutledge. "We will move the cup, and keep this area roped off. The players understand you are putting divers in the water. We will keep a careful watch. We thank you, Lieutenant. We have an awful lot at stake, including the national championship."

"I want to speak with every player, briefly, as they finish," said Rutledge. "I also want my men to talk to their caddies. I'll give you a list of other officials I want to interview. Before they leave the course."

Colburn nodded his cooperation. The greenskeeping crew was ready to move the cup. Colburn joined them.

The two deaths kept drifting in and out of Morris's mind. There was no rational connection, but this time there was no question of suicide. Not by drowning. Not John Whitlow.

"Walk with me to the clubhouse," said Rutledge.

"You'll have to walk through three hundred writers," said Morris. A huge crowd was pressing against the line of guards. "You better give them a statement." Morris had already called in a brief notice to the press room over Colburn's walkie-talkie. "You give the statement," he said. "I'll bum us a golf cart and join you."

A battalion of writers surged against the rope off the seventeenth green. Several were shouting questions at Rutledge. He stood behind the rope and ignored them. Cameras were already focused on him.

"Are you all ready?" asked Rutledge. The reporters were quiet. Rutledge originated the words with great effort: "A body was recovered from the lake in front of the seventeenth green at Atlanta Golf Club at one-thirty this afternoon. The body has been identified as professional golfer John Whitlow of Houston, Texas. Preliminary examination indicates he had been in the lake overnight. Cause of death has not yet been determined. It's very likely he drowned. That's all we know at the moment."

Writers began shouting questions at Rutledge, and even at Morris. A number of them were running for their typewriters. Rutledge climbed in the cart and Morris started for the clubhouse. They were soon swallowed up by the crowd strung along the eighteenth fairway.

"Why did you say you might have been 'the next to last person' to see Whitlow alive?" Rutledge kept looking straight ahead.

"There's no chance both of these deaths were accidents. Or suicides," said Morris. He had known from the moment the body came up out of the lake there would be no holding back of any information. "I saw Whitlow's wife last night." Rutledge had his dark eyes on him.

"She was with a guy. I didn't see his face but I'm sure he was a golfer. They were swimming in the Peachtree-Forsyth Hotel pool. About nine-thirty. Sans bathing suits." Rutledge's eyes did not blink. "I'm sure she saw me."

"Who was the golfer?"

"I didn't see his face. I saw them both underwater when I dived in the pool. I couldn't swear to it, but I'm sure he was Al Morgan. Just the way he moved in the water. He's an

77

older guy. Married. A bunch of kids. Having trouble with his game. It could be messy."

Rutledge only nodded. "What's his wife like—Whitlow's?"

"Maybe a couple of years older than he was. Twenty-five or so. Dark. Pretty. Tough. From New Orleans. They'd been married two years and separated once."

"What else do you know about Whitlow? That I should know."

Morris stopped the cart. They were free of the reporters. "He was a great young golfer, the best to come along since Tommy Fryer. But he had a pronounced sway in his backswing. After a year on the tour, he became convinced he would never win a major title if he didn't correct it. Publicly, he said to hell with the Masters and the U.S. Open, all he wanted was the money. But he took his swing to Rossi last December. Privately."

Morris was surprised to see Rutledge taking notes. "Whitlow didn't have the patience to stay with a rebuilt swing. He missed the cut twice on the winter tour, and went back to his old sway. Rossi was disgusted with him. And disappointed. He needed a teaching success on the men's tour. Rossi needled him as late as Wednesday, said he was still 'coming off the ball.' "

"Any reason you didn't tell me all that Wednesday night?" asked Rutledge, the slightest edge in his voice.

"It didn't seem to have anything to do with what happened to Rossi. It still doesn't. Nobody throws anybody off a hotel balcony over a backswing. And then drowns himself in a lake."

"Unless, maybe, he doesn't know or care what he's doing," said Rutledge. "Remember, this is your story."

"Yeah. You explain to me what it means."

"Who else didn't get along with John Whitlow?"

"The PGA tour," said Morris. "He was a brassy kid. A merciless competitor. No nerves. There hasn't been a putter like him since Travis Walker in his prime." Morris knew he was talking to avoid thinking. "Did you read today's sports page?" he asked.

"Only to check the Open scores," said Rutledge.

"I had an item on the wire. The players' agent, Everette Holland, is suing Whitlow for one and a half million dollars.

For breach of contract. Ev is not one of the greedy 'new breed.' He's the last honest agent in sports."

Rutledge was sitting straight up in the cart. "A lot of honest men come unglued for a lot less than a million dollars."

Morris felt hot and unclean. He needed a shower and a drink. He wouldn't get either for a while. He started the cart again and guided it to a stop in front of the clubhouse.

"Morris, I'll tell you something. I'm scared."

It was Morris's turn to look at Rutledge. He seemed to have slept in his gray suit.

"It's too late to worry about the dead. I'm scared of what happens next. You know these people, Morris. Upside down and under water." Morris did not smile. "I've taken over the club manager's office. I'm going to question the players. I'll tape it. I want you to listen."

"I'm a newspaperman," said Morris.

"You know golf," said Rutledge. "It's a separate world. And it all moves out of town in three days."

"Murder is your business." Morris said the word without a sense of reality.

"It's your friends who are dead," said Rutledge, swinging his weight off the cart, not looking back as he walked toward the clubhouse.

Morris felt his knee with both hands. It was early afternoon, and already it was swollen.

11 ▦

TOMMY FRYER'S FINE BLOND HAIR WAS TOO DAMP TO FLOAT above his forehead. He leaned on his putter and ignored the ball on the green.

It would drop him a stroke below three others tied at one-thirty-eight. The momentum of the tournament was recovering with the ritual of play. But the people were quieter, and the golfers hardly spoke.

"Dinner he makes it," LeBaron whispered to Morris, who was startled to hear so natural a proposition in the strange quiet.

Fryer looked at the leader board. Now he was looking at the sky. The long-range forecast was for rain. Morris could see lightning far in the distance. Fryer seemed to shiver, but he looked around the enormous gallery at the eighteenth hole without emotion.

A sixty-eight wouldn't be THE round, but it would do for the lead, thought Morris. Tomorrow he might take the grass right down to the roots. He was capable of it.

"Keep it in the hole," said Watson, his caddy, directly under them.

Fryer turned to look at him without belief.

He was hardly balanced over the ball before he sent it rolling, hugging the ground, gathering momentum into the slope, now dying of its own weight, barely turning, the grain of the green holding it against gravity, until it fell inevitably into the cup. Fryer turned, grinning. Watson lifted the pin and flat high over his head.

"Tomorrow they'll have to call him long distance to catch him," LeBaron said to Morris, who nodded in agreement.

"I'll see you in the clubhouse later, for a drink," said Morris.

"Could you tell us what the detective asked you?" Morris had dutifully asked the question of each of the leaders as he appeared in the press room.

Tommy Fryer was uncertain if he should answer. "I think you had better ask him," he said. "They were just routine questions."

Enough of the players had answered openly for Morris to know what they had been asked. Two questions interested him. All of them had obviously been asked where they were staying, and where they had eaten dinner Wednesday night. Rutledge meant it—he was afraid. But why Rossi and Whitlow? Or if Rossi, why Whitlow? Morris could not get the question out of his mind. Twenty-five years' difference in their ages. They lived a thousand miles apart. One playing. One teaching. Who could hate them enough to kill them both? And for what reason? It made no sense.

Morris wrote one word on his notepad: WHY. He underlined it. It was the only question. From the splash-second the paramedic hauled the drowned body onto the front of the green, he had asked himself that one word: *WHY?* It did not occur to him after that moment that Jim Rossi and John Whitlow had not been murdered. Before, he was prepared to accept the logic of Rossi as a suicide. Though it made no sense. Now he could not imagine how he had ever considered it.

Morris wrote another word on his notepad: *WHO?* But his mind was not yet ready to weigh it.

Fryer finished describing his round. Morris picked up his key shots and putts without having to think about them.

"I shot sixty-eight," said Fryer. "It could have been sixty-five. I'll shoot it tomorrow, or Sunday. With John gone, all we want to do is get the tournament over. Somebody has to win it. It might as well be me."

Morris moved deeper into the locker room. Lee Washburn sat over his golf shoes without malice. He seemed in rare control of himself.

"Well played," said Morris, of his sixty-nine. Again Washburn had let two shots slip on the last three holes. But there was no iron contempt in his long face to drive him deeper inside himself.

"Four off the pace is the same as even on this golf course," said Washburn. "I'm liable to par the last two holes one round and win the thing."

Travis Walker stood up in his bare feet. His own sixty-nine seemed to have put springs in his legs. "Lee, did you lose your ride? I never saw you sit around a locker room."

Washburn looked up. "What do you make of it? The investigation?" He included Morris in his question.

"The detective?" asked Walker. "He seems to know what he's doing."

"What do you think happened to John?" asked Washburn.

"I don't believe in that much coincidence. Whitlow could barely stand the sight of water in a glass."

Washburn looked to Morris. "I want to hear what the coroner says. But I don't think either death was an accident," said Morris.

"Do you know anything, Morris?" asked Travis.

"Nothing you don't know."

"I had to drive back out here last night," said Washburn.

He seemed relieved to be telling it. "I left my wallet in my locker. Quite a bit of money in it. I didn't see John. His locker was still open. I closed it. The detective wouldn't let me up about it. If I ever throw anybody in a water hazard, it'll be myself."

"Me, I'll cut my throat on a four-putt green," said Travis, laughing.

"What do the police do next?" asked Washburn, a grin failing him. He stood up carefully, holding his back.

Golfer's disease, thought Morris. One day the bad back puts you in the desert, at a posh resort, if you're lucky. And if you don't live up to your nickname, "Nasty."

"I talked with LeBaron," said Morris. "They are beefing up the security force. And bringing in a few units of the National Guard. You won't have room for a practice swing."

"To protect us?" said Walker, his iron grip on Washburn's shoulder. It sounded ridiculous. They both laughed.

"Whoever throws this twosome out of a hotel window will be easy to find," said Morris. "He'll be nine feet tall." Morris tried to laugh with them.

Travis lifted his socks from his locker. "I tell you one thing. I wouldn't want that pudgy detective looking for *me*. He's got a grip like my old man. When he looks at you, he seems to know what you don't want to say."

Morris walked deeper into the room, chilled by the air conditioning.

Art Howard leaned his elbows on his knees, swelling his stomach over his belt. He looked too exhausted to move.

"I can't remember one hole I played," he said to Morris. "I can't get these shoes off and my feet are killin' me."

Morris could still see the astonishment on his caddy's face at the way Art's irons were flying into the heart of the greens.

Suddenly Art was laughing. "Can you believe three sixty-nines dressing in the same room." He dropped his head again. "I can't remember one pass I made at the ball." He looked up, as if Morris had just appeared in the room. "I can't remember what that heavy little detective asked me. I can't remember what I said. You were here with Whitlow yesterday?"

"I was here," said Morris.

"I tried to think of the sound of Whitlow's voice, of what he said. All I could remember was how tired I was. Same as now. I don't know which four girls. I didn't see 'em. Sure I was at the Central dinner. You were in the elevator!" Art accused Morris.

Morris was amazed. Art was drunk. He had never known him to drink more than a beer, before this week. He wasn't even mixing his Scotch. He better save some for tomorrow, thought Morris. He was two shots from leading the United States Open.

It was 7:48 P.M. The digital preciseness of his wristwatch glowed in the near dark. Morris dropped his arm as he walked toward the lake. He could not see the water. It made a flat pool of night under the forms of the trees. He could not see the divers. He could hear them.

"Did you get the other one?" someone asked, his voice oddly young in the black wetsuit that disappeared in the shadows of the trees.

"It's in the van," said the older, heavier voice from the lake.

"Fellows, I'm John Morris. With the Associated Press." He used his best official voice. He might have been running for office.

"Watch it," said the young voice, lifting a long cylinder into the van parked between them. "Jesus. Some day. We've gone through about six of these." He let the spent cylinder of oxygen drop in the van.

"Find anything?" asked Morris.

"Not as much junk as you might think," said the larger figure, coming up from the lake, dangling two sets of flippers in one hand. "Mostly it's mud to your knees. And plenty of golf balls. A few clubs. No more golfers." He laughed without apology.

"We found a shoe, a loafer," said the younger one. "We're pretty sure it was his. Found it where he came out, in about six feet of water."

"Is one of the clubs a putter?"

"I think so. We're no golfers." The older man stuck out a meaty right hand. "My name is Mike Jenkins," he said. "My partner is Larry Martin." They all shook hands in the near dark.

"Where did you find the putter?"

All three of them jumped at the voice that came from under

the trees behind the seventeenth green. It was Rutledge. He did not have to introduce himself. The two divers obviously knew him.

Jenkins lifted a small armload of clubs from inside the van. Two were broken. The club he held up was a putter. The cabin light was now on in the van. Morris could see that it was a blade putter, the same as Whitlow's.

"No need to be careful," said Rutledge, "not with it covered with mud." He handed the putter to Morris.

"That's the type," said Morris. "Whitlow used this one, or one exactly like it."

"Right here," said Jenkins. He took a light out of the van and was shining it at the edge of the water, in front of the green. "We tied a piece of cord to that peg. There's a brick on the other end, in the lake, exactly where Larry found the putter." He lifted the cord gently.

"It was out there forty feet," said Jenkins.

"Forty feet!" said Rutledge, before he could control his voice.

"That doesn't count the six feet of water it was in," said Larry.

The dark was over them now absolutely, except where the light shone. Morris walked to the steep slope in front of the green. He laid his cane behind him on the green. He felt abandoned without it, his stiff knee all but useless on the sharp incline. He stepped down toward the water, leaving his balance in midair, his foot searching for the ground under him, twisting until he was falling, his stiff leg suddenly cold up to the thigh in water.

Rutledge and the young diver dragged him to his feet. "You always rehearse like a madman?" Rutledge choked back a laugh.

"Funny thing, I forgot I was holding the putter, but I nearly squeezed it in two," said Morris. "Maybe I was afraid of throwing it back in the lake. What if I had been Whitlow and had sunk three hundred thousand dollars worth of putts with it?"

"Forty feet is a helluva ways," said Rutledge. He turned to the two divers. "Bolton is waiting with a couple of steaks. He'll help you with the report. We'll bring the putter and the shoe."

They cranked the van, leaving the lake darker in the closing night. Rutledge flicked on a light. "Do you think he could have thrown it that far?"

"I don't think he threw it at all. If he had slipped he would simply have found himself knee deep in water. He trotted down here looking for the putter. He was in a panic about it. He would have been an easy target, bending over on that incline. He wouldn't have seen anyone behind him."

"A frightened man can do anything," said Rutledge, "even sling a putter forty feet."

"Even commit murder?" said Morris. It was the second time he had said the word.

"Do you think someone's afraid?" asked Rutledge.

"I only know two golfers are dead. I've been out here twenty-one years, and that's twice as many suicides and accidental deaths as I've seen. If you don't count automobiles and airplanes."

Rutledge swung the light toward the clubhouse. "I've been questioning your friends," he said.

"What did you learn?"

"I'm not sure. I know your friends now, but I still don't know golf." Morris did not miss the way he pronounced the word *friends*.

"Bolton is holding the tapes. If you want to hear them."

"Are they legal?"

Rutledge swung the light on him. "As legal as murder." His voice was cold—as cold as the wet trousers on Morris's leg.

12 ⌗

JULIA SULLIVAN WAS SITTING ON THE FOOT OF THE BED WITH HER legs crossed under her.

"Morris."

He closed the door behind him. She knew that she looked younger than she was, and vulnerable behind the large octagonal glasses. His own face was on the television screen.

"Look who's famous," she said, as the network cut to a commercial.

He put a large hand on top of her short hair.

"It sounded so strange on television, to hear your first name: John Morris, of the Associated Press. I'm used to us: two last names, Sullivan and Morris, like a vaudeville act."

Her hair was very fine under his hand.

"It's terrible about John Whitlow. It's damn unfair not to give him a chance to grow up. What happened to your pants leg? What's going on, Morris?"

The double bed tilted as he sat beside her. "It's easy," he said. "Somebody's killing my golfers."

"Jim, too?"

"Sure."

"I hate it." She sat quietly, with her head up. "But I'm glad he didn't jump."

"Whitlow didn't jump either," said Morris. "He couldn't swim. He was afraid of the water."

"Then who?"

"The police have narrowed it down to one hundred forty-eight golfers, thirty thousand spectators, and a city of one and a half million. And me. Everybody could have done it."

"Sure. You did it for the publicity." She leaned against him. His bulk was like a refuge.

"How could a man be thrown over the balcony of a twenty-one-story lobby and nobody see it?" asked Morris. "Sick luck," he said. "How could a golfer be pushed into the lake of a U.S. Open course, at dark, and nobody hear it? Easy," he said.

"Why don't we stop the tournament?"

"You mean, why don't we stop golf? What do we do, take our accidental deaths on to Chicago?"

"Maybe it's just an Atlanta killer." She shivered against him. The word, *killer*, took on a new reality when she said it.

"It's possible. I don't believe it. He has to be someone in golf. Or someone who follows golf."

"Why?"

It was the question Rutledge had asked an hour ago. "Because of Rossi," said Morris. "He was an occasional TV announcer. His books sold well, but he was still an anonymous person. I've been with him all over America, and I can't remember ten strangers coming up and asking for his autograph. Whoever killed him knew him.''

Morris did not add: and, I believe, had an appointment with him. He could see Rossi, his slight weight exactly balanced, turning his head, watching for someone on the balcony, minutes before he fell. He often kept appointments at odd hours during a tournament. Especially with players. But also with agents and writers and caddies.

''What's all that?'' Sullivan leaned pleasantly across him to look at the machine on the floor.

''Tape recordings,'' said Morris. ''You might want to throw me out. 'Tricky Dick' Rutledge taped his interviews of the suspects.''

''Dirty tapes?'' She laughed behind her glasses.

''The dirtiest kind. Rutledge questioned the players. And others. He didn't tell them he was taping them.''

''He wants you to listen?''

Morris nodded.

''You trust him too much,'' she said. ''But he's right. You know the players better than anybody.'' She pulled her legs up tighter under her. ''Do you think the killer's on the tape?''

''I can't get to the question, *who*,'' said Morris. ''I can't get past *why*. Rossi had strong opinions. He was right too much. He could be stubborn, but he was also fair. That can be harder to take than stubbornness.''

Morris lifted the tape recorder onto the bed. ''John Whitlow irritated everybody. The more success he had, the less attractive he became. All he needed was an Open title to be impossible. But, tell me this,'' said Morris. ''What did they have in common that would make anyone kill them both?''

''What about murder?'' asked Sullivan, looking up through her octagonal lenses.

''What do you mean?''

''Maybe Whitlow saw Rossi killed. Or the murderer thought he did.''

''It doesn't make sense,'' said Morris. ''He had all night and all day to call the police.''

''What's the word . . . blackmail?''

''Possibly, but you can't make a living killing your victims.''

Morris checked the time mechanism on the tape recorder against the time coded list of names. He could select the person he wanted to hear.

"I can go back to my hotel," he said seriously, "if you're tired of this."

"Don't you dare move. Except to change your pants. You're drenching our bed, and probably catching pneumonia."

"I fell in the lake," said Morris, pulling off the wet trousers.

"Sure you didn't fall in the bar?"

Morris ignored her, and ordered two steaks, rare, to be sent up.

Morris advanced the tape and turned on the sound. Rutledge's voice was higher than you thought when you were seeing him speak. You couldn't mistake Jackie Whitlow's airy voice. You could hear the door open. It was quite a tape recorder.

"Mrs. Whitlow. Lieutenant Rutledge of the Atlanta Police Department." Sergeant Bolton did not use the word *homicide*.

Rutledge hardly gave her time to sit down. "Do you know where your husband spent last night?" He offered no human comfort for his death.

"No." There was no hesitation.

"When did you last see him?"

"Yesterday. We had breakfast and I drove him to the golf course. I followed him the last nine holes. He never saw anyone when he was playing. He played beautifully. I waited in the parking lot until it was dark. He was always the last to leave. He was only truly happy on the golf course, or in the clubhouse. I went inside. He wasn't there. He must've caught a ride. . . . I drove back to the hotel, but he wasn't there. He never came to the room." Her voice did not falter.

"Were you having trouble?"

"I think you'd better tell me how John died."

"Drowned. We're almost sure. We'll have to make tests."

"Oh God!" All the disguise was gone from her voice. She made noises, but not crying noises. "He was terrified of water. He couldn't swim." Then she was unable to speak.

"Would you like a drink?" Rutledge might have been at a reception.

"Please. Anything." There were ice sounds. "How did he get . . . in the lake?"

"We don't know. That's what I'm here to find out."

"He hated even being close to the water." She sounded frightened.

"You didn't answer my question. Were the two of you having trouble?"

"No." She put the glass down on something. "We weren't your All-American couple." Bitterness suddenly lifted her voice. "It wasn't the first time he hadn't come home, but the other times we were fighting. He was no saint. Neither am I." She said it defiantly. "He was playing well. We rarely fought when he was playing well. Not even money mattered as much to him as playing well. Not that we didn't fight about money."

"What did you do last night?"

"You know," she said, her voice hard with awareness. "I ate dinner alone. A friend happened to be sitting at the next table. It was an accident. I don't care what you believe. What happened afterward wasn't an accident. I was angry. We had a few drinks. We went swimming." Her voice changed. "What we did in the pool was crazy."

"Who was he?"

"You know who he was. It just happened."

"Morris, what's that *click, click, click?*"

"That's Rutledge snapping his ballpoint pen." Morris backed up the tape.

"Was John having any unusual trouble? Anyone bothering him, threatening him?" It sounded like a serious question in a bad movie.

"He didn't have friends. Or enemies. The only people he knew were golfers. He lived to beat them all." Her voice tightened. "He was being sued. Maybe they killed him for the insurance money."

"Why do you say 'killed him'?" asked Rutledge.

"Of course he was killed." She seemed surprised that he might question it. There were sounds of another drink.

"Was he heavily insured?"

"His agent, Holland, insured him for two million dollars." She didn't stumble over the figure. "Half of it goes to me."

"Why did John stop his lessons with Jim Rossi?" Rutledge sounded tired, older.

"He couldn't play that way. He missed the cut two straight weeks. He was impossible to live with. He was going crazy."

"Did he and Rossi argue?"

"They fought. On the telephone. John said terrible things about him, that he was old, finished. Mr. Rossi was always nice to me, but I was glad when John went back to his old swing."

"When did you last see Rossi?"

"In the clubhouse, Wednesday. I didn't speak."

"Where did you eat dinner Wednesday?"

"At our hotel. The Peachtree-Forsyth."

"What time?"

"About nine o'clock. John joined me later. He was talking to his lawyers."

"Did he leave the hotel?"

"No, I don't think so. He wouldn't get off the phone, so I went down to the restaurant for a drink. John was terrified when he lost his swing. He blamed Rossi, but he didn't kill him. Someone killed them both. I'm sure you know that."

She put down her glass again. That was it.

"A tough lady," said Sullivan.

"And a rich one."

" 'No friends. Just golfers.' Is that the tour now, Morris?"

"That's it. And money. Monty would never have understood it. Remember when it was golf and friends? Even for Hogan."

The man on the tape was Dolan, all right, his voice as brittle as himself.

"Let's get it over with. I could die of pneumonia in this air conditioning." Morris remembered how he had sweated through his shirt.

Rutledge ignored him with his own voice. "Did Whitlow seem himself yesterday?"

"We didn't speak," said Dolan. Morris could see his dark eyes, deep set in the burned-out texture of his skin. "I didn't know him. I was off the tour last year when he broke in."

"Did you like him?"

"I couldn't stand him." Their voices were a battle of monotones.

"Why was that?"

"He won too easy. He came out here and never had it tough. He was a snotty, cocky kid. He could putt. It made up for his lousy swing. One day he would have eaten his share of dirt, like the rest of us. With that sway he would've. I'm sorry we won't get to see it."

Morris could hear Rutledge shifting in his chair. He knew he was trying to hold himself still.

"When did you last see him?"

"In the locker room, yesterday. About seven P.M. He was looking for his putter. I guess he was going to sleep with it. I told him I counted his strokes not his clubs."

"Who else was in the locker room? No hurry," said Rutledge.

Morris tried to count them in his own mind.

"I couldn't possibly see or remember them all. It's a big room." He took his time. "Travis and Kirkland." A pause. "Al Morgan and his bottle, that's one. Ward. Washburn was there, but he left. I don't know. Fryer. Yeah, Art Howard. Now there's a swing that could cure cancer. He was a good player once. I know there were others. I can't remember who."

Me, Morris said to himself.

"What time did you leave the clubhouse?"

Dolan's black eyes would be darker. "Probably eight o'clock. I had a drink at the bar. Drove back to the hotel, the Peachtree-Forsyth. Room eleven-twenty-five. Had dinner sent up. Went to bed early. Alone." The last word was bitten off.

"Did you know Whitlow couldn't swim?" Rutledge ignored the hostility in his voice.

"No. I heard it on the seventeenth tee, when they found him. Everybody in golf knew it but me. I'm surprised he didn't drown in the shower."

"Were you friends with Jim Rossi?"

"Not really." Dolan was careful to control his voice. "He could strike the ball. He was no putter. You could say the same thing about me. In fact, Rossi did. He liked my swing. Thought my grip was too strong. He taught like an old maid. I took two lessons from him. I couldn't hit it like a girl. On TV, he was okay. What could he say?"

"You saw him on the balcony before he fell." It was not a question.

"From the elevator." Dolan sounded concerned. "Five of us. Morgan, Washburn, Art Howard and the writer, Morris . . ."

It gave Morris a chill to hear his own name. For the first time, he felt embarrassed listening.

"... Morgan, I believe, noticed him first. He was just standing there."

"Alone?"

"Yeah. I didn't see anyone else."

"Was he walking?"

"No. Just standing there. Looking. Just waiting there."

"Were you all together at the dinner?" asked Rutledge.

"Well, no. It was an Airlines banquet. We wear their silly caps. There were several tables." Dolan was actually nervous. "Service was slow. People got up and went after their own drinks."

"What time did you leave?"

"Me? About ten-thirty. We didn't leave together. I may have left last, or first. I don't know."

That was all. They seemed to be walking toward the door.

"Oh," said Rutledge. "Was Whitlow drinking?"

Morris could imagine Dolan's mind, turning precisely, in frames; it was his greatest strength as a player, measuring his shots, selecting his clubs.

"Yes. He had a couple, maybe three drinks. He wasn't drunk."

The door closed.

"Your detective frightened him," said Sullivan. "I never heard Dolan afraid before."

Morris mixed them another pair of drinks. "One more tape before dinner?" he asked.

"It's like daytime TV. You hate yourself for watching, but you can't help it."

"... Did you get along with Whitlow?"

"I get along with everybody. There are those who hate my guts, and those who just hate me. All of them are willin' to drink my Scotch."

"Al Morgan," said Morris.

"I have a weakness for him. I can't help it. Bad as he is."

Morris rolled her over on the bed. "You liked the wicked type."

"Your tape's running." Julia was laughing at him. He let her up to rewind it.

"... I don't know if it's true, or if it has any meaning for you," said Morgan. "Whitlow told me. The only time I ever saw him really drunk. After he missed the cut this winter in

92

Los Angeles. He said Washburn's ball moved in the rough last year at St. Andrews, when he addressed it. That Washburn never looked up, like he didn't see it. Didn't call a stroke penalty on himself. He went on to birdie the seventy-first hole and beat Fryer by a shot. The British Open title is worth a bundle in endorsements. Maybe Whitlow was seeing things.''

''Why didn't Whitlow complain? Couldn't he call the penalty?''

''I don't know. He was really drunk in L.A. He swore it was true.''

''Did he tell Fryer about it?''

''I don't know. They weren't close.''

''That's baloney,'' said Morris to Julia. ''I followed Washburn on that hole. I don't believe Whitlow was even near him in the rough. But I couldn't swear to it.''

''Shhhh,'' said Sullivan.

''. . . When did you see Whitlow last?''

''In the locker room. Thursday. He was drinking my Scotch, out of my glass.''

''Anything seem to bother him?'' Rutledge was fumbling for a question.

''Yeah. He shot sixty-seven. He thought he shoulda shot fifty-seven. He was a greedy kid.'' There was a wait. ''He wasn't too happy with his agent, Ev Holland. Ev was suing him for a million or so dollars. Nothing to get excited about.''

''What did he say, exactly?''

''He was talking to Tommy Fryer. Ev's his agent, too. Or was. John said, 'Tell your friend to get his hand out of my pocket . . .' I didn't know Ev was that way.'' Morgan laughed. ''He got a rise out of Fryer. Takes a lot to get a rise out of Fryer. He told John to save his money for his lawyers. Told him not to build a shelf for the trophy yet. The boy wonders were after each other.''

''You still have a weakness for him?'' asked Morris.

''Ssshhhhhhh.''

''Do you know Whitlow's family?'' Rutledge avoided the word *wife*.

''I know his wife. That's family.''

Strange, thought Morris, Rutledge didn't pursue it.

''Did you know Whitlow couldn't swim?''

''I knew better than most. I tried to help throw him in a pool in Philadelphia. He'd won his first tournament. He nearly broke three necks, including mine. You couldn't believe how strong the Young Lion was." His voice quit laughing. "Or how scared he was of the water."

Rutledge asked him to describe what he had seen on the elevator.

". . . I spotted him. Rossi always looked funny, undressed, without his Hogan cap. I said something like: 'There's the Great Rossi.' "

"What was he doing?"

"Just . . . waiting."

"*Waiting*," imitated Morris. "Who for, Sullivan? That's the question.

"There was no one else on the balcony?" Rutledge seemed bored, hardly waiting for an answer.

"The four crazies," said Morgan.

Morris could hear Rutledge shifting again in his chair.

"Who?"

"Four girls. Groupies. They were on the opposite side of the lobby from him. You couldn't miss 'em. Long blonde hair, and they dress alike. I saw them on the course earlier in the day."

"Who are they?"

"Girls. Not kids. They follow the tour now and then, between jobs. I don't know their names. One of them is Jill. One, I think, is Lisa."

"How well do you know them?"

"Biblical *know*?" Morgan laughed. "Once I was with them. About three years ago, in Vegas, I think. A ready crew. But I stay away from them."

"Why?"

"They're into this, and that."

"Drugs?"

"Maybe. They can be a rowdy team. They'll be on the course. You can bet on it. You'll know them. They're always together. Just follow the leader. They love a leader." Morgan could not resist. "They have been known to love a runnerup."

Julia Sullivan laughed out loud, in spite of herself.

Morris switched off the tape recorder. "How can our detective find a double murderer? He can't find four blonde groupie girls or an old, alcoholic caddy."

Both of them jumped at the knock on the door. Morris

struggled with his leg to get off the too soft bed. The bellboy was there with their steaks. Morris overtipped him in relief.

Sullivan put down her fork and swallowed. "That tastes better than sin."

"It's age that does it," said Morris. "The sins of the flesh give way to plain appetite."

She threw a pillow over his head. "What about the sin of murder?" she said suddenly serious. "What did the players tell you about these interviews?"

"Pretty much what Rutledge asked them. Some wouldn't discuss what he asked. Tommy Fryer for one." Morris found him on the tape, and let it run while they ate. Fryer said he had not seen Rossi Wednesday night. He was with his wife in his own hotel, the Forsyth. She picked him up in the parking lot Thursday after his words with Whitlow. Nothing.

"You know what he didn't say?" Morris did not wait for a reply. "He didn't say he saw Jackie Whitlow skinny dipping with Al Morgan. I think our boy has a soft spot for her the same size as the one you have for Big Al. Quit eating my french fries." Morris raised his fork in defense of his plate.

Later, Morris remembered something. "Funny, Art Howard was all but drunk in the locker room, and tired."

"Art? You're kidding," said Sullivan. "He doesn't drink."

"He couldn't lift his head. Couldn't remember what Rutledge had asked him, or what he had answered. But you can't feel too sorry for a man who just shot sixty-nine." Morris fumbled to find Art on the tape.

"A sweet guy," said Julia. "He was born an old bachelor. Too tight to get married. Too tight to have a girl. Don't they have girls in Louisiana?"

Morris found Art on the tape. He was remembering that Morgan had spotted Rossi from the elevator.

"The 'Great Rossi,' " Art quoted. "Rossi was great at watchin' somebody else hit the ball. He didn't teach golf. He taught ping-pong. Givin' lessons up in the hotel air, to his own self. That was Rossi."

Morris rewound the tape. Art was the only one of them so far who *hadn't* said anything about Rossi's *waiting,* he thought. He also didn't mention Al and Dolan kidding him about his swing. Probably he heard it so much he didn't hear it at all.

Art did remember Whitlow looking for his putter. "That blade's so old you gotta get a tetanus shot to pick it up," he

95

said. "Whitlow couldn't sleep without it locked in the bank vault. He's sleepin' now, I guess." Art said he drove back to his hotel, alone. And went to bed, alone.

"Poor Art," said Sullivan.

Morris switched the recorder off while they finished the apple pie.

Sullivan lay back on the bed with a groan of satisfaction. He patted her flat stomach. "Where in God's name do you put fourteen ounces of steak and two beers?"

"It's an old Colorado trick. They only teach it in the mountains." She punched him in his meaty side.

Morris flipped on the tape recorder. Ev Holland seemed to be there, sweating, in the room.

". . . I was suin' him." His voice was almost a squeak. ". . . for one point five million dollars. We had a three-year contract. He told me Wednesday he wadn' gonna honor it. He told me to sue him. I was suin' him."

"Did he give a reason?"

"He wouldn't even talk about it."

"Do you have other clients?"

"Tommy Fryer was a client. But he's not renewin' after the summer. He told me a year ago. Tommy's okay."

"Was Whitlow insured?" Rutledge leveled the words at him.

"For two million dollars," said Holland.

"Who are the beneficiaries?"

"The corporation and his wife."

"What corporation?"

"My corporation: E. V. Enterprises. That's what I'm called, Ev."

Morris stopped the recorder. "That's not the business name Ev always uses. It's . . . L.A. Sports, for Louisiana. His partners live there. I wonder if Ev's pulled an end run on his partners, with the insurance. He's got rough partners."

Morris switched the tape back on. Ev said he had followed Whitlow through the seventeenth hole. Somebody else left him at the seventeenth hole, thought Morris. Ev said he hung around the clubhouse. Had a couple of beers. Back to the Royal Motel in the low-rent district. He said he hadn't been in the Peachtree Towers Hotel Wednesday. He'd been in his room, alone, he said.

"Poor Ev," said Julia. "Always alone."

"But not poor anymore," said Morris.

Now Rutledge was working his pen, *click, click, click*. He seemed too nervous to sit down. He kept walking around the room. Travis Walker must have been sitting, waiting. Morris laughed. The tough-guy detective couldn't squeeze out a question.

"I understand he drowned. Last night." Travis's voice was so remarkably familiar in the air. "I saw him in the locker room, after he finished his round." Travis was moving the interview by himself. "I didn't speak to him. I was still hot about the way he treated my old caddy, Old Thompson. On Wednesday. Thompson's a drunk, and his health is bad. Whitlow fired him."

"What happened?" Morris was surprised that Rutledge's voice was back to normal.

"Whitlow deliberately sprayed his practice shots. Old Thompson ran them down until he was sick. He's got no business caddying. But he was the best, once. He didn't deserve that."

"What kind of a fellow was Whitlow?"

"A hungry young kid. Maybe we all were once. Maybe he would have grown up." There was no conviction in his voice.

Travis did not remember seeing Whitlow's putter.

"Were you a friend of Rossi's?"

"Oh, yes. He hated my swing." Travis laughed. "Hell, it never bothered me. It got the ball where I wanted to hit it. I thought he was the fairest announcer in golf. His concept of the swing was old fashioned, but sound. I liked him. Can I ask you a question?"

Morris was again embarrassed to be listening.

"Do you think somebody killed them both?"

"I have no evidence to indicate it. I'm not a great believer in coincidence," said Rutledge.

"I never believed in it at all," said Travis.

Morris was pleased. Travis Walker could dominate the detective the same way he dominated the writers.

"Travis is the top of the line," said Sullivan. "Where do you place your order for his model?"

"I thought you liked 'em wicked."

"I'm bushed," she said, lying back on the bed.

"Two more quickies," said Morris.

*   *   *

Lee Washburn had not exaggerated. Rutledge wouldn't let him up about coming back to the clubhouse to get his billfold. Did he see Whitlow? Why did he close Whitlow's locker? Whom did he see? On and on. Washburn sounded plenty scared. Before that, he described seeing Rossi. He didn't describe him as waiting. But he said, "He was there, the same old Rossi, swinging an imaginary club, looking for somebody."

"Hear that," said Morris. "*Looking* is the same as *waiting*." All the rest was routine.

Into the room came the strangely high voice, equally as well known as Travis Walker's deep one. Morris could see his blond hair and square face. Yet Kirkland, the greatest player in golf, did not seem to unnerve Rutledge as Travis had. There was no *click*, *click* of his pen.

". . . Whitlow was carrying a drink through the locker room. I didn't see his putter. He was upset about misplacing it."

"Did he appear to be drunk?" asked Rutledge.

"I never saw him drunk in the two years he was on the tour. He was an intense young man. He wasn't interested in anything that didn't happen on the golf course."

"Did you know Rossi well?"

"Yes, I did. He interviewed me many times. He was good company. He knew the golf swing. Of course, we go at it with a little bigger arc, with more leg drive these days. Jim, as you may know, had worked with Whitlow. John had a pronounced sway in his swing. He would never have realized his potential until he corrected it. He didn't have the patience to work it out. Do you believe someone killed them both?"

Sullivan squeezed Morris's arm.

"I'm concerned. I don't have any evidence to justify it," said Rutledge. "Were you shocked at Rossi's death?"

"Yes. At first I thought he must have jumped. Maybe his health. But now . . ." He left the sentence unfinished. Then Kirkland said, "The day he fell, he was on the practice tee. He asked me something rather strange."

Morris heard Rutledge twist in his chair.

"He asked if I was satisfied with the pro at my club in Ohio. Jim couldn't have needed a job."

"What did you tell him?"

"I told him I had a good man. I wanted to ask him what he needed, but there were people around. Any club in America would have wanted Rossi. It bothers me I didn't make an effort to see him later."

Rutledge sounded puzzled. "Don't let it bother you. From what we know, he had a lifetime position at St. Simons."

The rest was formality. Morris turned the machine to "record" and began to erase what he had heard. He would listen to a few more interviews in the morning. He had taken notes. And he could remember what had been said, as if he had written the script.

"I'll buy you a drink if you'll set out the dishes," said Sullivan.

13 ⊞

ONLY THE ERRATIC LIGHT FROM THE MUTE TELEVISION SET washed over the room. Sullivan was asleep. Morris got to his feet, careful not to rock the bed. He pressed against the top of his digital watch. The red numerals, 10:17, appeared and lingered on the face. The hotel health room closed at eleven. His bathing suit was damp and pulled reluctantly up over his legs. He felt to be sure he had a room key in the pockets of his old slacks, and slid his feet into a pair of worn loafers. Sullivan slept with the colored lights from the television playing soundlessly over her face. Morris walked through the door, leading the way with his cane.

The kid in the locker room was still reading his textbook. It pleased Morris that the boy did not know him or any of the golfers. He only recognized them as faces in the locker room. He held up a towel as Morris signed Sullivan's name and room number to the sheet. He piled his shirt and old slacks and loafers in a locker without a lock. He had remembered to leave his watch in the room. He would take a turn in the pool and have a good ten minutes in the steam room.

Morris crashed the empty water into pieces. He made no count of how far he swam; he stopped and treaded water, and put his head under and shouted at the bottom, surprised as always at the sound it made.

Morris pulled himself out of the pool. His left heel trailed a thin, intact line of water, as if his leg had emerged, battle scarred, from a jungle watering hole. His dripping suit was even harder to drag down. He walked into the steam room with the strained ends of his towel knotted around him.

Sitting on the first wooden bench was Tommy Fryer, his long blond hair curling with humidity over his high forehead.

Morris inhaled the wet heat and sat down.

Tommy looked up, then recognized him. "How was the pool?"

"Empty," said Morris.

"Have you been working?" Fryer had a soft voice for a Californian. He might have been from Atlanta, except for the lack of an accent. He turned his body on the bench as if to get comfortable in the heat.

"Sort of."

"That's a long day. One thing about playing. Once you hole out, that's all you can possibly do."

Morris almost said, you can practice. But Tommy rarely did, and maybe he would never have to. But I would not bet on it, thought Morris.

"Does writing get easier?" asked Fryer.

"Yes and no. Writing the sentences goes faster. Most of the time. And you know more people." And whom to believe, Morris thought. "But hauling yourself around, a few pounds heavier every year, is the trick. When you get my age, your hangovers grow atomic clouds." Morris laughed. "But you don't drink, and be glad about it."

"Morris, can I ask you a question you might not want to answer?" Fryer seemed almost out of breath in the heat.

"Sure."

"You always write straight to the point. No matter who's winning, or blowing the lead. Do you ever pull for any one golfer?"

"Oh yes. Every tournament."

"Like who?"

100

"I wanted Hogan to win one more. I always want the Old Guard to win one more. They're my generation. But there comes a time when they won't again. Then you like to see them shoot a nice round. I like to see young players, who have earned it, win their first tournament. Sometimes it can be a mistake. A piece of luck. But not often. It's wonderful to see a great player get it going, and not be afraid of the course, or of the past, or of what challenge is thrown at him, and win a major tournament."

"Like I won the seventy-three Open," said Fryer without embarrassment, but turning again on the bench.

"Like you won the Open."

"You ever pull against anybody?"

"Not that I would admit. Especially to myself."

"Do you think John's death was an accident?"

"No."

Fryer put his head in his hands. "What do we do?" he asked.

"Leave it to the police."

"I feel sick about him," said Fryer. "I didn't like him. I never went out of my way to know him better, to understand him, to help him. He was going to be a great player, but that wouldn't have been enough." Tommy was running with sweat.

"Travis said, 'Maybe he would have grown up.' But you see, he would have had to do it himself. You couldn't have done it for him." Morris could not remember one friendly, unnecessary act he himself had ever done for John Whitlow and could not excuse himself.

"What was it about Travis? What did he have?" asked Fryer, lifting his head, looking at him through the steam as if to see into the mystery of another man's life.

"He still has it," said Morris. "Let it ride on the blade. Everything. And not hold back. Not even your pride when your nerves are gone."

Fryer was looking down with his head in his hands.

"You okay, Tommy?" Morris was concerned. Whitlow's death seemed to weigh on him, as if he somehow could have prevented it.

Fryer only nodded without lifting his head from his hands.

"I gotta get out of here," said Morris. "I'm melting into nothing." He touched Fryer on a surprisingly thin shoulder. "Don't stay too long." Fryer waved a salute without looking up.

Morris was thinking when the phone rang. He did not have to look at his watch to know it was too early for his wakeup call. He freed his hand from a tangle of arms, and lifted the receiver.

"We're having coffee at the morgue." It was Rutledge.

"I'll be there," said Morris.

Sullivan covered her head with the pillow. Morris lifted one end of it. "I know you're under there. Get up when the phone rings again. Ride to the course with me. I'll be by." There was some sort of grunt under the pillow.

Morris looked out the window. Rain clouds hung in the air below him. He put on his old beaten yellow sweater, and took his umbrella.

Streetlights were still on and the same driver was sleeping in the same cab. They better set the pins in dry places, thought Morris. He could almost touch the heavy sky. It was a two-dollar cab ride to the morgue. It's a longer trip in another vehicle, he thought.

The thin milk-colored latex gloves peeled off the coroner's white hands like last year's skin being shed. But they left his fingers and knuckles as old as his cadaverous head and caved-in chest. Only his eyes darted with life. "Young fellow drowned. No question about that. Breathed in about as much mud as water."

Morris avoided looking at the form on the table.

"Couldn't have been in better health. Maybe he once had a stomach ulcer, but it was healed over. He should have lived to be ninety. Well, he missed it by about sixty-six years."

"Any bruises? Anything?" asked Rutledge.

"Nothing. If he ever slipped in the tub, I didn't see a sign of it."

"He could have been pushed."

"Could have been. One thing. He had to go down head first. He must have opened his mouth on the bottom to scream, or breathe. All that mud in his throat. He couldn't swim? An athlete like that?"

"Water scared him," said Morris, "any more than enough

to brush his teeth. Was he intoxicated?'' Morris asked as routinely as if he were on the medical examining board.

Dr. William Moseley shook his head, seemingly at his own forgetfulness, toppling his white hair over his forehead. "No. He'd had a couple of stiff drinks. Maybe as much as three ounces. And he hadn't eaten in at least five hours. How do these boys play championship golf on an empty stomach? No wonder they get ulcers at twenty-three. You couldn't call him drunk, on his blood-alcohol content. But he could have been light-headed.''

"Light-headed enough to lose his balance on a steep bank, in the dark, in slippery loafers, and fall in the water, and drown?'' Rutledge recited the possibility as if it were a fantasy.

"Possibly. However he went in, he went in head first. We've got a rash of golfers falling head first. That's asking a lot of the law of averages. Sorry I can't be of more help.'' He held up his empty hands; they seemed to gather age with the effort.

"Nothing helps this investigation. *Drowned*,'' said Rutledge. "You the reporters will have to live with that, the same as you did yesterday with *fell*. Morris, if you don't mind, I'd like to stop by your hotel later for a cup of coffee, before you leave for the course.'' He nodded his thanks to Dr. Moseley.

"You taking up law enforcement?'' said the old coroner to Morris.

"I've been drafted. I prefer a friendlier game.''

"Oh, he's friendly, all right.'' Moseley indicated the door that the Lieutenant was closing behind him. "But you wouldn't want to get between him and what he needs.'' There was an ominous warning in the old man's voice. Morris remembered how Rutledge had questioned Jackie Whitlow before telling her how John had died.

"No, I wouldn't,'' said Morris.

"I'll drop you at your hotel,'' said Moseley, patting him on the back with a hand as light as a breath.

Morris buried his head in the newspaper. He had phoned in the autopsy report on Whitlow. It was worth a new sub for his P.M. lead. Reporters in the dining room were being paged, he was certain, by their newspapers. Their editors would be anxious about the autopsy. Only two reporters stopped at Morris's table, which was in the corner of the room next to the kitchen. He told them quickly what he knew.

The Lieutenant turned his broad body inside the door in one movement, but Morris did not miss him. He stood until Rutledge saw him. The room was loud and crowded. Three double tables of golf fans blocked the two of them from view. The waitress put down a second cup of coffee. Rutledge drank deeply.

"You missed a sideshow at the station. About twenty reporters. All of them writing the word *drowned*. Or filming it. What did they think? He had been hanged under water?"

"Did they ask if Whitlow had been drinking?"

"No. And I didn't get into it. He wasn't drunk."

"He would have been an easy target. A little tipsy. On a steep bank."

"Morris. We've got a killer to find. And we have two days to find him."

Morris was flattered by the "we." "Any evidence I haven't heard?"

"No, but you've known they weren't accidents or suicides as long as I have. Longer. You knew Rossi. I remember how puzzled you were that he would kill himself. There are only two questions: who killed them, and why?"

Morris drank his own coffee.

"With Rossi, the killer was blind lucky that nobody saw him. He couldn't have planned it. But something happened in his mind. He planned the second one."

"He had to know golf," said Morris. "He had to know Whitlow. Whitlow always took his putter to his locker. He was bound to miss it. He hadn't used it on eighteen. He would look in the shadows of the seventeenth green. The bank there is steep. The water falls off quickly. Whitlow couldn't swim. But somebody had to be cool. If he knew golf he knew Whitlow was a dangerously powerful young man."

"The killer panicked afterward," said Rutledge, "throwing the putter that far. Forty feet. That was a mistake."

"Maybe he didn't panic," said Morris. "As the golfers say, maybe he was 'pumped up' and couldn't help throwing it that far."

"Once he had committed accidental murder, it was easy enough to plan the next one."

"But why?"

"The killer may have had very sound motives for both murders. He may not have."

"He may be sick, you mean," said Morris.

"He's dangerous, either way."

"What can you do?" asked Morris.

"We're doubling the security at the tournament. But we can't be everywhere. Atlanta is a big city. I can't get three shifts of a hundred and forty-eight patrolmen to follow each golfer twenty-four hours a day. I tried."

"You only need three shifts of sixty-six," said Morris. "They cut the field today to the sixty-six low scorers."

"I forgot about that." Rutledge hit the table with his palm. "It's possible they cut the killer." He bit his lip at the idea.

"Then he is waiting for us in Chicago," said Morris. But somehow he didn't believe it.

"Did you learn anything in the tapes?"

"I'm not sure," said Morris. "I erased them. But I remember them. Habit of the trade. I only listened to certain players."

"Who?" Rutledge looked interested.

"The leaders. And the ones I thought would know Rossi. They would have to be established players. He only did the color for the Open and the PGA, and he came around as a fan at the Masters. You would have to be good to be in any of those tournaments."

Rutledge was nodding his head.

"Everybody on the tape could have done it. Except Fryer. He was with his wife."

"Always worry about who's 'with his wife,'" said Rutledge. "I'll pick up the recorder when you finish your coffee."

The noise and laughter in the room seemed to deny that two golfers had died in two days.

14 ✵

M ORRIS STEPPED OUT OF THE RENTED CAR AND WAITED FOR Julia Sullivan to join him.

"People actually use this time of the morning," she said.

"They even have a meal for it. It's called breakfast."

"My goodness!" Sullivan was looking over the low hedge onto the golf course. "There's an army here."

"The Governor called up a National Guard unit," said Morris. The drab green of their uniforms stood out, even against the trees.

"Better not cut across a fairway today," said Sullivan. "You might wind up on somebody's bayonet."

Morris looked again at the nearest Guardsman. His rifle, thank God, was not mounted with a bayonet. Morris's sweater felt good in the dampness. It was not raining yet, but it soon would be. The sky was so low it seemed to touch the highest pines.

The guard at the gate checked their passes and waved them through. Sullivan stopped just inside the fence. She looked alarmingly trim and young in her rain jacket. "Why don't they play it another year? It isn't fun anymore this year."

"No," he said, taking her arm.

"Sorry if I'm ruining what's left of your Open." She squeezed his oversized wrist.

"Come on. This early we ought to beat the breakfast crowd."

Lieutenant Rutledge was sitting just inside the dining-room door. Morris knew he had impounded Rossi's files on St. Simons Island. He wanted Morris to fly down with him, this afternoon. Morris put off deciding if he would do it. In the daylight, it all seemed somehow unreal. Morris stopped and introduced Julia. "She will answer to her first name, but rarely hears it. She claims we are 'Sullivan and Morris,'

106

failing vaudeville team. If you play your cards right, she might invite you up to her private mountain in Colorado. I talk her down to the golf tour about five times a year." And that, thought Morris, should hold his curiosity in check, at least for now.

The detective took her hand awkwardly, as if he had forgotten the ritual.

"I'm afraid our golf tournament has turned as sad as the weather," said Julia.

He nodded.

"Lots of troops out," said Morris.

"They'll be scattered across every hole. Just to be seen. Then we'll have a plainclothesman with each twosome. None of it will mean anything to the man we're looking for," said Rutledge. "But we've increased the odds, a fraction, against his trying it again."

Morris gripped the head of his cane. Somehow he felt the presence of fear in the huge room. Maybe it was his own.

"Let me know about St. Simons," said Rutledge. "I'll need you."

Morris waved his hand, and guided Sullivan toward an empty table.

"I wouldn't want that man looking for me." She shivered against him.

"That's exactly what Travis said. I hope he's making the killer that nervous." Morris frowned. They might have been talking about the tee times.

The Players Commissioner, Horton, insisted they sit at his table, with Joe Goodner.

"We're waiting for someone," Morris lied without trying to sound convincing. "Damn if we're ruining breakfast," he whispered. Rutledge had burned Horton with questions on the tape, about his election, and who was voting for him and against him. Horton had kept his cool. He had been on the scene of both deaths. So had Goodner.

To the left of their table were Patricia Walker and Helen Kirkland. They both waved to Julia, and then to Morris.

"Do you know what Pat said about Horton's election?" laughed Morris. Julia shook her head. "She said, 'We have to keep Edward; he always looks like a man who just parked his boat in the lobby.'" Julia laughed until Horton looked over at them, as if to see what the joke was about.

The television announcer, Don Murray, came in, and both Horton and Goodner stood up to welcome him.

"Saw your show last night; it was first rate," said Horton. "Joe did a good job, too. You all did."

"You didn't think it was bad form to run the tape with Rossi?" asked Murray.

Morris almost swallowed the ice in his water. He missed Horton's answer. He had forgotten about the Friday night preview of the Open. So Rossi had been taped. It was a film Rutledge should see.

Murray had a smooth complexion and wore black-rimmed glasses. His professionalism and quiet grace at the terror-struck Munich Olympics had made him the most respected sportscaster in television. He leaned toward them and asked, "Morris, what do the police think?"

"They can't say that either death was murder," said Morris. "I don't think they called out the Guard to stop a suicide."

Murray laughed with him. "I hope you thought our footage of Rossi was in good taste?" he said.

"I didn't see it. I'd like to. I think the detective, Rutledge, should see it."

"By all means. We can have a showing in our control trailer, any time you like. Let me know."

Strange, thought Morris, that Murray would put up with Goodner's foul moods. But he knew his business. Maybe Goodner was good theatre. He had lied to Rutledge on the tape, insisting he "thought the world of Rossi." It would be interesting to see the *total*, unedited footage of last night's television show.

LeBaron kissed Sullivan dead on the lips, and sat down, as if by appointment.

"Does this always happen at seven forty-five in the morning?" she asked. "I've slept my life away."

"The clouds are so low," said LeBaron, "it's gonna rain up. Get inside if we have a lightning storm. We don't want to lose anybody else."

Morris nudged him with his cane. "This is really a lightning rod," he said. He was embarrassed, having listened to Rutledge question LeBaron on tape. Frank, like himself, couldn't prove he was not responsible for either death.

The good breakfast smells were as welcome as the eggs and bacon.

*   *   *

Morris walked between the National Guardsmen who stood without speaking in the locker room, making everyone nervous of their own conversation.

"Did you ever see a sky like that? A man could drown in a sky like that." Al Morgan did not apologize for the expression *drown*. He was covered with a sheen of sweat from practicing in the rising humidity. "I'm runnin' like a creek outside, and dry as bone inside," he said. "The more water I swallow, the drier I get."

"That's what you get drinkin' that hair tonic," said Art Howard, who sat in the middle of his stomach, which bulged out around him on the bench. His small hands moved nervously over his belt and shirt. He was wearing his street shoes. Morris knew he was not scheduled to tee off for another hour and a half. He was too close to the lead to sleep late, thought Morris. That's the Open. Art and Travis Walker were tied at one-forty-one, three shots behind Fryer.

"Watch me shoot nine threes, and have the course wash away," said Art.

"You shoot the nine threes and I'll pay a grand apiece for 'em," said Morgan. "Rain or shine."

"I'll settle for the two thousand you owe me," said Howard. There was no fun in his voice. He stood up. Morris knew he and Morgan had been rookies together. He had never had a year like Morgan's in 1973, when he won two hundred fifty thousand dollars. Still, Art had won nearly a million dollars.

I wonder what he's done with it, thought Morris; he damn sure hadn't spent it on himself.

Al Morgan had blown his own money over four continents. But he was cheerful, and Art seemed bitter. How do you explain that, Morris wondered. He was not in the locker room to ask questions. He only wanted to feel the intensity of the Open.

Morgan lifted out a dozen new balls and slammed the door of his locker. "Come on, Dolan," he shouted across the room, "get your ornery self in gear. We got a golf course to play."

Dolan did not answer. It was the privilege of age. He would be trying to put the word *hook* out of his mind. But he would let it fly. Morris admired Dolan for never trying to

109

steer the ball off the tee, no matter where it landed. Dolan walked out of the room without speaking.

"What time are you off, Pete?" asked Travis.

"In thirty minutes."

Morris knew they placed Kirkland as far ahead of Travis as possible to spread the gallery. And many would be following Fryer, the leader, in the last twosome.

"We should send you and Pete off together," Morris was surprised to hear himself say to Travis.

"Sure," Travis laughed. "And see which one of us could break ninety."

They were friends, but when they were paired together, they wound up playing each other, and the course swallowed them both alive.

"Morris, you can't write it," said Kirkland, "but I can't make myself believe this is the Open. I don't know what I've been practicing for for two weeks."

"Who could blame you? The deaths. And you're not in love with the course."

"It's not an unfair test. Losing Rossi and Whitlow ages us all. Maybe this is the week I become an old man." Kirkland was thirty-seven.

"You're a fledgling," said Travis, who was forty-six. "You can make up five strokes in five holes."

"If Tommy gets it going, we'll all be shooting for what's left," said Pete.

"That's a fact," said Travis. "He goes off at one-twenty. He'll come in at one o'clock. Hit five practice balls, and birdie the first three holes." He paused. "He better." He grinned the most famous smile golf had ever known.

"Just remember, Travis," said Morgan, "if you get it three under, you'll be tied for the lead, and you know what happens in this tournament to the leader."

No one laughed, except Morgan. Their discomfort made him laugh harder. He walked out of the locker room laughing.

"Well," said Lee Washburn, who rarely spoke before a round, "nobody's killing the drunks who barely make the cut." The National Guardsmen shifted their weight in their boots.

Morris followed Morgan to the door of the locker room.

"Morgan, I didn't like what you said about Travis."

Morgan stopped, surprised. Morris never interfered with locker room talk.

"What business is it of yours? AP?" He said the letters contemptuously.

"I'm incorporating it as my business. It comes at a late age, but you might begin to watch your drunken mouth. While you are at it, be careful whom you call a cheater in the British Open."

"That wasn't me, that was Whitlow." Morgan did not sound so cocky.

"Sure it was. He just never accused Washburn to any other person while he was alive."

"I can't help that. Listen, don't tell that big ape. I'd hate to see him really mad." Morgan was truly nervous, looking over his shoulder at Washburn.

Morris moved up against him. "I think you are lying. If you ever repeat it again, I promise you I will print it." Morris looked down on him. "Do you have anything else to say?"

Morgan left the room without speaking.

15

FIRST THE WIND ROSE, SEEMING TO DRAG ITSELF THROUGH THE trees, feeding on its own velocity, drawing leaves and multicolored hats and dried pine needles after it, leaving only the whistle of its passage in the air. Then the rain came at once, sideways on the wind as much as down, in a falling, blowing river of water. The chill of it took the breath of the thirty thousand on the course, all of them drenched before they could unwrap their umbrellas, the driving, everywhere rain finding its way between their thin layers of spring clothes.

The caddies rushed for the great swollen bags lying helplessly on the grass, rainsuits zipped tightly in them, umbrellas lashed hopelessly against them. Caddies and golfers were running with water in an instant, their socks wet in their shoes. Finally raised, the huge circles of umbrellas could not stop the water blowing wildly under them. Even in the flying chill, Morris marvelled that Kirkland and Washburn carefully marked their balls with coins, and then tees, as the water ran through their fingers. The caddies could only jump with the rain and their own curses, snapping covers over already drenched clubs.

The first lightning struck, leaving its doom in the air. The crowd was pouring through the trees in plastic trails like exploded rainbows. A plainclothes policeman struggled in the solid, falling rain to keep the two golfers in his sight.

"Get those crazy cameramen off the towers!" Morris recognized Dr. Edward Harris, official meteorologist for the Open. His screaming couldn't match the velocity of the rain and lightning.

Morris could not begin to keep up with Kirkland, who was headed off the course toward a house along the fairway. There was no refuge from the five bogeys he had scored to take him out of the tournament.

Washburn stopped for a moment under Morris's umbrella. "You make it okay?" he shouted.

Morris yelled, "Yes."

"I'll hire a plane . . . bomb the course . . . if it washes out my three birdies!" Washburn was screaming every word. He was running now through the trees toward the same house that Kirkland had disappeared into.

They will be two guests to remember, thought Morris. He rode his cane under his umbrella toward the long refreshment tent ahead of him. It was no help against the lightning, but at least he could get away from the rain blowing sideways through the trees.

Travis's was the first face he saw under the tent. He was leaning out, looking up into a falling wall of water. Ducking back under, he blinked the rain out of his eyes. "Thank God we're not flying in it," said Travis. "But it would be a ride to remember." He grinned to a large woman holding a cup of hot chocolate. She looked suddenly weak with his closeness. Everybody wanted to hand him a cup of coffee. He took a paper cup from the proffered hand of an old man of at least seventy-five.

A figure passed, drowned in the gloom and rain without so much as a newspaper for an umbrella. He looked into the tent, and boomed in a deep Georgia voice, "Hell, it ain't rainin'. Let's get 'em, Travis!" Lightning struck as he said Travis's name. A roar of approval ran through the tent.

Travis now had his hand on the old man's shoulders, as if they had long been comrades together, and the cup of coffee they were sharing sealed the years between them. Morris was sure the old man would die for the powerful hand on his shoulder. Eyes like his had willed both of Travis's birdie putts into the cup on the first three holes before the rain.

Travis was now a stroke from the lead, and the water in his hair ran with youth. He twisted his shoulders to keep himself loose. The rain still had not broken.

"Hey, Jesse!" Travis had somehow learned the name of the young boy running the concession tent. "You got any more hot dogs?" Jesse flinched at the shouts of "hot dog" that were thrown at him. His hands fumbled the hot dog into the bun. "Little mustard," said Travis. "Mustard" was repeated five times like a call for plasma.

Up came the mustard. Travis bit into the cold bread as if it were a delicacy, and looked again at the rain.

Morris could see Art Howard squatting at the far end of the tent. His caddy, Sam, was drying the grips on his clubs. Art was one under after three holes, and two shots off the lead. Morris checked his watch. Tommy Fryer had not teed off before the rain. It was only twelve-fifty. The crowd under the tent was careful to give Sam room to work. Morris was sure most of them did not know Art's name, and he had been on the tour seventeen years.

Morris, already wet, struggled into his rainsuit, and worked his way to the back of the tent. "Well played," he said.

Sam smiled. Art pushed his tinted glasses higher on his round nose. "Yeah, rain," he said. "If I was shootin' bogeys it would be shining sun." He sat on the foot of his bag while Sam dried the grips.

A golf cart pulled in under the trees, beside the tent. It was LeBaron. Morris lifted himself with his cane into the wet seat. The cart roof only stopped the water that was falling in a straight line.

"Welcome to the Sun Belt," said LeBaron, the wet chill taking his breath away. Morris opened his umbrella in front of them, deflecting some of the blowing rain.

"Any players under there?" Frank was shouting over the noise of the rain.

"Travis and Art."

"We better send a van. Lightning might hit a cart."

"Thanks a lot!" shouted Morris.

Frank tried to call the clubhouse on his walkie-talkie. All he could raise was a tangle of static. He started the cart forward, easing his way through the people still streaming under the trees toward the parking lots. Finally he pulled into the caddy yard under the clubhouse overhang.

Morris furled his dripping umbrella, and propped himself out of the cart with his cane. "I thank you," he said. "I'm not sure for what." Water ran as furiously inside his rainsuit as off it.

LeBaron saluted him. He was back on his radio trying to locate a van.

Morris looked for the voice he heard further under the clubhouse. Lightning punctuated the sentences.

"Alfred, if it rains this round out, I'm carryin' the clubs, and you can play the front nine over. Not me, by God." Alfred was shaking his head at Al Morgan, all the time savaging the weather under his breath.

Morris had seen Al slide a sixty-foot putt impossibly downhill into the cup, as though he were twenty-three and didn't know the putt couldn't be made.

"Morris, you ever see a man shoot nine straight pars on an Open course without hitting the fairway." It was not a question. "Old Dolan got it up and down from the rough, the sand, the trees. It's time he four-putted or snatched one out of bounds."

Morris now saw Dolan for the first time, drinking coffee alone against the wall. He seemed to have retreated deeper inside himself with the sound of the rain. Even the thunder did not reach him. He and Morgan were lucky to have made the turn just as the rain broke. Morris looked out at the scoreboard with his binoculars. Both of them had shot thirty-five. And both of them were dry.

"Come on inside," said Morris. "I'll buy the coffee."

"I gotta stop this Georgia rain," said Morgan. "God is a bogey player. Leave him alone and he'll wash me out."

Dolan never spoke.

Morris kept a change of clothes in the press room. But it

114

was a long, wet walk to the gymnasium. He sat on the steps up into the clubhouse and pulled off his two-piece rainsuit. He was drenched on the shoulders and at the knees. One Irish coffee would do as much as a dry sweater.

It was impossible to move in the dining room. There was not even standing room between the tables. Morris checked his watch. He would have to file an early A.M. lead within an hour. It wouldn't be anything but a weather report.

The room was steamy with body heat. It felt good. The sound he heard over the noise, the name that was being paged, was his own. Maybe Sullivan was calling. She was here somewhere. It was not like her to page him. It could be from the press room. Morris struggled through the standing bodies to the receptionist's desk at the front of the clubhouse. He identified himself.

"Oh, yes, Mr. Morris. Lieutenant Rutledge wants you. In the manager's office."

Sergeant Bolton led Morris into the room without knocking. Rutledge was looking out the floor-to-ceiling window. The rain had stopped as if it had fallen in one piece. Light was already beginning to break through the sky. The practice putting green was still running with water, but the course was on high ground. Morris knew it would dry surprisingly fast. Rutledge turned from the window as if he were keeping an appointment.

"What time do you have?"

Morris checked his watch. "One twenty-one."

"I'm fast," said Rutledge. He held up a pairings sheet. "The last twosome was to tee off at one-twenty, until the rain came."

Morris nodded. The players went off in twosomes on Saturday and Sunday.

"Fryer's wife called. Five minutes ago. She doesn't know where he is." Rutledge wore the same gray suit. His pudgy body and face gave away nothing. He was snapping the ballpoint pen in his left hand.

All of Morris's quick thoughts could not keep the sick feeling from rising in his throat. Tommy Fryer. His choirboy good looks had not spoiled him. Nor his swing like liquid iron. Nor all his quick money. He was tough. He was frank. He was sick about John Whitlow. He didn't really know

115

Rossi. He was the one player who could not have killed them both.

"Has he checked in at the locker room?"

Rutledge shook his head.

"Where did Nancy call from?" asked Morris.

"The hotel."

"This time of day? That's unusual. She's always at the course when Tommy is playing."

"She was nearly hysterical. I understood he didn't wake her this morning. She slept until noon. He apparently didn't come in last night."

"That's crazy," said Morris. "I left him in the steam room. About ten forty-five. In the hotel."

Rutledge was looking at him as if he didn't know him.

"Did the starter, Bryan, miss him?" asked Morris.

"No. The rain hit before his twosome was to check in. I haven't told anybody he's missing. I want to be sure it's not just a hysterical wife. He may have been caught somewhere in the storm."

"He should have been on the practice tee. Or the putting green," said Morris. "Have you talked with Bobby Watson, his caddy?"

"No. I was paging you," said Rutledge. "Let's find him."

"Tommy has at least an hour, or an hour and a half," said Morris. "The course won't be playable before then."

Rutledge handed Sergeant Bolton his walkie-talkie. "Get Colburn and the man from the PGA . . ." He looked to Morris.

"LeBaron."

"Yes. Tell them to meet us in the caddy yard. Alone."

"Is Fryer as straight an arrow as they say?" asked Rutledge.

"He's a Mormon. Doesn't drink or smoke. Plays a little bridge, never for money. He married Nancy four years ago. They are inseparable. He's not as dull as that sounds. He'll give you his opinion. He's one of the great iron players of our time." Morris stopped in the crowded hall. "Nancy must be terrified."

"The hotel is sending a doctor to her room. Let's go," said Rutledge.

Morris held to the railing and swung his left leg down each step to the basement of the clubhouse. Rutledge waited for him. "Who is this Watson, his caddy?"

"An unusual boy. He has a graduate degree in math from Stanford. He and Tommy were in school together."

Morris's cane rang on the concrete floor. Guards stood in the club storage room and the caddy yard. Morris moved toward a powerfully built young man with red hair and fair skin irritated by too much sun. He was standing under the overhang of the building.

"Bobby, this is Lieutenant Rutledge," said Morris.

Watson looked up in surprise. He did not offer to shake hands, keeping his arms tight against himself as though to hold in his concern.

"Did you see Tommy before the rain?" asked Morris, touching him easily on the shouder.

"No." Watson had difficulty getting the word out. "We usually go down to the practice tee about forty minutes before a round. Tommy rarely hits more than a dozen balls. Sometimes he will putt afterward for twenty or thirty minutes. He just wants to loosen up before teeing off."

It seemed to make Watson more comfortable to talk. "I was waiting on the practice tee. He was about five minutes late when the rain hit, at twelve forty-five. You could see it was coming. I was sure he just stayed in the clubhouse. Where is he, Morris?" Suddenly Watson was struggling to keep his composure.

"We don't know. When did you last see him?"

"I had dinner last night with him and Nancy, at the hotel. About eight-thirty. He said he'd see me on the practice tee at twelve-forty. He always wrote down what he would shoot." Watson pulled a scoreboard out of his pocket. Fryer had penciled in a sixty-five.

The other caddies were moving toward them. Rutledge said, "Stay here with his bag. And don't spread any panic."

Morris gripped Watson's powerful forearm. He wanted to say something to reassure him. That they had time. That the course would be at least an hour drying out. He could only set his heavy jaw.

Morris followed Rutledge out into the open caddy yard. LeBaron and Colburn were approaching in separate carts. Morris climbed in with LeBaron.

"Take us to the parking lot," said Rutledge. Morris could see a helicopter drifting in the still gusty winds, now settling in front of the clubhouse.

Rutledge waved the two carts to a stop.

"Who's missing now?" asked LeBaron, "the Goodyear blimp pilot?"

"Tommy Fryer," said Morris, anticipating the shock on his face.

"He's not here at the course?" Colburn lost his princely poise.

"He's also not at his hotel," said Rutledge. "The two of you wait in the club manager's office. You better get the other fellow, the Commissioner . . ."

"Horton," said Morris.

"Yes," said Rutledge. "I may call you to stop the tournament. Sergeant Bolton has contact with our security people. I don't want any golfer or caddy to leave the clubhouse for town without my permission. Understood?"

Neither Colburn or LeBaron protested.

"I'll call Mary," said LeBaron, "and send her up to Nancy's room. She's already in the hotel."

"Good," said Morris.

Rutledge waited for him to lead the way into the helicopter, without asking if he were coming.

They couldn't talk over the noise of the engine. The front had passed, but the sky was still turbulent, bobbing the helicopter about like a thistle in a high wind. The trees and hills of Atlanta reminded Morris, from this height, of the trees and hills of Paris. It should be some landing, he thought; the Peachtree-Forsyth Hotel was seventy stories high. The clutch of downtown skyscrapers was suddenly under them. The pilot jockeyed both hands and feet at the controls, all the while looking down at the small square landing pad shifting with the gusts of winds. He hovered, then set them down in one movement, and cut the engine. The silence filled the bubble of glass they sat in.

"Wait here," Rutledge said to the pilot. He nodded and jumped out first, and began tying the craft down in the wind.

Morris counted eight men waiting on the roof.

"Five are mine, three are with the hotel," said Rutledge, as if he had read Morris's mind. He did not introduce any of them.

"We turn this hotel upside down," Rutledge said as the eight men gathered around him. "If Fryer is in it, we find him. Check every public place: restaurant, rest room, bar, shop. Check every room on his floor of the hotel. Don't bother his wife in twenty-three-ten. Not yet. Check his hotel bill. He was supposed to have eaten in the dining room last night. See if he charged it. Call your night staff. See if anyone on the desk remembers seeing him. And why didn't he get a wakeup call? Take us to the health room," Rutledge said to the short, powerfully built young man who was already leading the way.

"Jack, come with us," Rutledge said to the oldest man, obviously a policeman, who stepped forward.

As long as Rutledge was giving orders, as long as they all kept moving, making decisions, Morris did not have to imagine what they would find.

The elevator began to drop with a queer sense of movement without sound.

"What time does the health room open on Saturday?" asked Rutledge.

"At ten A.M.," said the heavyset young man, who was apparently with the hotel. "It doesn't get much traffic until the afternoon. You'd be surprised how few people use it at all. Most of those who do are regulars whose business keeps them here sometimes for weeks."

The elevator stopped twice to take on passengers. The hotel detective led them off at the eighth-floor level, down the corridor, directly onto the escalator.

Morris looked over the side the strange geometry of the lobby. He could not shake the memory of the Towers Hotel lobby as it had looked eighteen floors under him.

"Straight ahead." The hotel detective was pushing his stubby legs to lead the way. He braced himself to swing open the door into the health room.

The smell of chlorine was heavy in the damp air. The concrete floor was slick with humidity. Morris's cane echoed in the room like a code. He stopped beside the artificially blue water in the short pool. You could not see the bottom, even in the shallow end. Rutledge looked directly at him, but did not speak. It would not be a fun job, searching the pool, thought Morris.

"David!" the hotel detective called inside the swinging door to the men's locker room.

A rumpled, white cotton jacket that might have been on a medical intern appeared between two rows of locker stalls.

119

The tall black man had a stack of unused towels across his arm.

"This is Lieutenant Rutledge of Homicide. He has some questions to ask you."

The black man looked at the towels in his arms as if they were prima facie evidence against him. He was in the middle of the room, and seemed to need a wall to lean against.

Rutledge gave the house detective a look of disgust. Morris had never heard him use the word *homicide*. It was more unnerving, even, than *murder*.

"Nothing to be upset about . . . David?" Rutledge said his first name as a question.

"David Long." The man said it as if he had just learned it himself.

"Maybe you can help us. We are looking for a hotel guest. A golfer. His name is Tommy Fryer."

The black man's eyes filled with interest, rather than fear. "I know him," he said. "Don't mean I ever saw him. But he's been right here in this room. He's leading the Open, but I got my money on Mr. Pete Kirkland."

The way he said "Mr. Pete Kirkland" sounded exactly like Alfred; Morris could close his eyes and see the caddy saying it.

"What do you mean, 'he's been here'?" asked Rutledge. "This morning?"

"No sir. Only had two couples in the pool this mornin'. It's a shame the way the people don't use this health room. It'll be pickin' up in an hour or two. Mr. Fryer was here last night, and most every night this week. His name is down on the night sheet, signed up for a towel."

"Where's the night sheet?" asked Rutledge.

The black man walked past him toward a table at the far end of the room. He never stopped talking. "I 'spect I'd know him, if I saw him—Mr. Fryer. I've seen him on the TV. But Joe Lee dudn' know any of 'em. He wouldn't know Mr. Pete Kirkland if he was standin' right here in the room. Joe Lee takes over at four-thirty. All he knows is them heavy books from Gawga Tech."

"What time was Fryer here?" asked Rutledge.

David Long pulled a double handful of looseleaf papers out of a drawer in the table. "Can't exactly say. Joe Lee dudn' write down all the times like he's supposed to. Looks like he musta been here 'bout ten-thirty.''

Morris looked over Rutledge's shoulder. The Friday night names were entered erratically. Some of the guests had signed their own names. Including Tommy Fryer, in a loose, forward slant.

"Let me see Thursday night's sheet," said Rutledge.

Long found it with difficulty. Morris began reading the names. Scrawled almost exactly in the center of the page was the signature, Al Morgan.

"Let me have all the papers," said Rutledge.

Long handed over the unclean, ill-sorted sheets of legalized pages.

"What time do you come in?" asked Rutledge.

" 'Zactly at eight," said Long.

"What do you do first?"

"Make sure Joe Lee has mopped the locker rooms, and the steam room, and out by the pool. Count up the dirty towels and turn 'em in for clean ones. Clean out the lockers. Then I'm ready for business."

"You've done all that?"

Long nodded solemnly.

"Do you have a couple of bathing suits we can borrow?" Rutledge asked.

"Got four or five. Old. Been left here. Don't know if they'll fit. You welcome to 'em." Long pulled the suits from deep in another drawer in the table.

"You swim, Jack?" Rutledge asked the tall detective.

"Not so you'd notice it."

Morris picked up a huge pair of boxerlike trunks, in an outrageous, long-faded Hawaiian print. He laughed in spite of himself. "Just what I've been looking for," he said. The dead weight of the suit in his hands made him remember what they were truly looking for.

Rutledge lifted a large maroon suit in one hand. "It ought to do the job," he said, grimacing at Morris.

The two of them emerged from their lockers carrying their watches, keys, and billfolds in their hands. Both of them were formless and ridiculous in the trunks. Jack, the detective, laughed, taking their valuables.

Morris found it difficult to keep his balance without his cane on the slippery concrete floor.

121

"Check the lockers," said Rutledge, "while we take a look in the pool." Jack was still smiling at the two of them in the trunks.

Morris walked directly to the near end of the pool. He fell headlong into the water without allowing himself to think. The pool was only eight feet deep under the board, but you had to touch the bottom to see it. He was able to go the length of the short pool easily without surfacing. He stood up in the shallow end to breathe. A head surfaced, and went under again in an awkward thrusting of hands and feet. The Lieutenant came up out of the shallow water with a gasp of air. He choked until he got his breath.

"I haven't been in a pool in twenty-five years," he said. "Longer than that. The army, I guess."

"It's the only exercise I get, except walking," said Morris. "That's how I keep my weight at a tidy two eighteen." He laughed. He was sitting on the bottom. Water up to his neck always made him laugh. He thought of Rossi, who had been all seriousness on the ground, but in the water had been as childish as himself.

"If you'll handle this end," Morris said, "I'll take the deep end. Won't take but a minute." He shoved off the concrete wall and skimmed the cool, rough bottom with his fingertips, all the time fighting the thought of what he might touch with his hands. It took a dozen turns to be absolutely certain that the pool was empty of everything but too much chlorine. His eyes were burning. He blew a blast of air and too warm water across the top of the pool. Rutledge was sitting on the concrete edge, trying to recover his breath.

Morris joined him. "Thank God he's not in there."

"He's somewhere," said Rutledge.

"Lieutenant!"

Jack came through the swinging door holding a pair of plaid trousers. Morris could also see a blue shirt, and white shorts, and a pair of well-shined loafers. "This was in a pocket." Jack held up a room key in one hand.

Rutledge took it from him. "Room twenty-three-ten," he said, as if it were predestined there in his hand. He also took the trousers and measured them against himself. They were cut for a thin man well over six feet in height. He held onto the key, and dropped the trousers back across Jack's arm. Morris followed them into the locker room.

Rutledge pulled open the airtight glass door to the steam room, the suction drawing a swirl of steam into his face. He took a full stride inside. Morris stopped behind him, his lungs again breathing the familiar wet heat. Fryer was leaning forward on the end of the first bench, his head frozen in the heat onto his fists, his elbows propped inside his thighs. They stepped nearer to him. His long blond hair was painted alive against his dead white forehead. His eyes were fixed open. Even in the steam they could see his pupils dilated in a dark circle.

Neither of them spoke. Rutledge reached through the heat and gripped Fryer's wrist. Morris could see it was fixed rigidly under his chin.

"Get that attendant in here." Rutledge's voice was iron. "Tell him to shut off the damn steam."

Morris might have been a rookie cop. He walked back through the open glass door.

The tall black man, looking at the clothes still across Jack's arms, had grown older in his tracks. "Turn off the steam, Long. The Lieutenant wants to see you inside." Morris's own voice was without mercy.

Long moved as in a dream, turning the valve to stop the steam. His legs didn't seem able to carry him into the small room. He held onto the glass door and drew himself inside. "God-Jesus!" he begged when he saw Tommy Fryer. "Don't make me stay inside of here." Steam and sweat were already running down his face.

Rutledge looked at him through the sweat running into his own eyes. "You *made sure* the place was *cleaned up*, the steam room was *mopped out*." Rutledge's voice was trapped within the four walls.

"I didn't look. 'Fo' God I swear! I was out late an' got up sick. Couldn't keep nothin' on my stomach. Didn' even look inside-a here. Laid my head on my table, took a nap, 'til the two couples came to the pool. 'Bout ten o'clock." He was standing, but he might have been on his knees. The sweat was running down his neck, staining the crumpled white collar of his jacket.

"Who turned on the steam?" Rutledge was now looking directly into his eyes, which wandered in his face as if searching his own mind.

"I couldn't be sure. I can't remember if I did, or if I didn't. All mornin' the door was steamed up like always. Maybe I did. I don't remember doin' it." His voice was a plea, as if the life of Tommy Fryer might have turned in his hands on the valve to the steam room. He wouldn't look at the stiffly huddled form on the end of the bench. The steam was now settling, but the room was still damp with heat.

"Out," said Rutledge.

Long backed out as if afraid to turn his head on death in the room.

"Get our people," Rutledge said to Jack. "Seal off the area. Get this man downtown. Read him his rights, and get his statement." He said it as if Long were standing across the street in another hotel. "Find out who he was with last night. Get 'em downtown. Get this boy Joe Lee at Georgia Tech. Get him over here before you move anything. Get a written statement. I want this room taken apart."

Morris and Rutledge showered and dressed without speaking. As long as he was moving, Morris did not have to think.

"Where's the telephone?" asked Rutledge.

The hotel detective, who had not spoken, pointed. "On the floor, beside the table."

The Lieutenant dialed a number. "Doc," he said, "Rutledge. Bring your gear to the Peachtree-Forsyth Hotel. The health room on the tenth level. Take the escalator from the eighth floor. You'll need a vehicle. We've got another golfer." The iron was still in his voice. Apparently Dr. William Moseley did not ask the name of the golfer. Rutledge hung up.

He dialed again. "Bolton. Fryer's dead," Rutledge said, without identifying himself. "No player leaves the clubhouse until I get there."

Bolton must have asked how he died.

"He's in the steam room. Not a mark on him," said Rutledge.

"No way he used dope," Rutledge answered. "He was a Mormon. Didn't drink or smoke. But he didn't die of steam heat. Not at twenty-seven. We're looking for something that overdosed him. And somebody. In my opinion. Or we're looking for a job.

"Moseley's on his way. We can't wait for him to tell us

what killed Fryer. Or what's going to kill the next one. I want every locker and every golf bag searched. Better find out what they're carrying in their pockets. For the players' own protection.

"Hell no, it's not legal. Get their permission. Anybody who refuses to cooperate will get to know me better. A damn sight better. Put Colburn on the other extension. But stay on the phone." Rutledge waited.

Morris wrapped his hand around the thick wrist supporting the telephone. "Careful Lieutenant. Cancel the tournament, and the golf world leaves town. Unless you are ready to arrest somebody."

"What happens if we delay it?" Rutledge had one hand over the receiver.

"Nothing. The Western Open in Chicago doesn't start until Thursday."

Rutledge spoke into the phone. "Fryer's dead. I don't want the tournament cancelled. Neither do you. Keep it suspended, even if the course dries out. I'm *asking* every player and caddy and key official to allow their bags and lockers to be searched. And themselves. Including you! For your own protection. No player leaves the clubhouse until I get there. I'll be less than an hour. Let me speak to Bolton, alone.

"Collect any medicine, pills, spray, gum. Any *substance* from the players and caddies. Turn their bags and lockers inside out. I don't know what we're looking for. Admit it. Tell 'em. Tommy Fryer didn't die of old age. Don't push anybody who refuses to cooperate. Leave 'em to me. Check Colburn and LeBaron. Holland, if you can find him. Goodner. You know the ones we're interested in. Keep the stuff separate. I'll have the lab on twenty-four-hour duty. I want it all tested. Let me speak to LeBaron." Rutledge waited again.

"Understand this. If there's a killer, he's a friend. Tell that to anybody who complains about being searched. You can help us delay this tournament. I don't want it cancelled." Rutledge listened, and handed the phone to Morris.

"Can we trust him?" asked LeBaron.

"Maybe," said Morris.

"We've come too far. Too many one-whore hotels. Too many fifteen-hundred-dollar purses. Now we play for seven million dollars. Every sponsor's calling me. Chicago's in a panic. If we cancel here, do we cancel the tour? No, by God, we won't. I'm sorry, Morris. That's how I feel.''

"Oh, no, you're not," said Morris. "I feel the same way.'' Both of them hung up.

Morris could imagine how the scene would be on the other end when the news spread about Fryer: the committees, the players, the TV network, the reporters, the National Guard, what people there were left among the trees after the storm. The storm was a blessing. The tournament had already been stopped.

Morris dialed the press tent. He dictated Fryer's death in short, blunt sentences. He reported the Open was suspended. He did not use the word *cancelled*. He did not know how Fryer had died. He rang off.

Rutledge touched Morris on the arm. "Let's get it over with," he said.

The escalator ride down was too short. The elevator was there waiting. Morris did not compose what he would say.

Nancy Fryer stood up when the door opened. She did not cry when she saw Morris's face. She gripped her small hands into fists. She did not want anybody to touch her. She would only sit down after Mary LeBaron sat first.

"Where is he, Morris?" Her voice seemed disembodied, as if it had originated in the air.

"He's downstairs. In the health room. We don't know how he died yet.'' Morris kept speaking. "It was not painful. He seems to have gone to sleep.'' His own use of the word *we* committed him to Rutledge's conspiracy to find the murderer.

"Asleep," she said, with no emphasis.

"What time did he leave the room?" Rutledge asked.

She seemed to welcome the abruptness. "I don't know. I must have dozed off. He always took a late sauna. For his back. It helped him sleep.'' She did not bite off the word *sleep*. "He always set our alarm. He didn't trust hotel operators. I can sleep until noon. That's what happened.'' Her voice was small and controlled. "I knew. I knew as soon as I saw the time.''

"We have to look through his things," said Rutledge. "Frankly, I don't know what we are looking for. We'll also have to talk with you later.''

"About what?''

126

"Jim Rossi. John Whitlow. Other questions."

She seemed to want to talk. "Tommy liked Mr. Rossi. But no one ever helped him with his swing. Not even his father. He was not that close to John. Tommy thought he needed to grow up." She closed her eyes.

"I'll take you to my room," said Mary. Nancy allowed herself to be lifted from the bed.

"I'll give her something. She'll be all right. I'll stay with her," said an older, heavyset man with a leather bag in his hand. Morris had not noticed that he was in the room.

"You're staying in this hotel?" Rutledge asked.

"In a way. With Sullivan," said Morris.

"You'll need some dry clothes. We're flying to the course. And then to St. Simons Island. I have a plane waiting at the airport."

"Rossi is the key," agreed Morris. "Whoever killed him, owed him. Something. It wasn't a logical something. Not the way he was killed. The other two make no sense. But their murders were engineered. Maybe we have three murders and two murderers."

"It's possible. It's too complicated to believe in. Murder is a simple invention," said Rutledge.

"What killed Tommy?"

"I have no idea. There are no obvious insults to the body. Doc can't give us another accidental death." Rutledge's voice seemed to lean on Morris for help.

"Rossi has to be the key," repeated Morris. "Unless we have two murderers. And, as you said, that's twice as hard to believe. Why kill an old teaching pro if you really mean to eliminate the leaders of the U.S. Open? But my editors will probably eliminate me for leaving the Open with dead bodies all over the course and stacking up in the hotels."

16 ✣

FRANK LEBARON POURED THEM EACH A STIFF SCOTCH OVER ice. Morris swirled the drink in his glass. Rutledge bolted his own in one movement. James Colburn lifted his glass with a slight tilt of his head. Eight generations of Virginians had endowed him with an economy of motion.

"James, how long could the USGA operate without its revenue from the Open? Free of debt?" asked LeBaron.

"Two weeks. Possibly three."

"Then it couldn't operate at all."

"Not as we know it."

"It's your organization, your tournament," said LeBaron. "And your decision. The PGA tour needs the Open. Needs the confidence of the public. I have a near panic on my hands. Sponsors in Chicago are in a state of shock. They're afraid we'll cancel out. There are millions of dollars at stake."

"May I speak candidly?" asked Colburn, holding his glass motionless in his hand.

"Please do," said LeBaron.

"The professional tour is of no concern to me. I've always thought of it as a circus, a corruption of a thoughtful game." He did not change expressions. "One does admire the skill of the players. But then most of them are trying to be the next John Whitlow."

"Maybe it's because they didn't inherit their money from a generation of better, tougher men." Morris kept his voice as even as the Virginian's.

"Oh, yes, my grandfather," said Colburn, "gave me my first set of cut-down, wooden-shafted clubs. I still polish them once a year. All of his life, he was a delightful man to play golf with. He was also President of the USGA. I despise what the Open has become. But I won't have it cancelled while I hold office, if they fill the lake with professional golfers.''

"I prefer they fill it with presidents," said LeBaron. "I suppose we should be thankful, murder seems to have brought out the real Colburn under all those fraudulent Virginia vowels." He did not keep his voice under control as well as Morris.

Rutledge refilled his glass and drank easily, as if they were discussing an opening for bridge.

"We will suspend play for a day, or two days," said Colburn, ignoring LeBaron. "Perhaps they will apprehend the murderer. Logic indicates there must be a murderer. We have no true evidence that we know of." He did not look at Rutledge, who emptied his glass.

"I can deliver the USGA Executive Committee," said Colburn. "It will be a *near* vote to resume play. But not the same thing as a *close* vote. This golf club has invested four hundred thousand dollars in improvements to the course. The USGA will fail without its Open revenue. The television network is committed to meet its schedule. They will hate finishing in midweek. But murder is not altogether unattractive to them. We will play the seventy-sixth U.S. Open to a final conclusion. If we can count on the players?" The last was as much an insult as a question.

LeBaron's face seemed to draw to a point. "Colburn, when you see me again at this club, speak to me only if it's business. Don't use any word that isn't necessary." LeBaron then began to recite, as if he and Morris were alone in the room: "I can handle Horton. He's terrified of losing his re-election as Commissioner. Only Kirkland and Travis can manage the players. Frankly, I don't care what they decide. We'll salvage the tour if they abandon the Open."

Colburn lit a cigarette to dismiss them.

"Let me walk through the locker room," Morris said to LeBaron, "and see how it sits. I'll leave it to you to put the decision to them to play or quit."

"You've got thirty minutes," said Rutledge. "The plane's waiting."

"What am I supposed to do, breathe through my ears?" Travis Walker complained. He put his bottle of nose drops in his locker. "When it quits raining, I'll quit breathing, if we're still playing on grass."

"It's okay for my lips to fall off as long as you can breathe," said Kirkland. "Those guys even took the Band-Aids out of my bag. No way I could talk them into leaving my chapstick."

"The police station ought to smell better," said Lee Washburn. "They went out of here with a truckload of mouthwash."

"Yeah," hollered Al Morgan across the locker room. "That's the idea. We'll all smell so raunchy nobody will get close enough to drown us."

He raised a few nervous laughs.

"Did you have to stop play where you were?" asked Morris.

"Oh, no," said Morgan. "LeBaron pitched a fit. The cops said, pick up. He said, hole out, and then pick up. I think he would've gone after 'em with a sand wedge. They let us hole out, but with just the clubs we could carry in our hands. Couldn't touch our bags. On TV it's gonna look like a drug shakedown in a Central American airport."

The laughs were shorter.

But each of them had finished the hole he was playing before the search, thought Morris. The third round could be completed. It didn't have to be replayed entirely.

The air was suddenly quiet.

"Morris, how do you die in a steam room?" asked Travis.

He shook his head. "I have no idea. There wasn't a mark on him."

"You saw him?" said Washburn, the silence even heavier in the room.

Morris nodded. "I was with him last night. He seemed tired, but fine. I left him in the steam room. He hadn't moved when we found him."

"We were in there all week," said Dolan. "I missed last night. My back wasn't stiff for the first time in eight years." Dolan dropped his shoes as if for emphasis.

"We'll never see a sweeter iron player," said Art Howard, removing his dark glasses, and wiping his face with a towel, blinking his eyes against the dim light.

"What happens to the Open, Travis?" asked Kirkland. "How can we lose three golfers and keep playing?"

"How can we not play after seventy-six years of Opens?"

"All we can do is wait," said Kirkland. His lips were badly chapped. Morris could see it hurt him to speak.

"We can't leave town," said Travis, "not without problems with the police. Somebody's got to tell us what happened to Tommy."

"What about Chicago next week?" asked Morgan.

"Do we play there?" said Washburn.

"What about the rest of the tour?" Dolan looked into each of their faces.

The room was quiet again.

"We can finish here in a day," said Kirkland. "If we play, what are we, greedy?"

"If we don't play, what are we?" asked Travis.

The players broke into separate conversations.

Travis spoke very low, so that only Morris and Kirkland could hear him. "I was glad it was you, Pete, who came after me. I always thought you could pass the game along to Tommy, when the time came."

"Listen, Travis. You're going to play forever. And there'll be another great young player." Kirkland's voice was heavy with emotion.

Morris turned, expecting to see Fryer sitting, drinking an ever present orange juice in front of his locker.

The twin-engine state plane was taking on gas. The front had passed, but it was not a promising sky to fly in. The pay phone rang in the one-room building.

"Yes," said Morris.

"It's an unusual time to take a vacation," said Julia Sullivan. "I got your message from Frank. I noticed it was not an invitation. St. Simons is my favorite island." The false cheer went out of her voice. "Why Tommy?" she said. "The world's gone mad."

"Someone has," said Morris. "We've got to stop him. Rutledge wants to see Rossi's files. He thinks I can help him. We'll be back by morning. Catch a ride with Frank to the hotel. I told New York I'd be out of touch, but they'll be calling all night. Take the phone off the hook if you have to."

"I'll just wait for the next hearse." Her voice was not pretty to hear. "How did he die, Morris?"

"They don't know. I left him sitting there last night, Sullivan. He looked tired, but he was fine. When we found him, he hadn't moved."

"Morris, can't we leave? Go home?" She got her breath. "I'm sorry. Of course you can't. I'll be here. Miss me," she said.

"I already do." They hung up.

"The plane's ready," said Rutledge behind him. Morris followed him through the glass door.

As soon as the plane was in the air, Rutledge flipped on his tape recorder. "Have we learned anything?" he asked.

Morris almost came out of his seat. "Last night's TV show. About the Open. Did you see it?"

"Yes," said Rutledge. "I also talked with Don Murray, the announcer who did the show. He told me he mentioned it to you this morning. Rossi and Joe Goodner went after each other. Over the course, over Kirkland, even over Bobby Jones. Murray edited out the worst of it. He played the soundtrack for me. Rossi and Goodner had no use for each other. Men have killed each other for lesser reasons."

"I'm sure Goodner was going to lose his TV contract," said Morris. "Rossi wanted him out."

Rutledge made a note to himself in his pad. "Did Goodner and Fryer get along?"

"I don't know of any particular incident between them," said Morris. "Goodner resented all the young players, after he was finished. He didn't admit anybody had hit the ball properly since Hogan. And himself, of course. Shouldn't you be at the course? Taking statements from everybody?"

"It's being done," said Rutledge. "You tell me. Who *couldn't* have met Fryer in his hotel? Until we know what killed him, we can't know what time frames are important. Of course, they'll have my head if we don't learn something from Rossi's files. But they'll have it anyway."

"New York knows I'm out of my skull," said Morris. "We lose the leader of the Open for two days running, and I'm flying four hundred miles to look through the files of a teaching pro who killed himself."

Rutledge pulled on a cigarette and snapped his ballpoint pen in and out in his left hand. They were the only two passengers in the Beechcraft. Morris leaned back in the near dark, his left leg stretched full length down the aisle between them. "You still haven't found Old Thompson?" he asked.

"Don't remind me. We have a stationful of drunks, none of them caddies. Everybody came to the course today in rain gear. You couldn't identify anybody in that storm, not even four blonde girls."

"I can almost understand some maniac killing two superstars," said Morris. "For money, or envy, or some unknown hate of himself, maybe. But why Rossi?"

"That's why we're on this plane," said Rutledge, shutting off the tape recorder. "They still kill people for money, all right," he said, his eyes closed. "Fryer was under contract to your friend Holland, the same as Whitlow. *I* might have killed them both, for two million dollars."

"He's somebody in golf," said Morris. "Somebody who knows our habits. Somebody you *expect* to see every day."

Rutledge was asleep. Morris looked down at Georgia, the great distances between small towns, and even highways. It might have been an uninhabited country of green pines, except for the straight discipline of fences. The open land gave him a depth of sadness he could not explain, yet he could not stop looking down on it. There was no hint of the lives that were lived along the distant roads.

Morris woke as the plane banked in the air for its approach to St. Simons. The green-on-green Marshes of Glynn stretched out of sight around the rim of the mainland; then they were down.

Rutledge awoke. "Rossi's secretary is meeting us," he said, working his powerful right leg as if it were numb with sleep. "I want a cup of coffee, and I want the friend who hated Rossi. But we mustn't get ahead of ourselves."

A lone figure, a woman, was waiting outside the small airport building in the flat heat of the island. Morris was surprised that she was young. His mind had arbitrarily anticipated a precise old maid.

"Detective Rutledge?" She extended her hand between them.

Rutledge took it awkwardly. "This is Morris of the Associated Press. John Morris." Her hand was cool in the heat.

"No baggage?" she asked, looking behind them.

"Just this." Rutledge patted his briefcase and tape recorder. "We could use a bit of coffee, and then we better get straight to work."

"I've some freshly made at the office. Oh, my name, Mr. Morris, is Caroline. Caroline Winters. Do you know St. Simons?" They might have been down to invest in real estate. Nothing about her hinted what had happened to Rossi.

"Yes," said Morris. "I did. Years ago. I hope it hasn't changed too much."

"It's changed," she said. "Not yet too much. I grew up here." They were getting in her car, a simple Chevrolet. "I suppose I don't hate every change, like some of our natives. We have several new golf courses, at least one of them bankrupt. Without the Island Course, I would never have known Jim Rossi. I would regret that very much. The office is out the island, toward Fort Frederica and Christ Church. You remember the way?" She looked back at Morris.

He nodded that he did. He was puzzled that she was directing her conversation to him.

"Miss Winters," said Rutledge. "Does Rossi's suicide make any sense at all?"

"No," she said. "Jim Rossi did not kill himself." She only glanced at them both, sure that they agreed with her. "He had no reason to. He had sound investments, a large income. He loved everything about teaching golf. He was a generous man, and could afford to be. You knew him well, Mr. Morris. He often spoke of you. He always read your stories. He had several newspapers flown in so that he could follow the golf." She concentrated on her driving. The traffic was far heavier than Morris remembered it.

"He taught golf very seriously," said Caroline. "He didn't care about your age, or your level of skill. He would teach you as long as you worked, and took his advice."

"What if you didn't take his advice?" asked Rutledge.

"Sometimes it caused hard feelings," she said, "even with highly skilled players. He would warn me to expect an angry call from someone he had dropped. Ted Dolan was one, some years ago. John Whitlow dropped us. I've made notes. Jim Rossi was honest and fair, but not everybody liked him." She looked back at Morris, seemingly for reassurance that she was not being disloyal.

"If he kept records of all of his lessons," said Morris, "the file must take up the northern end of the island."

"Not really," she said. "He used tape recordings. His notes on each student's progress take only a few sentences. I've pulled the tapes on all his lessons with tour professionals for the last five years. There haven't been a great number. Nothing like the women pros who depended on him; they're terrified about their games, and sick about Jim."

"Did he have financial dealings with golfers?" asked Rutledge.

"He lent money to many of them."

"And to writers," said Morris. "You could always count on Rossi to help finance your divorce."

"He was a generous man," said Caroline. "I have his financial papers: his loans and gifts to anyone in golf. The paperwork is rather complex, but I can guide you through it. Then I have his correspondence, and records of his phone calls from the office. Most of it won't have a bearing on what you are looking for. I can help save you time."

"What are we looking for?" asked Rutledge.

"The man who killed Jim Rossi." She took her eyes off the road to look at them both. "I want him found, and tried, and, I hope, executed." She looked back at the road. "I'm sorry if that sounds cold blooded. It's how I feel. Here's the office." She turned between two mounds of palmettos into a clearing of live oaks. A small cypress and glass building was fitted under and between the dark twisted limbs of the tree.

"Have you heard about the death of Tommy Fryer?" asked Rutledge.

"Yes." She stopped the car under a limb weeping with Spanish moss. "It was on the radio. Fryer never took lessons from Jim. I'm sure of that. But Jim admired him. His swing and his personality. Jim thought he should practice more. He often said that one day he would regret it."

"He's beyond regret," said Morris.

"Did Whitlow come here?" asked Rutledge.

"Yes, he came here several times. Before and after the past Christmas holidays. But he had trouble with his game, and went back to his old swing. Jim had warned him it would take a year, or two years, to relearn his swing. Jim also told him he could be the next great player if he would sacrifice the time and money to do it. He couldn't. I don't think he tried very hard."

"How did Rossi take it?" asked Rutledge.

"Very hard. He was almost bitter about it. He thought it was such a waste. But he didn't hold a grudge. He would have been sick at what happened to Whitlow. You must stop this man, whoever he is."

"Were you and Rossi lovers?" asked Rutledge with no warning.

"No. No fault of mine. I don't think he even suspected how I felt about him. Golf was his life. Poor Margaret invented her own world to live in, most of it terrifying. She's in the East with her sister now. I don't know if she will ever be able to live alone. Come on inside."

Being in the office was like sitting in a very low tree house. The limbs from the live oaks were visible in every window. There were only three rooms: a reception area with deep, comfortable chairs, and Caroline's desk in the corner; Rossi's office, which was mostly glass, with stop-action photographs of the golf swing on the two solid walls; and the long viewing room, which was lined with filing cabinets. It could be closed off with draperies for looking at slides and motion pictures of the golf swing. The ceiling in the viewing room was high enough for the actual rehearsal of the swing. There was even a patch of astroturf on the floor. Several golf clubs stood in a rack in the corner.

The coffee was rich and hot.

"Let's start with the financial papers," said Rutledge.

Morris was surprised at the extent of Rossi's generosity. Much of it to older players whose names were a hazy recollection even to him. "Rossi couldn't have known them," said Morris. "They were finished before he was even on the tour." Two of the old-timers were big names in their day, Open champions, Whitley and Jernigan. Morris had not known they were in financial trouble. He had written about them both. Rossi had mailed them each checks of fifteen hundred dollars for the last five years.

" 'For services rendered,' " quoted Caroline. "Of course, there were no services. Jernigan writes a short, very formal, thank you, every fall. We never hear from Whitley."

"I'll be damned," said Morris. "Here's a check I saw Thursday. To Alfred Mancha, one of the last of the old caddies. He carries for Al Morgan. Rossi had just died. Alfred wondered if the check was still good."

"I know about Al Morgan," said Caroline. She lifted

another folder onto the table. "We carried all loans forward for tax purposes." There were five single-spaced pages of them. Opposite Al's name were a list of amounts and dates, and the total figure, seven thousand five hundred dollars. "He once owed us more than that, but paid it all back three years ago. We sent him fifteen hundred dollars just last month."

"This one is ridiculous," said Morris, pointing down the list of names and loans. "Travis Walker couldn't know he owes Rossi seven hundred fifty dollars." Travis had netted five million dollars last year. "Talk about your easy touches," said Morris, "only I never heard of Travis keeping any records of his loans."

"I'm sure Mr. Walker simply forgot the seven hundred fifty dollars," said Caroline. "Jim never allowed me to send a statement to anybody. If they forgot, they forgot. That loan was twenty-four years ago."

"About the time Travis married," said Morris. "If Jim didn't collect, why didn't he throw the records out?" The sight of the old forgotten debt irritated him. Did anybody ever kill a man out of sheer irritation? Probably, he thought.

"That's the agent, Everette Holland?" said Rutledge, of a name on the list.

"Yes."

He had the largest outstanding debt, twelve thousand five hundred dollars. But he had paid it down from twenty thousand in the last five years.

"Ev said something to me that I didn't understand," said Morris. "He said it would be impossible for him with Rossi gone. Now I understand what he meant."

Caroline had his file. "Mr. Holland formed a partnership with four other men, eight years ago. He borrowed twenty thousand dollars from Jim for his share of the financing. You can see he has made regular payments. He's a very nice man."

"How much was Rossi worth?" asked Morris.

"I don't know the size of his total estate," said Caroline, "but, judging from his income, it would have to be several million dollars. He earned a great deal of money teaching golf, and in book royalties. But his real estate investments made him a wealthy man. His attorney, here on the island, handles that."

"Who inherits the estate?" asked Rutledge.

"I don't have a copy of his will, but I've seen it. It's left in trust to his wife. Some to his sister. There's a separate trust for golf. Small amounts for many of the players and caddies in these files."

Morris turned to Rossi's teaching records. "Who is 'W'?" he asked. It was a recent entry: W—lessons to start, July 3.

"Jim was tremendously excited about that," she said. "W stands for Washburn. It was just a shorthand. Sometimes he forgot who the letters stood for. I always tried to make a note. Jim was sure Lee Washburn had the ability to become the greatest player on the tour. He was to come down after the Open. You can listen to Jim's comments. He had already begun a tape."

Caroline stopped. "I pulled the tape, but I can't listen to it. His voice is so alive. It doesn't seem possible he is dead." For the first time, her defenses seemed threatened.

"Here are four lessons with 'T.W.,' " said Morris. "Now tell me that's not Travis Walker. What a fraud." He laughed. "Travis swears he never took a lesson from anybody but his old man."

"It was three years ago, after his father died," said Caroline. "Walker insisted on secrecy. He flew here in his own plane at night. They were on the tee at six A.M. It was all hush-hush. You would have thought Jim was giving him plans to the B-1 bomber."

"Nothing he would rather fly," said Morris. He was sorry the lessons had not helped. But not even Rossi's camera could stop time. "He must have had fun, tinkering with the most famous bad swing in the history of golf."

"I don't see Pete Kirkland's name or initials," said Rutledge. "Did he ever come by?"

"No." She turned through the telephone records, which she had kept with a meticulousness that must have pleased Rossi. "You can see Kirkland often called. They talked about golf courses he was building. Jim had almost total recall of every major course in the world. Kirkland would describe problems he had, and compare them with certain famous holes. Jim would suggest ideas. He loved doing it. You can listen to notes he made to himself afterward."

Rutledge was turning the pages of loans and gifts, which

were listed by date. "Ted Dolan," he said. "Twenty-five hundred dollars, this April. Did he ever come back?"

"Yes," she said. "About four years ago. They argued constantly over his swing. Jim wouldn't teach him anymore, but he helped Dolan get a top club job last year. He was upset when Dolan walked out on the job this winter. They didn't seem to be close, but they had been contemporaries on the tour. He could never get Dolan to change something about his grip. You can hear it on the tape."

"Was he helping anyone else find a club job?" asked Morris.

"Yes. He had called a number of clubs recently. I don't know for whom. I usually didn't get involved until he was asked to write a formal letter of recommendation. He didn't seem to be having any luck."

Morris counted fourteen calls, to clubs from Georgia to California. "We need these clubs and numbers," said Rutledge.

"Wait and we'll copy all the pages you need at once," she said. "There's a Xerox machine we can use on the island. It doesn't matter how late we finish."

"Did the TV commentator, Joe Goodner, ever call, or write, or come by here?" asked Morris.

"Definitely not. I think he was the only man Jim Rossi openly disliked."

"Why do you say that?" Rutledge asked, looking up from the pages of loans and gifts.

"Goodner tried to get him fired from the broadcast team. We got several letters from Don Murray. You have to read between the lines. But Jim knew what was happening. Jim had signed a new three-year contract. He felt sure they were dropping Goodner."

"How do you know that?" asked Rutledge.

"He told me. I have a copy of his new contract." She found it, as well as three letters from Don Murray.

"I see Edward Horton called several times recently," said Morris.

"Horton?" she repeated. "Oh, yes, the players' commissioner. Yes, I have some letters." She got them from the files. "His contract is coming up for renewal. He and Jim were not close. Jim often disagreed with him, but you can see he supported him.

"The man Jim loved with the PGA was Frank LeBaron. I know you are friends," she said to Morris.

He nodded. He did not trust himself to speak. The three of them, LeBaron, Rossi, himself, were kids together when the tour was still young.

"Here's a call. Last Friday," said Rutledge. "To Art Howard. Was he taking lessons? Or borrowing money?"

Caroline couldn't place him at first. "I remember. We were returning his call." She was checking her notes from last week. "He wanted an appointment. During the Open. I suppose about his game. Jim agreed to see him during the tournament. They didn't fix an exact time."

She flipped through the records of loans. "I'm sure we never lent him money. I know Jim liked him. We kept trying until we were able to return his call."

Morris looked at his watch. Two hours had flown by. "Let me start the tapes," he said. "When I hit something I think you should hear, I'll holler." Rutledge agreed, barely lifting his head from the records.

Morris threaded the tape of John Whitlow's lessons. Rossi did not waste a syllable. He dictated in rapid, surgical phrases the technical causes of Whitlow's sway. He described other slight flaws in his setup and grip. His tempo was fast, but Rossi felt it suited him. By the third dictation on the tape, Rossi knew that Whitlow would not stick with the new swing. It was strange to hear his voice, saying, "The next time he misses the cut, he will revert to his old swing. He will never reach his full potential." The words were clipped, but without emphasis, as if they were said by some new computer prophet. Morris listened for the disappointment Rossi had to feel, but it was not on the tape.

Rutledge listened to a replay of the tape without comment.

Three hours later, Morris could no longer distinguish between the voices on the tapes. Only at his dictation about Lee Washburn did Rossi reveal his involvement. His pronunciation became as smooth and fluid as Washburn's take-away. "Only a tendency to close the clubface is between Washburn and the most enviable swing in modern golf." Morris rewound the tape for Rutledge to hear. Rossi had always been conservative with his opinions. His estimation of Washburn's potential was almost historic. Washburn himself was making a powerful commitment, to risk altering his swing in mid-summer, at the height of the big-money tournaments.

It was nine P.M. They had a small mound of papers to be copied. Descriptions of forty golf swings were whirling through Morris's mind. The coffee was gone. Rutledge's dark complexion could not hide his fatigue. Caroline Winters slid down in her chair with her feet stretched out in front of her.

Rutledge stood up with the stack of papers. "We'll take you to dinner. I think we've done all the damage we can do on this island."

Morris was sure Rutledge would not say her name. "Caroline, we thank you," he said himself. She lifted a hand in response. Morris felt a sudden sense of panic. He did not know what he had expected to learn. They had found out much that he did not know. But what did it mean? Somehow he had expected to learn more. How did what they had seen and heard fit together? And what did it tell them?

Neither of them slept. The plane moved smoothly as though the dark had quieted the air.

"What do we know?" asked Morris. His voice strained above the engines. He realized he did not know the man who turned to hear his question. He could be married, single, divorced, widowed. Corrupt. The Lieutenant's square face in the faint cabin light, his calm, eased Morris's mind. The unanswered questions did not seem so desperate to him.

"Your friend Rossi was a complex man," said Rutledge, speaking directly ahead as if to himself. "He was generous. But he kept a record of a twenty-four-year-old debt. He knew the golf swing. But he only taught it on his own terms. He put Joe Goodner on his broadcast team, and Goodner tried to have him fired." Rutledge waited. "Rossi's wife was ill. His secretary loved him, but he did not respond. She *says*. He lived on an island, but his mind reached into the lives of the most powerful men in golf, and in broadcasting. One of those lives came back to kill him. One of *these* lives." Rutledge lifted the briefcase in his lap.

He waited again. Morris did not speak. The detective opened his briefcase and turned through his notes. "The girl, Winters, is right. Jim Rossi was not a man to kill himself. Oh, no. It was as if he meant to dominate the minds and swings of the players who came after him. Was that unnatural?"

141

Morris was as surprised at his language as at his question. He considered it. "All teaching pros have their methods. But it's true. Rossi was inflexible." Morris could hear Jim reciting every aberration of every player's swing—distantly, almost coldly, always disapprovingly, without inflection. And yet, on Wednesday, he had remembered Travis Walker's baggy pants of 1954. "He was fair in his television commentary. He never flattered a moderate effort. He was right too damn much." Morris was quiet. He could not say it aloud; it was too trivial, too personal, but he remembered again the only moments he had ever seen Rossi forget himself, when they would hit the small, original motel pools, the water cold in January, even in California, both of them laughing spurts of air under the surface.

Rutledge watched him carefully. Then he spoke again from his notes. "John Whitlow was unable to change his golf swing. He said nasty things about Rossi. 'Friends' made sure that Rossi heard them." Rutledge turned a page. "Rossi gave money to old, washed-up players who could not help him. No one even remembers their names. He gave money to caddies and to some active players. But mostly he made loans. He didn't try to collect them, but he kept careful records. Ev Holland, the agent, owed him as much as twenty thousand dollars. He still owes half of it. Holland's only clients, Fryer and Whitlow, have been murdered."

Rutledge did not pause over the word *murdered*; he might have said *honored*, thought Morris.

"I'm sure Holland had a multimillion-dollar policy on Fryer, just as he did on Whitlow. We'll find out tomorrow. Something we already know—the policy on Whitlow is in the name of a corporation owned solely by Holland. His partners will be surprised to learn that."

Morris was surprised that Rutledge knew it. He did not try to imagine how Ev had gotten the news of Tommy's death.

Rutledge began again. "Rossi often found club jobs for touring players who wanted them, or needed them. He was looking for such a job, for somebody. He once gave 'private' lessons to Travis Walker. He advised Kirkland on the designs of golf courses. He was not close to Edward Horton, but supported him for re-election as players' commissioner. Rossi had an appointment with a middle-aged pro, Art Howard, during the Open. Two other over-the-hill pros owed him

142

money, Al Morgan and Ted Dolan. The most gifted and frustrated player on the tour, Lee Washburn, was coming to him for help." Rutledge closed his notebook in the near dark.

"You can't simply *list* a man's life," said Morris, suddenly irritated. "When you do, his generosity and his selfishness read like the same act."

"They do when the order of things includes his own murder."

They flew for a long time with only the sound of the engines in the dimly lit cabin. Both of them were exhausted. Neither of them slept.

"Where do we start tomorrow?" asked Morris, his eyes closed.

"At the morgue," said Rutledge.

17 ✠

MORRIS STEPPED OUT OF THE CAB FROM THE AIRPORT. THE night air gave him a false sense of energy. By the time he walked into the hotel, he was all fatigue. It was Sullivan's hotel. He was dead, but he did not want to be alone. Maybe it was the great distance that had separated Rossi from the world that frightened him. He cracked the room door. Luckily the chain was not fixed. He slid off his shoes in the dark.

Sullivan always slept rolled in a ball. "Who's that?" she said, not really awake.

"The UPI."

"I only use the Associated Press," she said unclearly. She was still rolled in a ball.

"It's okay to use them. You wouldn't want your daughter to marry one."

He stretched out on the bed. She was now too still to be sleeping.

"New York's been calling. Ringing every hotel bed in town."

"I bet."

She was awake but still in a ball. "The city's gone mad. The Governor. The Mayor. The National Guard. Even the federal government. Everybody's been interviewed except the murderer."

"I wouldn't be too sure," said Morris.

"Oh?" She turned over in spite of herself.

"Whoever he is, he's no stranger."

Morris's mind was spongy with fatigue. "It's too complicated to puzzle out. But whoever killed Rossi knew him well. Maybe owed him money. Or hated him. Or both. He's someone we know, someone we see every day."

"If they arrest everybody in golf who knew Rossi, who we see every day, they'll have to start a penal colony. Let's start it in the Virgin Islands."

"What killed Tommy Fryer?" Morris said, almost to himself. Fatigue rose up in him. He was dreaming before he was asleep.

The clock in his head went off silently, and Morris was awake. It was still dark. He was more tired than before he slept. He rolled quietly out of bed. Sullivan never unfolded herself. The bathroom light shot into his eyes. The blade was old in his spare razor, and raked his face.

Light was now breaking between the buildings. Morris had to wake a driver in his cab. He gave directions. The driver was too sleepy to speak.

The old man was standing alone outside the city morgue. Morris dreaded getting out of the cab.

Dr. William Moseley offered his thin hand. The coroner's face was incredibly tired under his fine white hair. "I see our detective," he said, looking past Morris.

Rutledge was walking toward them, not hurrying, as if they were having a civic club breakfast. Rutledge raised his thick left hand without speaking.

"I've been here all night," said the old man. The lack of color in his face was terrible to see. "I need coffee." They started toward a cheap all-night restaurant. The old man drifted slightly between them, but kept moving his thin legs. Rutledge still had not spoken. Nor Morris.

Moseley took the coffee as if it were a sacrament. Then he spoke very slowly, in a voice without substance. "Don't send

144

me any more boys," he said. He took the coffee again between his ash-white hands. "I'm too old for any more boys. I mean it." He looked at them as if they were personally responsible for the last two deaths.

"Difficult to know the exact time of death," said the old man. "All that heat accelerates deterioration of the tissues. But I would fix it between eleven and twelve P.M. Maybe nearer twelve."

"What time did he eat?" asked Rutledge, his voice cracking from its first use.

"About nine o'clock, nothing unusual. Not a mark on him. No cardiovascular disease. His heart simply stopped beating about midnight." Moseley raised his cup for a refill of coffee. After the lone waiter retreated, he continued. "No heavy metal, or any poison showed up. No overdose of barbiturates. We are running even more sophisticated tests. They will take time." He waited, drinking his coffee.

"The heart of a twenty-seven-year-old athlete doesn't just quit beating," said Morris. His own scratchy voice did not soften his suspicion.

The old man was not offended. "No. There are drugs that could stop it. Digitalis has been used. But usually administered over a long period of time, to a heart patient. It would show up readily in the blood." He waited again. "I've been in pathology for fifty-three years. I've been a coroner for thirty-five. I know my job. It's not an exact science. It very nearly is, but the physical makeup and tolerance of every man is different. In criminal pathology you also need an instinct for what happened. Maybe I'm too damn old. Maybe I stayed one case too long." He seemed to sink in his chair with age and indifference.

"You mean that's it," said Morris. "*Heart failure?*" He did not try to contain the sarcasm in his voice.

"Maybe," the old man said. Still he was not offended. He drank from his coffee. He seemed to rise up as he set down the cup.

"What do you mean?" asked Rutledge.

Moseley's white hair fell over his dead white forehead. "I talked with three heart specialists at Emory University. One of them came down. We weighed every combination of circumstances and drug. What could stop his heart, without enlarging it, without damaging it? And not leave evidence of itself? Really only one thing." The old man drained his coffee. "Shock," he said. He looked them both in the eye.

"You don't mean he was frightened to death," said Morris, sarcasm now rampant in his voice.

"Shock would have the same effect," said Moseley, undisturbed. "There are many circumstances that can throw the body into shock. Loss of blood, of course. And certain drugs will do it. But he was uninjured, and any drug in an amount lethal to his heart could be easily traced. Or almost any drug."

He did not wait for Rutledge to question him. "Early this morning, Dr. James Sutherland asked me if the boy had a history of hypothyroidism. I see no evidence he suffered any disorder of the thyroid. I have not contacted his family. It will be easy enough to establish."

The old man's politeness was as genuine as his great age. "Let me try to explain a drug to you, gentlemen. Excuse me if I oversimplify. The thyroid is a gland at the front of the neck. It regulates body metabolism. The thyroid produces a large amount of a substance we call T-4, and a tiny amount of a substance we call T-3, or triiodothyronine. You don't have to spell it to understand it." The old man's lips thinned in a near smile. "Almost all of the physiological effects of the thyroid gland are performed by the agent T-3. Most of the body's T-3 is actually formed outside the thyroid in peripheral tissues, from T-4 that comes from the thyroid. Do you follow me?"

"More or less," said Morris, embarrassed over his own sarcasm.

Rutledge was taking notes with his heavy left hand slanted across the table in front of him.

Moseley continued, "If a person were given a massive overdose of T-3, it would completely bypass the body's natural regulation of the drug. T-3 promotes the synthesis of protein. Speeds up metabolism, as the body actually burns up its own tissues. An overdose would irritate the heart muscle until it beat faster and irregularly. It would also dilate the blood vessels, creating a large vascular bed for the heart to fill, as if you increased the size of a vat you were pumping into, causing the heart to strain to fill it. If a person were in a steam bath . . ."

Rutledge looked up from his notes.

". . . The heat would also cause the blood vessels to dilate further, and the blood volume to be lowered as water escaped. The concentration of T-3 would thus be even further increased in the blood. The heart, exposed to such an amount of T-3, and an increased workload, might go into shock, and fail of ventricular fibrillation. Before there had been time for any abnormal pathological changes, such as enlargement of the heart, to have occurred. The heart would fail and the body would die. And there would be no abnormality."

"What about the presence of that amount of T-3 in the blood?" asked Rutledge. "Couldn't you measure it?"

"Difficult to say. A certain amount occurs normally in the body. There is only one method of measuring it. That's to run a radioimmunoassay on a blood sample. We are doing that. But it will take sixteen hours. It's a complex process. We actually measure the presence of T-3 by radioactive count, plotted against a standard curve. A lethal amount should be obvious. But not necessarily. What might be a dangerous amount at room temperature could be lethal in a steam bath. As I said, pathology is not an exact science."

"How long would it take an overdose of T-3 to take effect?" asked Morris.

"Hard to say." Moseley pulled his thin hands over his white face. "A maximum effect should occur within four to six hours after ingestion. He would experience a rise in temperature, warming of the skin, vasodilation, rise in heart rate, possibly shock, ventricular fibrillation . . . and death. The steam room would accelerate the process."

"Anyone in the clubhouse locker room could have put it in his orange juice," said Morris.

"Did Fryer seem to be in trouble, to be sick, in the steam room?" asked Rutledge.

Morris ran his hand through his black and gray hair. "He kept his head in his hands. And he turned on the bench, as if he might have been uncomfortable in the heat."

"What did he say?"

"We talked. About writing. About golf. About Travis Walker. He was upset about Whitlow. He blamed himself for not being more helpful to him. It was nonsense. Nobody could help Whitlow grow up. I told him that. He was running with sweat. But then he was in the steam room when I got there. I did ask him if he were feeling all right."

147

"What did you say exactly?" asked Rutledge.

"He had his head in his hands. I said something like, 'You all right, Tommy?' He didn't answer. He just nodded his head without lifting it from his hands. I told him I had to go. And not to stay in there too long. He waved without looking up."

Nobody spoke.

The old man was talked out. The coffee no longer helped.

"Is there any reason other than hypothyroidism to prescribe T-3?" asked Morris.

"To test for it," said Moseley. "The thyroid should shut down if you give the body an oversupply. Then . . . it's very poor medicine, but certain careless, 'high society' doctors have given patients small supplies of triiodothyronine, to speed up metabolism and weight loss. It would usually be given with an ordinary—and dangerous, too—appetite depressant. It's very bad medicine."

Morris and Rutledge both sat up with their elbows dominating the top of the table.

"How is it prescribed?" asked Rutledge.

"In tablets. An irresponsible doctor might prescribe ten fifty-microgram tablets to be taken, one a day. Twenty such tablets, dissolved and administered at one time, would produce a serum level far above normal, high enough to run completely off the standard curve, which measures eight hundred nanograms per one hundred cc of serum. It could be fatal, even to a young athlete of twenty-seven. The tablets are easily dissolvable."

"Amphetamines are typical appetite depressants," said Rutledge.

The old man nodded his head. He sat in an erect collapse.

Rutledge snapped his pen, in and out, in his left hand. "Has the lab turned up anything of interest in the drugs taken yesterday from the golfers?"

"Plenty of cigarettes. A bit of marijuana. Booze. Librium. Valium. Codeine. Muscle relaxants. A mountain of junk. Golfers must all be hypochondriacs. We'll be testing for weeks," said Moseley.

"I'll send over a list of no more than fifteen names," said Rutledge. "In an hour. Test their stuff first. Will that speed it up?"

148

"Oh, yes," said the old man. "Much of it we just smell or taste. If we don't drop dead, it's okay." He laughed.

Morris was amazed how young his laugh sounded, as if it came from some lost place inside himself. "The pro-ams," said Morris. "Who plays in them before every tournament? 'Fat Cats.' Businessmen. Lawyers. *Doctors*. It costs as much as fifteen hundred dollars for them to play one round with the pros."

Rutledge looked up, then touched the old man on the arm. "You go home and sleep. We won't send you any more boys. I promise."

The police station, in its declension of repair, retreated from Decatur Street, as though itself a fugitive from society.

Television reporters mounted an electronic barrier on the dull concrete steps to the entrance.

"Good Lord," said Rutledge.

Morris had already filed a report of their flying trip to St. Simons Island. He included nothing of what they had learned. He could not even speculate that there had been three murders. Not on the Associated Press wire. Not until Rutledge said they were murders.

"Lieutenant!" Cameramen jockeyed for position. All three television networks needed footage, even if it was the same footage. Meter readings were taken. Rutledge might have been auditioning for a low-budget thriller.

"How did Tommy Fryer die?" A major network reporter fired the first question.

"He died of heart failure. The exact cause is still being investigated."

"What do you mean, 'exact cause'?"

"The final autopsy report has not been completed," said Rutledge. His bulk, his lumpy suit, stood formidably in front of the cameras.

"Was he murdered?" The words were thrown down on the unclean steps.

"You tell me," said Rutledge. "Maybe golf is just a dangerous game."

The reporters lost their carefully nourished composure. Questions scrambled other questions, words and tempers flew around the perimeter. Reporters crowded in front of a camera.

149

"Back off!" shouted a muscled cameraman. "Didn't you hillbillies ever question a cop?"

"Dammit, shut up!"

Rutledge did not move, or speak.

Morris's own pulse quickened as if evidence against the murderer had been increased in midair. He breathed in slowly several times. What has been increased, he thought, is the risk, the risk to Rutledge. The detective parried all of their questions. Morris maneuvered his own bulk with his cane until he was beside a local AP reporter.

"What has he got?" the reporter asked.

"A gut feeling," said Morris. "No hard evidence. Yet. They're pushing me in New York. Tell them we'll have the one break that matters. *Who did it*. When he knows who did it."

The reporter nodded.

Morris moved away, ignoring the frantic hand on his arm. To hell with New York.

"Why?" insisted a reporter. "*Why* were they all killed?"

Morris watched Rutledge, who stood unmoving in the center of eyes and lenses.

Rutledge ignored the multiple calling of the question. He walked through the ragged line of reporters and policemen, looking back once, powerfully down on the cameras, a scene that would doubtlessly be thrown on millions of television screens.

Morris was sure Rutledge was looking for him. He wedged his way with his cane to the station door. Two cops looked at him, and at each other, and let him inside. Rutledge stood waiting. Morris followed him into his office. It was larger than he had imagined. And more bankrupt of content. The ugly wooden chairs must have survived an earlier, uglier building.

"This room was built for a Captain of Homicide," said Rutledge, throwing his coat on his chair, its swivel sprung perpetually backward. "I'll be lucky to retire a Detective Sergeant. Sit down. We don't have long. They'll want me in there." He nodded toward the bowels of the station. "I'll be on my hands and knees to City Hall inside thirty minutes. We've got to move, Morris. If we let them cancel the tournament, they take the murderer with them. Maybe he never has to pay." Rutledge leaned over the desk. "We keep him here. I don't care who he kills, he doesn't get away."

Rutledge pushed a pad of paper toward him. "Write me fifteen names. One of whom is the murderer. We'll compare lists." He was clicking the button on his pen in and out, as if to prime it.

Morris lifted his own pen. It was as cold as judgment in his hand. Sixty-six golfers were left in the field, all of them with caddies. There were tournament officials, announcers, the press, thirty thousand fans. His mind was delaying. It wasn't that difficult. The innocent people he weighed did not stop him. But when he wrote the name of the true murderer, he would somehow fix his guilt in time, as if he himself were an accomplice after the fact. Morris squeezed his forehead. He began to write without determining the order of the names.

Al Morgan. Broke. Game failing. Owes everybody, including Washburn. Alcoholic. Gambler. Age 40. May be finished. Saw Rossi from the elevator minutes before he was killed. Owed him money. Seduced Whitlow's wife, *after* he was dead. Fryer saw them in the pool. Was at the course when Whitlow drowned. Was in the same hotel with Fryer. Claims Whitlow saw Washburn cheat in British Open to defeat Fryer. That Whitlow threatened to expose him. Why would Whitlow or Morgan lie?

Joe Goodner. Hated Rossi. May have been losing his job as a TV commentator. In the Towers Hotel when Rossi died. Said he saw Art Howard with Rossi two hours before Rossi died. Art denies it. Who's lying? Why? At the course when Whitlow drowned. Staying in Fryer's hotel. Bitter, his golf career cut short by injury. Golfers dislike him. Aging, he resents talent and youth.

Old Thompson. Drunk. Health ruined. Fired by Whitlow. Was in the hotel minutes before Rossi died, asking for his room number. Not seen when Whitlow drowned. Not seen when Fryer died. Not yet found to be questioned. Sick, but still powerful, desperate, and maybe dying man.

Ted Dolan. Age 46. Quit secure club job in January that Rossi had gotten him. Owed Rossi $2,500. Hook killing his game. Broke. Desperate. Can't tolerate blond kids dominating the tour. Cast-iron temper. Saw Rossi from elevator before he was killed. Skipped that fact in interview with Rutledge. Paired with Whitlow before his death. Did not speak during round. Refused to answer when Whitlow asked about his missing putter, just before he drowned. Hated Whitlow, and his easy success. Stayed in same hotel with Fryer. Shared steam bath with him earlier in the week. Skipped steam bath Friday night. "First time his back hadn't been stiff in eight years." No life outside the tour.

Everette Holland. Was losing his only clients, Whitlow and Fryer. Was suing Whitlow for $1.5 million. Insured Whitlow, probably Fryer, for millions. Himself major beneficiary. Denies being in Towers Hotel when Rossi died. At the course when Whitlow drowned. Following him during his round. Whereabouts not known when Fryer died. Finished as agent. Now rich.

Art Howard. Like Morgan, age 40. Losing his careful game. Missing cuts. Lives alone. No family. Cruel nickname, "Dr. Zero." But respected, liked. Known to be close with his money. Did not seem to resent Whitlow, Fryer, siege of blond kids on tour. A loner. Maybe finished as a player. From elevator, saw Rossi before his death. In locker room with Whitlow before he drowned. Stayed in hotel with Fryer. Did not owe Rossi, or take lessons from him. Had appointment with him during tournament. Did he keep the appointment? He says no. That he only planned to discuss his swing with Rossi. Why would he lie? Goodner says he saw them together in the lobby two hours before Rossi died.

Lee Washburn. Maximum talent. Regular winner, but only one major tournament, the British Open. Never realized potential at 32. Should be Travis Walker or Pete Kirkland of his time. Unsatisfied. Violent temper. Close only to his wife. Great natural swing, but was to take lessons from Rossi. Did not mention that fact to Rutledge. In elevator, just before Rossi died. In locker room, before Whitlow drowned. Returned to locker room that night for wallet. Stayed at Fryer's hotel. Tremendous income on tour. Ruthlessly ambitious.

Morgan made a point of insisting that John Whitlow saw Washburn's ball move when he addressed it in the rough at St. Andrews, and that Washburn did not call a stroke penalty on himself. He went on to defeat Tommy Fryer one stroke for the British Open title. If Whitlow saw the ball move, why didn't he call the penalty? Was he threatening Washburn? Washburn has never been accused of cheating, by anybody. Why would Whitlow lie? Why would Morgan lie? What if they weren't lying? Morgan owes Washburn big money.

Edward Horton. Lives only to be Commissioner of Tournament Players. Office up for vote. Attending party in Rossi's hotel just before he was killed. At course when Whitlow drowned. Suite in Fryer's hotel. Fryer was on policy board. Would have had influence in election of commissioner. Political creature. Totally interested in himself. An effective commissioner. Exact relationships with three victims not known.

Frank LeBaron. Loner. Except for his wife, myself. Been on tour as tournament director 21 years. Exhausted. Perfectionist. Scrambled in tour's lean years. Would do *anything* to help keep tour afloat. No real temper. Plenty tough. Rossi considered him his closest friend. Was in hotel when Rossi was killed. Had been with USGA president, James Colburn, until just before time of death. Was at the course when Whitlow drowned. Staying in Fryer's hotel. Obsessed with keeping tour alive.

John Morris. Reporter for AP. Covered tour 21 years. Saw Rossi from elevator. Then was drinking alone in rooftop bar. Saw Rossi fall to lobby. *Alone* in elevator when Rossi fell. Had known Rossi longer, better than anyone but LeBaron. In locker room before Whitlow was drowned. Helped him look for putter, in his bag and in press room. Saw him trotting toward 17th green in the dark. Had written tough story about Whitlow's treatment of his ex-caddy, Old Thompson, day before his death. Saw Morgan with Whitlow's wife after his death. Shared steam room with Fryer when he was dying, without knowing he was ill. Aging, 46. Lives alone. Fixed salary. Could be resentful of millionaire golfers. *Could be unaware of his own actions*.

Morris looked up from his notes. Rutledge was staring into the air over his desk, clicking his pen as though in time with his thoughts. Morris pushed his pages of notes across the desk.

Rutledge read them without looking up. He read them again, seemingly a word at a time. Finished, he handed over his own single sheet of paper.

Morris looked down at the simple list:

Ted Dolan, Everette Holland, Joe Goodner, Al Morgan, Art Howard, Lee Washburn, John Morris, Frank LeBaron, Old Thompson, Edward Horton, Travis Walker, Pete Kirkland, *four girls*.

The four girls were underlined. Morris's own name was printed in the same childlike block letters as the others.

"Morris, as a suspect, do you use vodka as an appetite depressant?" asked Rutledge, his face threatening to smile. It was the only humor Morris had ever heard in the detective's voice.

"Careful," said Morris. "Our murderer only kills his friends." He dropped the sheet of paper in front of Rutledge. "You're hallucinating if you think Travis Walker is a suspect. It's meaningless enough to list Kirkland."

"Funny," said Rutledge. "Kirkland didn't tell me, but he was in Rossi's hotel when he died, and he was in the locker room before Whitlow drowned. And so was Walker."

Morris made no effort to hide his own boredom at the reply. "Why do you list the four girls?"

"What did they *see* on the balcony? Or what did they *do*?"

"Is the killer's name written here?" Morris pointed at the pages scattered in front of them, as though by fate.

"It's there," said Rutledge.

Morris could see the two of them, thick in their suits, looking across the desk at each other. "What if I'm the man?"

"I'll pull the switch myself," said Rutledge, without blinking.

18 ⌗

The doorman at the Towers Hotel ignored the taxi to lavish his presence on a brown Porsche. Morris paid the driver. It was noon. He needed a change of clothes and a drink. He would reverse the order.

He hesitated to approach the raised lounge in the lobby. People stepped around him, pointing, watching the outside elevators climb the layers of balconies. There should be a scar in the air where a human form fell, thought Morris.

"Why not?" he said aloud, and started toward the circular staircase up into the bar.

The hotel had managed a feat of repair in the four days. The parrots were back inside their deep cage, its bamboo flawlessly together. Yet they were strangely quiet, as if something remained of what had broken in. Morris looked up. The fairy wings of Plexiglas were still shattered, giving reality to all that had happened.

"I'll buy you a drink." There was not a more familiar voice in America. The lounge was dark. Morris could see it was nearly empty. Travis Walker pushed back a chair at his table. He was sitting alone. Morris had not seen him alone, in a public place, in fifteen years. Morris did not know how tired he was until he sat down.

"We're old, Morris."

"I'll be younger when my drink gets here." It was strange to be alone with Travis, with no one pressing to get his attention.

"When have we had a drink?" asked Travis.

"Us? I remember when you couldn't afford one."

"I used to drink only in private clubs where you couldn't sign for it, and they wouldn't take cash." He laughed. His laugh was half an octave lower with age. "I only see you in press tents, Morris. Where somebody always asks if I'm giving up the tour. I don't blame them. Who wants to hear a replay of a round of seventy-five?''

"Your sixty-nine, Friday, was your lowest Open round in five years," said Morris.

"You're kidding! Five years! Where'd they go? Now everything's a sidehill putt. For a par. How come we never drink anymore?'' Travis was ever so slightly slurring his words.

"You live at thirty thousand feet," said Morris, "flying to the next city."

"Yeah, Friday afternoons when I miss the cut."

"Is there anybody you're not in business with, Travis?"

"Just those who don't have flush toilets." He laughed, and held up his glass to the waitress, who did not recognize him. "I still love to strike the ball," Travis said. "I can't imagine the Open without me in it." The words came out more plaintively than he seemed to intend. "Why can't we hire a designated putter?" He laughed.

"I've used a designated writer," said Morris. "Remember when you took the fourteen at Pebble Beach? And made us all toast every stroke with a drink? I never did make an overnight file. Thank God for Blackie, who covered for me. He invented your line: 'How did I shoot a fourteen? Easy. I sank a twenty-foot putt to keep from shooting fifteen.' " Both of them were laughing.

"Who's killing our golfers, Morris?" The fun was gone from the air.

"A friend," said Morris.

Walker sat erect in his chair. "What do you mean?"

"He's one of us," said Morris.

"How do you know?"

"He has to be. To know the things he did. To have been accepted without question on the scene of three murders."

"What did he know?" asked Travis.

"Habits, for the most part."

"Do they have any idea who he is?"

"They know within a few names," said Morris. The girl was bringing his second drink. Rutledge had not warned him what he could say, or not say. What did it matter? The killer already knew everything.

"This detective, Rutledge, seemed to know what he was

156

doing," said Travis. "But then we lost Tommy. Who's next?"

"Whoever is next will have to work at it," said Morris. "See your shadow over by the bar?" The cop was making no effort to conceal himself.

"Oh, yes," said Walker. "I'm glad to have him. I'm no hero. Who are the suspects, Morris?"

"I can tell you two of them." Morris's voice was not kidding. Travis leaned toward him. "Both are sitting at this table."

"You're serious."

"Sure."

"Hell, I was at a party with Pat when Rossi was killed." Travis looked up at the top of the lounge. "It must have been some scene."

"It was," said Morris. "Your party was just a few floors below Rossi's room. You wouldn't have been gone long." He smiled.

"Morris, you sound like a damn detective." Travis was not offended.

"In my opinion, Rutledge has your name on his list for two reasons. One of them is, you could be the killer," said Morris.

"What's the other?" asked Travis, tilting his drink in the near dark.

"He doesn't want the tournament cancelled. The killer would leave town. If the most famous name in golf is a suspect, and agrees to stay, how can the others leave?"

"The most famous name in golf is not to be confused with golf's greatest player." Travis's voice was not bitter.

"Kirkland? He won't be going anywhere either," said Morris.

Travis almost choked laughing. "I can see me in jail. But Kirkland?" He finished his drink and raised his glass for another.

"Morris." Travis did not slur his name. "Nobody's cancelling the Open. Rossi grew up with us. Tommy could have been the king. Whitlow would've stayed a jerk all his life. They all had a right to be whoever they were. If your detective wants the Open, he'll have it."

"Remember," said Morris, "you're tied for the lead."

157

"I don't kill so easy." Travis was again slurring his words. "It doesn't matter now. This Open belongs to the killer. He can have it. But he killed my chances of winning. I could have held together Saturday for nine more holes. Maybe. Maybe I could have gone eighteen today. It would have been close. My nerves are finished, Morris. There's no chance I can hang together for twenty-seven holes. Your detective needs it, Morris, we'll play it."

Travis looked up again at the broken Plexiglas in the roof of the lounge. "At least he went fast. But Rossi would have hated the mess he left."

Morris could not take his eyes off the shattered fairy wings. "Are you sure we should play it? Is it worth the risk?"

"Oh, we'll play. To hell with the risk. When does the USGA make a decision?"

"This afternoon, maybe. It's up to Colburn. He has his executive committee in his hip pocket. It's the players he's concerned about."

Travis frowned at Colburn's name. "I'll see you at the course."

"Morris," Travis said, as if he were standing and already leaving the bar. "What about the funerals?"

"Only Rossi's body has been released. His family held private graveside services yesterday, in New Jersey. LeBaron sent flowers in our names. He'll dunn you. The other two? I doubt Rutledge will release their bodies until the tournament is over. He's afraid of a mass exodus to the funerals. He wants the players here. He wants the killer here."

"How did Tommy die?"

Morris knew immediately that he would lie. He didn't know why. "They're still testing. It must have been some kind of drug. Don't trust anybody, Travis."

Morris stood up. He tried to leave money. Travis kept handing it back as if it were contaminating the tabletop.

"Morris, you now owe me a drink." He was barely slurring his words.

The taxi driver kept calling in for directions. He couldn't get it straight, where you turned off Roswell Road to reach the Atlanta Golf Club. There was an electrical storm of advice on his radio. The road was marked. They couldn't miss it. Morris looked out into the deep trees now filled with expensive houses. It would have been quicker to go by the expressway, but he wanted to see what Roswell Road had become. A lone figure of a man, hardly erect, walked along the shoulder, looking back, not raising his hand, but indicating with his hunched shoulders and his defiant look that he would accept a ride.

"Stop!" said Morris. The driver looked wildly into the back seat, holding his mike, not braking the car, as if he could only believe in the voice on his radio. Morris pushed him on the shoulder. "Stop the cab," he said.

The driver checked the rearview mirror and brought the cab to a reluctant stop. "What do you mean?" he asked.

Morris did not answer. He could see the man behind them was not hurrying. He kept to the same pace, still turning to look at automobiles that overtook him. It was Old Thompson, all right. No mistaking his walk, thought Morris. He was wearing the same broken coat and plaid shirt as he had on five days ago when John Whitlow had fired him on the practice range. The way he kept turning and walking, he was in no position to hire a cab. Morris opened the back door just as he came even with them.

"Thompson."

The old caddy was amazed at the sound of his name.

"Come on, get in," said Morris.

Old Thompson looked at the driver as if he expected to be ordered on his way. The driver was back on his mike asking for directions.

"Where've you been since Wednesday?" asked Morris.

"Sick," said Thompson, in a raspy, alcohol-ruined voice.

"You know the tournament has been suspended."

Thompson hesitated. Finally he nodded his head.

"Why go to the course?" asked Morris.

"I need a bag." He couldn't keep his hands settled in his lap. He knotted them in his ragged coat pockets.

"They want to talk to you," said Morris. He deliberately avoided the word *police*. Thompson looked at him, kneading his fists in his torn pockets.

"Talkin' can't help none of 'em," he said.

"You know about John and Tommy?"

He nodded his head, the tiny veins ravaging his wind-scarred face, his hands now making knots of fingers in his lap.

"Did you see Rossi Wednesday night?" asked Morris.

Thompson drew up inside his coat. "No, I left. I was sick. Sometimes he gave me money. Gave us all money. Never asked for it back. I meant to see him at the course."

"Were you still in the lobby when he fell?" asked Morris.

There was hollowness in Thompson's eyes. "Only heard it. Didn't see it. Thank God I didn't. Didn't know who it was. I got out quick. I heard them say his name in my room on the radio."

"Where are you staying?"

"Old hotel. More a roomin' house. The Sidney Hotel." He laughed, a croak in his ruined throat. "So many has jumped there, they nailed the windows shut." He seemed embarrassed to be laughing. "Mr. Rossi was okay," he said. "Never forgot me. And I never caddied for him. Did he jump in that hotel?" Thompson's voice was unbelieving.

"No," said Morris bluntly. "Someone killed him. Also Whitlow and Fryer."

Thompson shrank back from Whitlow's name, deeper into his own shoulders. "Why they want to talk to me," he said. But it was not a question.

"You were in Rossi's hotel. Whitlow fired you Wednesday. What about Thursday? Did you speak to Tommy Fryer? They wanted to know the same kind of things about me," said Morris. "Just tell them the straight truth." Morris said it as if they were conspirators.

"Same man did it all?" said Thompson. "Couldn't't'na been me. I been laid up sick. Never left my room, except to eat somethin' Saturday. They said Mr. Fryer died in a steam room." There was fear in his voice.

"Do you know anybody who hated Rossi?" asked Morris.

"Plenty of 'em owed him. Not like me, that he give bits and pieces. Owed him big."

"Who?" asked Morris.

"I can't prove nobody. I just know they did." Thompson shut his mouth tightly and looked straight ahead.

"Lieutenant Rutledge wants to see you," said Morris. "Nothing to be afraid of. He's talked to Travis, to all of us. Do you need money?"

160

Thompson kept looking straight ahead. "I can't pay my way outta my room, unless I get a bag. If I can get to Chicago, I can find some kid to carry."

Morris handed him a twenty-dollar bill.

Thompson sank back in the seat. Age and fatigue dragged his coat down on his shoulders. "I knew he couldn't swim. I never drowned him." Thompson looked out the window at the passing line of trees. "Only reason to kill all of 'em," he said, almost to himself, "they was rich."

The driver turned left toward the golf course, talking away on his radio, paying no attention to what was said in the back seat.

Morris counted out the money for the cab. The rain was gone. He was not as tired. He suddenly felt as if they all were moving in one direction. What had Old Thompson said? Only reason to kill them, they were all rich. Simple as that. What had Rutledge said? Murder is a simple invention.

Morris showed his identification to the guards on the club-house door. They accepted his explanation of Old Thompson, who followed him inside. Club members passed them silently in the hall, the carpet swallowing up the sounds of their shoes. Sergeant Bolton walked out of the manager's office. Morris stopped him.

"Sergeant, this is Thompson, George Thompson, the caddy." Neither of the two offered to shake hands. "You might get him a beer and a sandwich, while he waits for the Lieutenant. What time will he be here?"

"Not long," said Bolton. "Maybe an hour." He still had not spoken to Thompson, but guided him into the manager's office. The caddy's shoulders had lifted at the idea of a beer.

Morris looked into the main dining room. Light and grass and trees poured in the floor-to-ceiling windows. All of the thousands of people with their moving inventory of colors were missing. Inside, it might have been closing time at a popular restaurant. Chairs were uniformly empty at the tables. LeBaron was drinking coffee alone in the far corner of the large room.

"You look like hell," said LeBaron, who seemed curiously rested.

"I do that," said Morris.

"Morris, do you have any doubt all three of them were murdered?"

"No, now all we have to do is prove it."

LeBaron lifted his eyes over his cup.

"Lieutenant Rutledge is getting there," said Morris. "If he can keep the Open in town."

"He's sure it's someone in golf?"

"He's sure it's one of *us* in golf."

LeBaron was amazed. "You mean I'm a genuine suspect?"

"What the hell is a fraudulent suspect?" said Morris. "I was in both hotels when Rossi and Fryer were killed. So were you. Both of us were here when Whitlow drowned. That's genuine enough for a grand jury."

"Only we didn't do it," said LeBaron. "Not that there weren't times Whitlow needed drowning."

Morris tapped his shoe with his cane. "What about the 'people's president,' Colburn. He was with you, just before Rossi was killed."

"True. But he got tangled up with one of his committees. They'll vouch for that.

"Here we are, Morris, explaining to each other how we all could and could not commit murder."

The two of them looked across the table with frank curiosity. Both of them laughed.

"If I kill anybody, Morris, it'll be a sportswriter asking, 'Would you please go over your putts,' and we're all waiting to hit San Francisco, and the golfer just took forty-one putts."

"It will be justifiable homicide," said Morris. "Do we play the Open, Frank?" His voice did not commit himself.

"We play," said LeBaron. "Colburn can deliver the USGA. They have to play. They're broke. The club's out a half-million-dollar investment in the course. The network loved televising Vietnam—what's three murders to them? But Travis and Pete have to back us. With them, I can handle the golfers. What about you? I doubt we could bring it off without the old AP."

Morris spoke to keep from answering. "I saw Travis in the hotel. He wants to play. He'll be here this afternoon. I haven't seen Pete." Morris tried to imagine how Kirkland would react. He had his own, strong opinions. If he thought the Open should be cancelled, he would leave. Period. No matter who stayed. "I'm worried about the risk," said Morris.

"All we have to lose is the public," said LeBaron, "and

the tour. Then Colburn can have the game back as an old-club perversion between gentlemen.''

"Is the panic that thick?"

"I can't go near my hotel room. Chicago is frantic to know if we'll play there. So are the rest of them."

"What does the state of Georgia say about the Open?" asked Morris.

"The Governor is in the press room now. And the Mayor. The news is all bad, but they can't resist three hundred reporters. The Mayor has turned white. It may cost him the next election. I offered to be there. Colburn said it was his show."

"I better look in on my boys." Morris stood up with his cane.

"Morris." LeBaron raised his voice.

"If we play and someone else is killed, it ought to be me."

"I'll keep that in mind," said Morris.

LeBaron went back to his coffee and his paper.

Leaving the clubhouse, Morris on impulse turned into the caddy yard. The bags in the storeroom waited in long rows of colors like formula racing cars. The caddy master recognized him. Two National Guardsmen waited at ease out of the sun.

"Any of the caddies here?" asked Morris.

"Just Bobby Watson." He indicated the far end of the storeroom. "He's helping the police with Fryer's gear." Morris could see him now, squatting down between the bags. A cop with a pad was obviously taking inventory.

"Okay if I speak with them?"

"Sure." The caddy master looked as if he wanted to follow along.

Morris did not recognize the cop. Now he could see there were two of them, both strangers to him. "John Morris, Associated Press."

They nodded as if they knew him. Watson offered his hand.

Every item from the bag was laid out on the concrete floor: clubs, gloves, balls, tees, a rainsuit, an umbrella. It was all spread out as if for inspection. Watson signed a receipt listing each object. He turned his back on the two cops.

"No one will ever swing his clubs again," said Watson. "Thank God he won the Open once. The other tournaments

163

don't matter now. You're probably the only man in America who could name them." Watson stopped talking to compose himself. "You think you could get his clubs placed somewhere?" The clubs seemed terribly important to him.

"The golf museums will be fighting for them," said Morris. "You let Nancy know where you think they should go. She'll respect your opinion." The sun made them both blink as they walked into the open.

"It doesn't make any sense," said Watson. "Nobody could hate Tommy. Even when he beat you, he left you something."

"He was a generous winner," said Morris, "but he had his opinions."

"Hell yes, he said what he thought. He wasn't intimidated by Travis or Pete. They knew that. The great courses didn't frighten him. He enjoyed the crowds. Whoever killed him had to be crazy."

"You don't have anybody in mind?" asked Morris quietly.

Watson hesitated, then shook his head. "I miss him already. He told me this was the last year I could caddy for him. I got into it on a lark. We were fraternity brothers. The places we saw. He was something, Morris, the last day of a tournament, when there wasn't enough oxygen in the air to breathe. He said next year I had to go 'legitimate.' The word he always used. I wanted this last Open. We would have won it. We might have walked away with it." He reached in his pocket for a cigarette. "Well, it's over now. Nancy's tough. She'll survive. I don't want to think. Just go back to California, and do mathematics."

Morris listened. The grounds were strangely quiet. "Bobby, you hesitated just now. Who did you have in mind? It might be important. I'll be careful how I repeat it."

"I don't know what happened between them, but Tommy was upset with Al Morgan. You know Al. But it was more than his booze, his needling. I don't know what it was. Maybe it was nothing."

"You talked with the detective, Rutledge?" asked Morris.

"Yes, but I didn't tell him that. He asked me to stay in town, until the tournament is finished. Or until they cancel it. Nancy's family, and Tommy's are here. I'll be with them. God, I hope it doesn't drag out. We all need to get away from what's happened."

164

Morris gripped Watson's shoulder with his huge hand. There was nothing else that either of them could say.

Morris walked toward the press room in the gymnasium. He could hear the noise inside before the door opened. The guard nodded his head without speaking. Writers were standing and shouting questions at Colburn. The Governor and Mayor were seated between more guards. It was impossible for Colburn to pick out one question to answer. He made no effort to do so, but stood carefully in the white heat of the lights without sweating, or moving. His composure drove the reporters to greater fits of questions.

"Is the tournament cancelled! What are you, butchers?" shouted a Chicago paper into the noise. Other questions were yelled out. The sound drowned the words. Morris was suddenly angrier than he could remember. He was sick of murder, and what had happened to the National Open, and to all of them in this room. He wanted to swing one of his big hands in a tight fist. Morris stood, leaning on his cane, holding one massive arm over his head until there was quiet. Something in his own face made it unnecessary to shout. "Gentlemen, one question at a time."

"The tournament is suspended," said Colburn. He had apparently said it before. "The police are advising us on the progress of their investigation. The deaths of three golfers has astounded us, and grieved us." His voice never changed its inflection. "The police have not yet called it murder. We don't know more than that. I do know the Open is a trust, to the living and the dead. A National Trust. We will make our decision on continuing the tournament within that context. Gentlemen, I do not think we can add anything of significance to what we have already told you."

The Governor and the Mayor stood up and moved quickly for the door. Colburn walked behind them, without hurrying. Most of the reporters moved for their typewriters. Some of them stood shouting questions. Morris waded between them to the AP table. "Any messages?" he asked the computer operator.

"Yeah. They all say, 'call New York.'" The operator was unmoved by the urgency of the messages.

Morris sat down. He typed:

Atlanta, Georgia—Police narrowed the search for the alleged killer of U.S. Open leaders John Whitlow and Tommy Fryer to twelve names. One of them mine, John Morris, of the Associated Press. The same man is believed to have killed teaching pro Jim Rossi. According to a police source, six of the twelve suspects are prominent professional golfers playing in the Open . . .''

Morris did not name them.

"Here,'' said Morris to the operator, when he had finished. "This ought to give them something to do in New York besides call me.'' Well now, he thought, somebody has identified it as murder.

The Atlanta bureau chief jumped up to read the bulletin. "Jesus, Morris.'' When he looked around, Morris was moving between the jangle of cheap typewriters.

The sunlight seemed artificial in the air. The day should be clouded over and damp cold, thought Morris, shivering in the June heat. He was not halfway to the clubhouse when he made up his own mind about the tournament. "We'll play the son-of-a-bitch,'' he said aloud.

A cop stopped him at the clubhouse door.

"Mr. Morris.''

"Yes.''

"The Lieutenant wants to see you, in the parking lot.'' He pointed to an unmarked vehicle.

A door opened as Morris approached. Rutledge stepped out of the car. He waved Morris to him.

"I want you to meet four young ladies.'' Rutledge sounded pleased with himself.

Morris bent awkwardly over his cane, and looked inside at the four girls, three of them in the back seat. Each one's hair was straight and blonde and long. Their outfits were coordinated in a variety of colors, the predominant one being red.

"Look carefully,'' said Rutledge.

The girls avoided his eyes. They were not as young as their hair and their clothes. They were pretty, but hard around the edges, a look of brittle makeup around the eyes. Morris straightened up.

"Okay, take 'em back to the station,'' said Rutledge.

166

"Who are they?" asked Morris, stepping back from the moving car.

"Three are from L.A. One is from New Mexico. Working girls, actually."

"I've seen them. I'm sure I've seen them here, and on the tour," said Morris.

"They say they met at the tournament in Las Vegas, about five years ago. They work a while, follow the tour a while. They like a *high old time*." His voice was as brittle as the faces of the girls.

"High enough to commit murder?"

"They were charged with manslaughter in Phoenix two years ago. Seems they were in a pool with an older man. He didn't swim that well. They were *teasing* him. Wouldn't let him touch the side of the pool. He tired. Maybe panicked."

"And drowned?"

"Lucky for them he died of a heart attack. Just *good time girls*." Rutledge's voice was dangerously even.

"What did they see on Rossi's balcony?"

"The youngest one, Chris, she's twenty-five, a well-traveled twenty-five. She saw him go over. 'Fall out,' she described it. Then she screamed. The other girls thought she had fallen, and looked at her. They didn't see him. They *said*."

"What else did this Chris see?" Morris was surprised at the tightness in his throat.

"She buried her face in her hands. She *said*. Before doing that, she *thinks* she saw something moving behind the vines, the what-do-you-call-it . . ."

'Philodendron.'

"Yes. She didn't see a face. Just movement. She buried her head, and then they panicked. They ran for the elevators. The other girls didn't know what they were running from. They were lucky. An elevator was coming down. The girl, Chris, told them what she had seen. They were frightened. But shrewd. They took the elevator below the lobby, and left through the parking garage."

"Why were they there?" asked Morris.

"*Good time* girls. Looking for a party. They only remembered the first name of the man who had invited them. And that he was staying on the eighteenth floor. They said. His name was Glenn. They never found the party."

"Do you believe them?"

"They denied seeing anything at first. A night at the station, separated, helped their memory."

"Is that legal?"

Rutledge smiled without humor.

"Do you think they could have thrown him over?"

"Sure. Four strong girls. For kicks, maybe. But they didn't do it. They're scared, but not scared enough."

"They could be hiding what they saw."

"It's possible," said Rutledge. "For money, maybe. If so, they picked a dangerous man to threaten."

"Somebody had to be there."

"He was there all right," said Rutledge. "Let's go inside."

Morris took one step and stopped. Standing, he seemed to take on greater bulk. Rutledge waited without speaking.

"I've made a decision," said Morris. "You tell the twelve of us that one of us killed three people. Tell us together. And I'll do everything I can to keep the tournament alive."

"Why tell them?" Rutledge was too surprised to conceal his curiosity.

"So we can protect ourselves. And so the players can make a choice: play or withdraw. Or hire a lawyer and sue for slander. Let it be their decision."

The two of them were sweating from the heat rising off the asphalt.

"Okay, I'll tell 'em."

He had no choice, and yet Morris could see the idea began to appeal to him.

"Let the pressure build," said Rutledge. "It might be interesting."

"You sure you have the right twelve?"

"Oh, yes. Just the number for a jury. We'll let the boys judge themselves." He was actually smiling.

"You forget. I'm one of the boys," said Morris.

Rutledge looked at him without answering. He started toward the clubhouse. Morris's cane sank ever so slightly into the hot asphalt.

"Get me the pro-am pairings of all the tournaments since January," said Rutledge. "I want the name of every medical doctor who was paired with the six golfers on my list."

"That shouldn't be hard. LeBaron will know how to get them."

Rutledge stopped. "Forget LeBaron. *You* get the list."

Morris remembered LeBaron was also a suspect. Disloyalty rose up in his mouth until he spat. PGA headquarters ought to have the names on file somewhere.

"The blood report on Tommy will be ready tonight," said Morris. "It might be negative. We could be jumping the gun. Maybe he wasn't given this T-3 at all."

"Yeah. Maybe he was frightened to death by a downhill putt." Rutledge turned toward the clubhouse door.

"One more thing," said Morris.

"What do you want, my badge?"

"I want to leak the names of the twelve of us. As having been cross-examined by you as apparent suspects. Or material witnesses. Hell, an hour after we have been in that room our names will be leaked anyhow."

"First, we get an agreement to finish the tournament," said Rutledge. "Then you're on your own releasing their names." He gave his short, strangled laugh. "Can you sue yourself for libeling yourself?"

It would be a long day for the Associated Press legal department, Morris admitted to himself.

"Will they play?" asked Rutledge, his voice again all iron.

"They'll play. There's too much at stake. What do they gain not playing? All twelve suspects, except Goodner, go to Chicago. Remember, you only *believe* we've had three murders. You haven't arrested anybody."

They opened the clubhouse door and stepped inside.

LeBaron waited with Travis Walker in the club manager's office. He closed the door behind them. There were no formalities.

"Morris, will you back us if we play?" asked LeBaron. They looked at each other as if they had just met.

"I can't speak for the Associated Press. We'll move plenty of opinions. I myself will support the tournament. But I will only report the facts."

"Good," said LeBaron.

"The Players' Executive Committee has voted to play," said Travis. "Horton's in the bar. But the Commissioner will go along. Believe that."

"Has the USGA voted?" asked Morris.

"Colburn's had ten votes all night," said LeBaron. "He

only has an eighteen-man executive committee. He's in the dining room, working on a statement.''

LeBaron mimicked him, ''The Open belongs to those of us who love it. It's a National Trust, for the living and the dead. Sorry about the dead.'' It was not a bad imitation of the Virginian.

Morris poured them all a drink.

''You have the rest of today and, I guess, Monday,'' Morris said to Rutledge.

''You have the rest of today,'' said LeBaron, handing Rutledge a Scotch on ice. ''We play twenty-seven holes of golf tomorrow.''

Rutledge stood up in amazement. ''Why don't you play *tonight?* That doesn't give us enough time.''

''We're with the USGA,'' said Travis. ''We play twenty-seven holes and leave this town tomorrow.''

''Even the politicians want it that way,'' said LeBaron. ''But they won't be here, in case another leader goes down the drain.''

''Present company excepted,'' said Morris, touching Travis instinctively. He and Washburn and the kid from Alabama were tied for the lead.

Travis did not smile or flinch.

Morris picked up the telephone and dialed New York.

Whitfield answered.

''What are you working, a twenty-four-hour shift?''

Whitfield ignored him.

''The Open's on again,'' said Morris. ''Twenty-seven holes tomorrow. There'll be more guards than spectators. I'll have something else this morning.''

''What are you onto?'' There was a rare curiosity in Whitfield's voice.

''I'll call.'' Morris hung up.

''We've lost a day. Or two days,'' said Rutledge. ''Did you get the people I wanted?'' he asked Travis and LeBaron.

''The players are waiting in the locker room,'' answered Travis. ''They're not too happy about it. They want to know why we're here.''

''The others are in the dining room,'' said LeBaron. ''Travis and I will round them all up.''

''We need five more chairs,'' Rutledge said to Sergeant Bolton, who disappeared to find them.

"It should be an unusual meeting," said Morris. "The judge, the jury, and the plaintiff."

Rutledge did not smile, as if it would squander time.

The players scattered themselves into the chairs Bolton was handing into the room.

Ted Dolan, Indian dark with tobacco in his jaw, led the way.

Pete Kirkland had a rare puzzled expression on his burned lips.

Art Howard reached awkwardly with his short arms for a chair, his eyes invisible behind his dark glasses.

Al Morgan held a drink in his hand. "I'll tell you why I called this meeting," he said. "Whoever draws the short straw goes next." Nobody laughed.

Lee Washburn, his mouth drawn thin and angry, sprawled his long legs in front of himself.

Travis Walker was unable to escape the fame in his own face. Morris was sure he knew why they were here.

LeBaron delivered four men into the room.

Edward Horton twisted his too small mouth in his handsome face. The Players' Commissioner was obviously unhappy at being sent for by his own tournament director. LeBaron ignored him.

Joe Goodner took a chair along the rim of the group.

"What's the matter, Goodner?" said Morgan, "afraid somebody might ask you to swallow a microphone?" The players laughed.

Everette Holland looked straight down with his round face, as if he were embarrassed for anyone to see his eyes.

Old Thompson raised his head, and moved his own eyes around the room, stopping to look carefully at the detective. Morris could smell the beer that followed him to his seat.

Bolton closed the door as he left.

Rutledge walked around the club manager's desk into the half-circle of men. He could step and touch any one of the twelve. All of their eyes followed him. His lumpy suit emphasized his bulk. Morris was careful not to move his own larger body and break the spell.

"Gentlemen. One of you killed three men."

The careful remoteness went out of the room. Horton was standing. "What do you mean?" he said. He stepped on

171

Morgan's glass, breaking it against the chair leg, nearly losing his balance.

"Damn a man who spills good Scotch," said Morgan, slapping it off his shoe.

Old Thompson was the other man standing, shaking with rage, or fear, or need of a drink.

Kirkland looked around him, seemingly amazed. Travis sat back in his chair.

Rutledge waited. Horton and Old Thompson, exposed in the air, sat back in their chairs.

Now they were all looking at each other and not at Rutledge. Their faces, and bodies, and the hang of their clothes were so familiar to Morris that he could sense no evil in the room. Only anger.

"Listen . . ." said Horton.

Rutledge ignored him. "The killer was lucky," he said. "Then he was clever."

Morris moved his eyes from face to face.

"We aren't in this room to arrest him . . . not yet." Rutledge waited. "The USGA has voted to finish this golf tournament, tomorrow. Six of you are players. We're here because I want you to live long enough to play the twenty-seven holes."

"There is no proof anyone has been murdered," said Horton, standing up as if to leave. "You've mismanaged this investigation from the first. I want a lawyer if I remain in this room."

"Then leave," said Rutledge. "The first golfer killed was no longer a touring player, very much like you, yourself, Mr. Horton."

Horton wavered toward the door, and then sat down.

"Anyone here's welcome at the morgue," said Rutledge. "I'll have Doc Moseley walk you through Tommy Fryer's blood tests. Then you tell me what to call the way he died."

He's bluffing, thought Morris.

The body heat in the room increased. A deep flush of color had come back into Ev Holland's round face. Morris caught himself swallowing at the new tension in the room.

"I asked eleven of you here for one reason," said Rutledge. "To help you protect yourselves."

Again their looks went around the room. Al Morgan held the broken bottom of his glass without smiling. Art Howard pushed his prescription shades higher on his round nose.

"I wanted the other *one* of you to know, we will follow every step you take for the next two days." Rutledge's dark face broke unevenly into a smile. "The two of us will talk later." He walked back around the desk. "I'm afraid it's going to be somewhat embarrassing for the rest of you. Morris is putting all your names, and his own, on his AP wire. That's between your lawyers and his. Any questions?"

"Why are you so sure it's one of us?" asked Morgan, still balancing the broken glass in his hand.

"All of you had the opportunity. Some of you had a motive. One of you took advantage of both," said Rutledge.

The unrest in the room was fixed tightly in every chair. Then Kirkland stood up. His tenor voice was even higher. "We'll finish the Open with as much dignity as we can. I hope the families of the three golfers will understand. And the public." He looked at Rutledge. "I hope you are closer to catching the killer than this amateur theatre hour would indicate." Kirkland walked out of the room without looking back.

Morris watched each man as he followed him.

Dolan had not spoken or shifted his tobacco in his jaw. Howard, sweating, adjusted his dark glasses a last time on his nose. Morgan dropped the bottom of his broken glass in the wastebasket. "Twelve good men and true," he said. "What's a little murder between friends?" Horton stepped angrily around him. Washburn seemed unexpectedly pale and vulnerable despite his height. Goodner stopped in front of Morris. "Print my name and I'll see you in court." Morris did not blink. Travis walked out alone.

Old Thompson, now deep inside his shoulders, stood with nowhere to go. "I'll give you an address," Rutledge said to him. "They have a bed and food. Sergeant Bolton will see that you get a ride." Thompson shuffled out of the room, an old man, undefiant.

LeBaron's thin face was damp with sweat from the closeness of the room. "I've got to file," said Morris. "I'll meet you later." LeBaron nodded, and left.

173

Morris poured himself a drink. "Strange," he said, "for a minute, it was as if I had never met any of them."

"Yeah. Murder is like that," said Rutledge, filling his own glass. "People do it, every day. But it's like it happened in another country." They both finished their drinks.

Morris dialed New York.

19 ※

"**I**'M CAREFUL WHO I LET IN MY ROOM," SAID JULIA SULLIVAN. "Which of the twelve murderers are you?" She unlatched the chain on the door.

A thin, older man waited behind Morris. He made no effort to come inside.

"Who's that?" asked Sullivan, closing the door.

"A cop. Name's Benson. That's the only word he's spoken, 'Benson.' I think they taught it to him young, and he hasn't gotten over the sound of it. Are you nervous, holing up with a suspect?"

"Not with Mr. Benson outside." She pushed her fist in his chest. "Is it true, Morris? Is one of you the killer?"

"Rutledge thinks so." Morris filled one of the inexpensive, uncomfortable chairs.

"Do you?"

"He asked me to make a list of names. Mine was the same as his. Except he included Travis and Pete. And four girls who didn't do it."

"What girls?"

"Groupies. You've probably seen them. They were on the eighteenth floor, and one of them saw something, when Rossi was killed. She doesn't know what she saw, or she isn't saying."

"Groupies, and your name, Morris. Is this man a real detective?"

"My name was on my own list. I knew them all, better

174

than anybody. I was close enough to commit the three murders. I was even in the steam bath with Tommy. Maybe I killed them and don't remember it." He pushed his hand through his thick hair, resting his cane across his knees.

"You've never forgotten anything in your life, John Morris. Except the words to the marriage ceremony." She punched Morris until he laughed out loud.

The telephone rang.

"Probably for Mr. Benson," she said. She handed the phone to Morris. It was a return call from PGA headquarters in Florida. Morris slipped his notepad out of his back pocket. A secretary was quoting from her files. A Dr. Percy Moore had been on Ted Dolan's pro-am team in Los Angeles. Morris took down both his home and office numbers.

A Dr. Hubert Franklin had been paired with Al Morgan at Tucson. Their team had won the pro-am, in fact. Morris took his hospital and home numbers. The PGA knew, somehow, that he was a surgeon.

A Dr. William Morrison was supposed to have played in the same foursome at Greensboro with Lee Washburn. But he was called from the first tee. An emergency. Morris took down three numbers: his office, his hospital, his home.

"That's them?" asked Morris.

"Since January," said the girl in the PGA office.

Morris thanked her. He dialed Rutledge at his office.

"How many phones in your home?" Rutledge asked.

"Two extensions."

"Good. Stay there. I'll be right up. There's too much confusion here." They hung up.

"Our detective is on his way," said Morris.

"*Your* detective," said Sullivan. "Why are you so interested in what doctors were paired with which golfers?"

"Because of the way Tommy Fryer died. Maybe. The tests aren't completed. It's possible one of our six golfers came in contact with a certain drug, one not easy to come by. I think we'll soon have three nervous doctors on the telephone."

"What about you, and Frank, and Ev, and the others? You see dozens of doctors on the tour, and may not even know they are doctors."

"True. Rutledge knows that. He's playing the odds. I think I understand his logic. Pro golfers are spoiled everywhere they go, even by doctors. Especially by doctors who are golf nuts. They'll give a pro more time than they give their brokers. And, sometimes, unfortunately, they'll give him any drug in their bag. Maybe they charge him an autograph on a cocktail napkin. I've seen it done.''

"What drug killed Tommy?" asked Sullivan.

"Triiodothyronine. Maybe.''

"You could choke to death saying it.''

"T-3, for short,'' said Morris. "It affects the metabolism. An overdose can affect the heart.''

"Why would a doctor give anyone such a drug? What golfer ever heard of it?''

"Good questions,'' said Morris. "Irresponsible doctors have prescribed small dosages for weight control. T-3 helps the body burn away its own fat. It's dangerous medicine.''

"Then you're looking for a fat golfer?"

"Or maybe one who diets his weight off. These three doctors have been paired with Dolan, Morgan, and Washburn—since January.'' He handed her his notepad.

"That lets Washburn out, Mr. Body Beautiful. Unless he was getting the T-3 for you, Morris.'' She stayed out of his reach.

"Dolan and Morgan have to fight their weight. Dolan fights harder than Morgan.'' Both were powerfully built, thought Morris.

There was a knock at the door.

"Mr. Benson is not a man to waste words,'' said Sullivan. She opened the door. Rutledge nodded, not stopping to speak, accepting the names and telephone numbers from Morris.

"What time is it in L.A.?'' he asked.

"Three hours behind us. Four P.M.,'' said Morris.

"We'll start with this Percy Moore.'' The way Rutledge said his name was a libel.

"Dolan used to jog, kept the weight off the hard way,'' said Morris. "I don't remember his doing that this winter, though.''

Rutledge dialed Los Angeles. He indicated Morris was to pick up the bedside phone. A maid answered in Spanish and broken English. The doctor didn't seem to be in.

"You might try the man at Greensboro,'' said Morris. "He should be home by now.''

He wasn't. Rutledge talked his way past a tired receptionist at his office. Dr. Morrison came to the phone.

"Doctor, Lieutenant Rutledge in Atlanta. Homicide. You've read of the deaths we've had at the Open."

Now he had the doctor's attention.

"I understand you were paired with Lee Washburn in the Greensboro pro-am."

"Oh, yes," said a careful voice. "Nothing's happened to Lee?" He said the name *Lee* as if they had been Ryder Cup teammates.

"No. But this is important. Did you prescribe or give appetite depressants to Washburn?"

There was silence. Morris could hear the doctor breathing. "That's been some time ago. Does Lee say I did?"

"I'm not asking him, I'm asking you." Rutledge's voice was merciless.

"No. I'm sure I didn't. I don't believe I took my bag out of my car. I was called from the tee, an emergency." His voice gained in confidence.

"You did not give, or prescribe, any drug to Lee Washburn? Think about it. Murder is not a casual subject," said Rutledge.

"Are you accusing me of murder?" The doctor was incredulous.

"The drugs in question may involve murder." Rutledge offered no apology.

Dr. Morrison was not intimidated. "You have my answer."

"Where will you be in the next six hours? If I need to reach you?" Rutledge ignored his hostility.

"At home. I'm not on call." He offered nothing else.

"Thank you," said Rutledge abruptly, and hung up.

"Nice friendly call," said Sullivan.

Rutledge ignored her. He dialed Los Angeles again. This time the doctor, Percy Moore, was at home.

Rutledge began his explanation quickly. The same facts. The same language. He asked, "Did you prescribe, or give, appetite depressants to Ted Dolan?"

"Ted Dolan?" The doctor repeated his full name as if he might have confused him with someone else. "Has anything happened to Mr. Dolan?"

Rutledge did not answer.

"I don't prescribe medicine, except to my own patients. Amphetamines can be dangerous."

"Think about it carefully," said Rutledge. "We have three murders on our hands."

"Why are you calling me?" The doctor's voice was as much startled as outraged.

"We'll come and see you if we have to. You're sure you gave no drugs to Ted Dolan?"

"No, I would remember it."

"Will you be at this number for the next six hours?" Rutledge bore down with his voice.

"I'm on call," said Dr. Moore.

"Leave a number if you go out," said Rutledge. He hung up without a thank you.

"I hope you're never sick in Los Angeles," said Julia.

Rutledge was already dialing Phoenix. He got past the receptionist. Now he was talking to a nurse. "So he's resting between surgery. This is Atlanta Homicide. Get him on the telephone."

"What do you want?" Dr. Franklin did not identify himself. He had apparently been listening on an extension.

Rutledge gave it to him even quicker. And cruder, with practice.

"I did not prescribe, or give, any drug to Mr. Morgan," said the doctor. "Mr. Morgan seemed inclined to depress his appetite with Scotch, as I remember it."

"Be certain," said Rutledge, with no hint of humor in his voice. "Triple murder is not amusing."

"If the best lead you have is myself, in Phoenix, Arizona, your investigation is hilarious."

"Will you be at that number long?"

"Until I'm finished. Two hours, maybe. You have my home number, I suppose. I knew Tommy Fryer, a bit. A nice young man. I hope you catch whoever is responsible. But it sounds like you're scrambling in the dark, long distance."

"Thank you," said Rutledge, without apology.

"You almost hung up like a human being," said Sullivan, with ice in her voice.

"It's not easy to make a man sweat two thousand miles away," said Rutledge. "What do you think?" He looked at Morris, who hung up his own phone.

"He's lying," said Morris, looking at his notes.

"That Dr. Franklin?" said Rutledge, standing up.

"No, the second one. Percy. Dr. Percy Moore."

178

"Why do you say he was lying?"

"A doctor pays fifteen hundred dollars to play golf in a pro-am. He takes lessons for three weeks before the tournament. Tells everybody in his club what pro he's paired with. Maybe even looks up the pro's record. He sure as hell knows if he ever won a U.S. Open. The pro says two words to the doctor, like, 'good putt,' and he turns it into a thirty-minute story, how he gave the former Open champion Ted Dolan a putting lesson right on the ninth green. And this Dr. Percy Moore fumbles for Dolan's name, as if maybe he wasn't sure who you meant. He lied right there."

Rutledge was dialing Los Angeles as if his fingers could hurry the connection.

"And who said anything to him about amphetamines? You only asked if he had prescribed or given Dolan an appetite depressant. You didn't say what kind."

Rutledge put his hand over the receiver. "There's an opening in Homicide. Can you type?" His voice was almost cheerful.

"Dr. Moore." He did not wait for an answer. "This is Lieutenant Rutledge. Drugs you gave Ted Dolan have killed at least one man here. You want to tell me about it? Or keep lying?"

Morris could hear the doctor breathing three thousand miles away.

Rutledge let the pressure build with the silence.

"Look," said the doctor's voice, not directly into the telephone, as if his eyes were searching for help somewhere in Los Angeles. "Maybe I gave him a few amphetamines. There's no crime in that. I'm a licensed physician."

"A few amphetamines," said Rutledge, using the words like acid burns.

"I take them myself," said the doctor, with failing enthusiasm. "Kills the appetite a bit. It's not acute medicine."

"It becomes more acute when the medicine kills the man, and not the appetite," Morris said, before he thought.

"Who's that?" asked the doctor, the new voice increasing his panic.

"You're the only one here talking about amphetamines," said Rutledge. "We're talking about triiodothyronine." He pronounced the syllables like a court sentence.

"Oh, God," said Dr. Moore. "He got them. He used them to kill someone? I can't believe it. I only brought ten tablets. Ten fifty-microgram tablets. One a day for ten days. Even if you took them all at once, it shouldn't be lethal. Unless . . . ." His voice trailed away.

"Unless what?" said Rutledge.

"Unless the patient had a heart disorder." Dr. Moore was almost breathing his words.

"Who suggested the T-3?" asked Morris.

"He did," said the doctor. "Mr. Dolan seemed to have had experience with it. Frankly, I . . . I never prescribed it for weight loss. It can be risky."

"But you weren't afraid to risk Dolan's life?"

"He asked me for it. I didn't have it with me. It's not the kind of drug you carry with you."

"But you got it for him?"

"Yes . . . I brought it Sunday."

"Why did you lie to me about it?" asked Rutledge.

"You frightened me," said Dr. Moore. Morris could imagine him sitting, unable to stand. "I panicked. I did nothing wrong. I'm licensed to prescribe the drug. As I see fit. I warned him that he should be extremely careful with it. One tablet a day, for ten days."

Morris managed to take down both ends of the conversation in his homemade shorthand.

"I'll have a record of this conversation flown to you," said Rutledge. "Read it. Have your lawyer read it. Then I'll want a full deposition taken from you, under oath, as to the drugs you gave Ted Dolan in January."

"How do you know my tablets were used?" The doctor's voice was all weakness. "I . . . Has Mr. Dolan been killed?"

"No," said Rutledge. "We will be flying out to take your deposition in the next two days." Rutledge gave him his own full name and rank and telephone number. And then hung up.

Rutledge pulled open his briefcase. "Dolan . . . how did you describe him?" He looked at Morris. " 'Ted Dolan. Age forty-six. Quit secure club job in January that Rossi had gotten him. Owed Rossi twenty-five hundred dollars. Hook killing his game . . . Cast-iron temper. Saw Rossi from elevator before he was killed. Skipped that fact in interview with Rutledge. Paired with Whitlow before his death. Did not

180

speak during round. Refused to answer when Whitlow asked about his missing putter, just before he drowned. Admitted he couldn't stand Whitlow, and his easy success. Stayed in same hotel with Fryer. Shared steam bath with him earlier in the week. Skipped steam bath Friday night. Said the first time his back hadn't been stiff in eight years. No life outside tour.' ''

Rutledge looked up from the paper. "No life anywhere, Mr. Dolan. Your own life for three others is a rotten swap, but it will have to do.''

His voice was not pretty to hear. Morris stood up, forgetting for the first time in years there was no bend in his left knee. He dropped his cane and it rolled under the table. The pain helped focus his mind. Sure, Dolan. What did he have after forty-six years? Bursitis and a snap hook. A powerful man with a tremendous war record, the only one on the tour. An iron temper. He held it in until it would burst out of him, rarely, frighteningly. Couldn't keep a caddy. Divorced. Family grown, gone. Finished. "Why didn't he kill somebody five years ago? Why don't we all kill somebody?" said Morris aloud. He sat down again on the bed.

Sullivan put her hands on his thick shoulders.

Rutledge checked his watch. "Doc said sixteen hours for the test. It's five P.M. That means ten o'clock.'' He was speaking almost to himself. The iron malice that he had used to sweat the doctors was still in his face.

Morris had seen Rutledge change, each time he had gotten what he needed. Maybe he was steeling himself to pull the switch on another man's life.

"Why?'' asked Morris aloud.

Rutledge did not look up from his thoughts.

"Dolan was finished.'' Morris attempted an explanation. "He quit the job Rossi had gotten him. Walked out on it. He borrowed twenty-five hundred dollars from Rossi afterward. His swing was erratic. He went to Rossi again in desperation, maybe for money, or for help with his hook. Maybe Rossi was disgusted with him. Wouldn't help him, or couldn't. Dolan had no life outside the tour. He lost his senses, and lifted Rossi in his hands, and threw him down eighteen floors.'' Morris waited. "Afterward, if he couldn't win the Open, no shaggy-headed kid would. Sure.'' Morris looked up. "I wonder why I'm having trouble believing it?''

Rutledge said, without mercy, "Forget who *might* have done it. I'm talking about who *did* it." The pronoun *I* did not escape Morris. "Everybody gets nervous when you start strapping old friends in the electric chair."

"What about proof?" asked Julia Sullivan. "Tommy Fryer died of an overdose of thyroid medicine, you assume. You won't know for five hours. Dolan had *access* to the medicine. But that's a long way from proof of murder. From proof of three murders."

"Motive. Weapon. Opportunity. Husbands and wives have been electrocuted on less evidence," said Rutledge. "The other two murders? I don't know. He may never talk. But you don't have to electrocute a man but once. A pity."

Morris looked at him as if he didn't know him. He couldn't place the careful, thoughtful detective he had watched and heard for five days. All Morris could see in Rutledge now was an instinct for the jugular. In his time, Dolan could drown an opponent in his own sweat. Or drown him in a water hazard, maybe? thought Morris. Or throw him off an eighteen-story balcony? Or burn his heart away in a steam room?

Rutledge stood up. "Dolan won't be out of our sight until I pick him up. Do you want to be there?"

"Yes," said Morris.

Rutledge waited at the door. "Thanks," he said, but he did not say Morris's name. He closed the door behind him without looking back.

"Cops," said Sullivan. "I thought you had a trial in there somewhere. Did it used to come before or after they arrested you?"

"Our detective changed identities," said Morris. "He was another man the minute we made up the list of suspects. He was no longer looking for a killer. He was looking for somebody."

"He could have picked you," said Sullivan. "There is almost as much circumstantial evidence against you as against Dolan."

Morris squeezed his heavy knuckles. "What did he tell me, if I proved to be the killer . . . 'I'll pull the switch myself.' He meant it. The old coroner tried to warn me: 'Never get between him and what he needs.' Rutledge needed a killer. Well, he has one."

"Do you think they can convict him?" asked Julia.

"I wouldn't bet on it. I've seen Dolan prop himself up from the inside too many times. It'll be iron against iron. Dolan will be some witness. Jesus. We sound sorry for him. Maybe he killed Rossi with his two hands. And the others." Morris tried to see Rossi, folded like a ruined sack; the mud sockets for eyes of John Whitlow; the steam rising around the cold death of Tommy Fryer. He saw Dolan, waiting in his room for what had to happen.

20 ▦

"YOU AWAKE?" SAID JULIA.

"Yes." He did not open his eyes.

"Did you sleep?"

"I dreamed Monty was driving us across Texas. West Texas."

"Not the wreck?" She pushed his hair off his forehead.

"No." Morris no longer dreamed of the wreck, when his knee was ruined. "We were just driving, across Texas."

"I miss him, too," said Sullivan. "But it doesn't bother me now. It hasn't for a long time. I just kid you. I'm glad you miss him. Where were we going across Texas?"

"West. Everything was west. All his clubs were in the back seat. I don't know how he shifted gears with us up front, in that old car. What happened to us all, Sullivan?"

"Colorado's still west," she said.

"What time is it?"

"Ten-thirty."

"Can you reach the phone?"

She handed it to him.

"I don't trust our detective," said Morris. "He knows everything I know. Why call me?" He dialed the number in his notepad. It surprised him to hear Dr. Moseley answer, very formally.

"John Morris, Associated Press."

"Oh, yes." The formality, and some of the age, fell away from his voice.

"Is it too early to know the result of your tests?"

"We know," Moseley answered. He seemed to be muffling the phone with his hand. Then he said, "Lieutenant Rutledge is here. I can tell you. The T-3 ran off the curve. The boy's heart was churning in it. The steam didn't help. Shock. Death."

Morris let the fact of it sink in. So it was murder. "Unlucky for the killer, having you in Atlanta."

"Old Moseley. I thought he died." The coroner gave a brief, airy laugh. Then he was quiet. "If you ever see me again, it'll be out at Piedmont Park. You'll have to play the course with me. You remember it. Chicken wire fences still keep your ball from going over the greens into the street. You'll know me." He wheezed another laugh. "I'll be the one not carrying any woods. Never could hit 'em."

"What did you find in Dolan's bag?"

Again a hand muffled the other receiver. "There were two bottles holding a few tablets of triiodothyronine. Two different trade names."

"Were the names of the doctors typed on them?" asked Morris.

"No dates or names. But we can probably trace the torn labels."

"What about amphetamines?"

He didn't hesitate. "Oh, yes. A number of them."

Morris let the silence grow. "Congratulations doesn't seem to be the right word. But you've done a remarkable job. Could I speak to Rutledge?"

Morris was instantly sorry he had not said good-bye, that the old man had passed the phone without speaking.

"I'll be at your hotel in fifteen minutes. Dolan's in room eleven-twenty-five. My men are outside." Rutledge hung up.

Morris put down the phone.

"No mistake," said Julia.

He shook his head lying on the pillow. "No luck for Dolan."

"Poor Dolan," she said. "I never really knew him." She said it in the past tense, as if he were already dead.

"Who were we supposed to hope had done it?" asked Morris. "Some maniac," he answered. "Not Dolan. Not just a hard, bitter man, whose life is over."

"Ann. Wasn't that his wife's name? Left him, how many years ago?"

"Maybe ten." Morris dialed New York.

Whitfield was on another line. Morris waited for him. He began to dictate:

Atlanta, Georgia—Former United States Open champion Ted Dolan was arrested here Sunday night, and charged with murdering 1977 Open leaders John Whitlow and Tommy Fryer, and teaching pro Jim Rossi. Dolan, 47, a native of Tulsa, Oklahoma and a veteran of 22 years on the tour, was to have competed Monday in the final 27 holes of the Open . . .

Morris dictated the technical properties of the drug found in Fryer's bloodstream, and in Dolan's golf bag. He included the name of Dr. Percy Moore, who had been paired with Dolan in the Los Angeles pro-am. Morris quoted the doctor, but was careful not to state that his drugs had killed Fryer. But the good doctor better have paid his malpractice insurance. Whitfield did not interrupt him once.

"Hold the story until I call back and confirm," said Morris. "They are picking Dolan up in the hotel right now. I'll get a quote from him."

"We'll go around the world with this one," said Whitfield. "Sorry it had to be one of your guys." He hung up.

Morris pushed his legs off the bed and slipped into his shoes. "My cane?" he said, suddenly aware it was out of reach.

Sullivan got on her knees and reached under the table. Crawling on the floor, she looked like a young girl. She stood up with the cane. "I'll race you," she said.

Morris took her and the cane in his arms.

Julia was crying. "Maybe he'll be found insane," she said. "I'm sure he will be." She handed him the cane.

"I'll be back," said Morris.

He stepped off the elevator at the eleventh floor, carefully advancing his cane between the automatic doors. Two detectives recognized him, and pointed toward Sergeant Bolton, standing in the hall.

Bolton stood awkwardly, with no place to lean his thin arms. Now he had his hands in his pockets. Morris looked closely into his eyes. Bolton had not changed. He had the same youthful sadness in his face.

The Sergeant raised one finger, indicating they were not to speak, then looked past him to Rutledge, who was coming alone from the elevator. He walked powerfully toward them, ignoring their eyes.

Rutledge began whispering before he stopped. "I'm going in quick. The light switch is on the right. Hit it when I'm into the room." He slid a key in the door. "Bolton." He did not look back. "Be ready."

Rutledge reached under his own coat. His palm and fingers nearly covered the automatic pistol in his right hand.

Morris squeezed his cane as if in self-defense.

Rutledge turned the key. He crouched quickly forward into the dark of the room. Bolton, his awkwardness flowing into motion, slid behind him, one hand clawed around a pistol absurdly out of place in front of him. The other hand flicked the room into muted pockets of light under lampshades.

Morris looked past Bolton onto the bed.

"Up, Dolan!" Rutledge kicked the bed, careful not to point the automatic at him, but letting him see it in his hand.

Dolan lay strangely precise under the thin spread, his head in the center of the pillow. He was awake, his eyes focused. The room must have been dark only a minute. Dolan pulled himself into a sitting position. Blood was now running strongly in his face. He turned, ignoring Rutledge and Bolton, with the iron pistol in his thin hand, and looked with surprise at Morris.

"Morris, what are these idiots doing?" His voice was familiar, but hurried, his breathing too shallow to sustain his words.

"Up!" repeated Rutledge, now threatening him with the small bulk in his right hand.

Dolan ignored him, still looking at Morris, as if seeing him could deny what was happening.

Rutledge kicked the bed again sharply with his foot. "Up!" He stepped forward, locking one hand on Dolan's thick wrist.

186

"Come with us, *easy*. Or the other way." Rutledge kept his voice threateningly low.

Dolan sat still, his breathing under control, his face struggling with fury.

Rutledge released him. Dolan stood up, vulnerable in his bare feet and striped pajamas. Bolton passed his empty hand along the trousers folded over a chair, then threw them to him. Dolan caught them, and began pulling them on over his pajamas.

"You're under arrest for murder," said Rutledge. "You have the right to counsel, you have the right to remain silent . . ." His voice was a monotone.

Dolan continued to pull a blue and white golf shirt over his head, leaving his artificially dark hair in free-lance directions.

"Morris, get me a lawyer." Dolan spoke to him as if the police were violating both of their lives. "Put this statement on your wire," he said. "Atlanta owes me one million, five thousand dollars. The five thousand I stood to win tomorrow. The one million is for false arrest, for destroying my name. You got that, Morris?" His voice was as deadly as the detective's.

"Okay, Sergeant," said Rutledge.

Bolton stepped forward, clamping handcuffs around Dolan's heavy wrists. Dolan was too surprised to object, until he felt the cold metal between his hands. He turned slowly to look at Rutledge, as if he had just entered the room by error. "Squatty man. You've made your big mistake." Dolan turned his back on him and moved toward the door, stopping beside Morris, whose form seemed to grow in the muted light. "Get me a good lawyer, Morris," he said, his eyes moving with confidence.

Morris was surprised to hear himself speak. "Don't underestimate their evidence. I know. I've heard it. And I've written it. Do you want to be quoted about suing for false arrest?"

"Damn right. I wouldn't spit on them, or their evidence."

Bolton guided him out of the room.

"Tough guy," said Rutledge. "We'll see how tough."

Morris stood away from the detective. There was nothing to be said between them. Morris looked at the door. Rutledge was gone.

Two cops entered and began going carefully through the room.

"Can I use the phone?" Morris asked. The cops shook their heads. Morris rolled with his sailor's gait out of the room, touching his cane for balance, organizing his dictation.

Sullivan waited with the door cracked. Morris put both arms around her without speaking. Then moved toward the telephone.

Whitfield took his description of the arrest, of everything that was said.

"Same old Dolan," Whitfield said. "Only this time it's not a triple bogey. It's a triple murder."

"The Atlanta bureau can round up all the quotes of 'shock and dismay,' " said Morris. "Be sure they contact the other eleven of us who were suspects."

"Give me your own reaction," said Whitfield.

Morris did not have to think. " 'Dolan is innocent until proven guilty. The evidence against him is substantial, but circumstantial. He had an outstanding war record. He has been a strong figure in golf, a U.S. Open champion in the best tradition. It's now in the hands of the state.' I've had it," said Morris. "And I've got to find a lawyer for him." He hung up. He looked at Sullivan. "Did I leave out anything?"

She shook her head, then asked, "Why didn't Dolan sound more afraid?"

"I don't know. He was in mild shock, at first. His breathing was shallow. Then he was ready to strangle somebody, but kept himself in control. It was as if he had taken a forty on the back side. He was that mad, and that normal. Maybe he doesn't realize what he's done. Or what they say he's done. What room is LeBaron in?"

"Sixty-fourteen."

He dialed the room. Frank answered.

"This is Morris. They just arrested Dolan. For murder." Morris described the evidence against him, and the arrest.

"I don't know how to feel," said LeBaron. His voice was tired. "But the game lives. And I'm glad." He paused. "How do you explain it, Morris? Dolan's always had a temper, but for twenty-two years he's been letter-straight with the rules. He's bitched. He's fired caddies. He's never filed a formal complaint on the tour. Now he kills three golfers.

188

Maybe he's sick, has a brain tumor." LeBaron's voice wore down into silence.

"He asked me to find him a lawyer. Do you know anybody?"

"Plenty of lawyers. I doubt any of them are criminal lawyers. I can find out. At least get you a name."

"You'll tell Colburn, and Horton."

"Yes. Should we call off the National Guard?"

"That's up to the state."

There was a silence. Then LeBaron asked, "What are the chances they arrested the wrong man?"

"It doesn't seem likely," said Morris. "But what is more unlikely than three murders? Why do you ask?"

"I don't know," said LeBaron. "I guess I would have trouble believing it, no matter whom they arrested. We've known Ted over twenty years."

Morris tapped his shoe with his cane. He waited to feel a sense of relief that it was over. It did not come. He was tired. As tired as LeBaron's voice. "Let me know if you come up with a lawyer. I'll be in the bar. Or the dining room. Warn him that Dolan's broke. I don't know what he can pay."

"We'll get him a lawyer," said Frank. He hung up.

"What 'doesn't seem likely'?" asked Sullivan.

"That they arrested the wrong man."

"How does an innocent man react when he's arrested?" asked Julia.

"I expect the same as a guilty one. The electric chair doesn't know the difference."

Sullivan shivered against him. "Can't he plead insanity?"

Morris remembered the confident movement of Dolan's eyes. "I don't believe he would go for it. If he's insane, he doesn't know it. But then, of course, he wouldn't. I'm tired, Sullivan. But I'm more thirsty than tired."

"Let's get out before the phone rings. But you have to have something to eat."

They had no trouble finding a table in the main dining room. Morris was sure he had ruined the dinner plans of at least two hundred reporters. More words would be written about Ted Dolan tonight than in all the ten years since he won the Open.

The first two drinks made it possible not to think. As

189

always, they were comfortable together without speaking. Morris was amazed how hungry he was.

Julia put down her fork after her first bite. "If Wellington had known they were going to name this beef after him, he wouldn't have worried about his reputation."

"Did he worry about it?"

"Of course not. I'm the one who's worried about my girlish figure. Uh-oh. Here comes your telephone call."

The tall, efficient hostess leaned over the table. "Your call, Mr. Morrs. You can take it here in the office."

"Yes," he said.

"Mr. Morris, this is Howard Neel. One of my law partners is close to your friend Frank LeBaron. Both of them have called me. I understand the police have arrested Ted Dolan for murder."

"Yes. About an hour ago. He asked me to find him a lawyer. I hope Frank told you, Dolan's won very little money on the tour this year. I don't know what kind of fee he can pay."

"We won't worry about that. The Golf Club is concerned that he be adequately represented. So am I. I've practiced criminal law here for twenty-five years. I'll give you some names to call as references."

"It's not necessary," said Morris. He could ask Frank about him tomorrow.

"Mr. LeBaron read me the text of your wire story. Does that represent everything you know about the evidence against Dolan?"

"Yes, it does. The Los Angeles doctor, Percy Moore, admitted giving the drug T-3, to Dolan. But it was in an unsworn statement. I was careful how I worded his evidence."

"Does Dolan have an immediate family?"

"He's divorced. His children are grown."

"Shall I go to see him?" asked Neel.

"Please do." Morris liked the unhurried sound of the lawyer's voice. "Tell him I'll come by tomorrow. If they'll let me see him."

"Is he a close friend of yours?"

"I've known him, on the tour, for over twenty years. He's not that close to anyone."

"How did he take it, the arrest?"

"It shook him, at first," said Morris. "Then he seemed more angry than afraid. He insisted he intended to sue."

"Yes," said Neel. "Well, I'll go by the station. I'll want to talk with you when it's convenient."

"Any time. I'll be at the course tomorrow. And thanks."

When Morris sat down again, some of his fatigue seemed to be absorbed by the chair. Sullivan was now eating a tall dessert. A chocolate smear on her chin made him smile.

"You look relieved," she said.

"Yes. A lawyer named Neel. Howard Neel. His partner's a friend of Frank's. Seems substantial. Dolan could do worse, I think. Are you starting a chocolate factory on your chin?"

"I'm eating fast. Before they bring the bill for General Wellington. Why don't you buy me an after-dinner drink and take me home."

"You're more expensive to keep on the road than Travis's jet."

"I recommend it, being a kept woman." She laughed.

Morris was sure he was dreaming. Sounds were going in and out of his head, but even with the telephone in his hand, he was not awake.

"Mr. Morris."

The voice was familiar. He opened his eyes in the dark. "Yes." Morris did not disguise the sleep in his voice.

"I apologize for calling. This is Howard Neel, Dolan's attorney. I tried to sleep. I couldn't."

Now Morris was awake. Objects in the room were taking on shapes in the dark. "Go ahead."

"I met with Dolan. They gave us more time together than they probably meant to. Can we talk off the record?"

"Sure."

"Stay in this business twenty-five years, and you have gut feelings. Some of them mistaken, but not so many. A disturbed mind can feel you, can fool itself."

"Do you think Dolan's psychopathic?"

"No, I don't. The evidence against him is powerful, but circumstantial. I'll have to dig all the way to California to defend him. I feel the truth of what happened will come out, in time. What bothers me is tomorrow."

"What do you mean?"

"Sometimes a good surgeon won't operate. You may have all the symptoms, but he just doesn't feel you're sick enough. That's my impression of Dolan. There's evidence against him, but he's just not sick enough to have killed three people. What happens tomorrow if the wrong man is in jail?"

"There's still security at the course," said Morris.

"They've called off the National Guard. And the extra police support. There will just be routine security. And maximum security didn't help Tommy Fryer."

"Funny. LeBaron worried about that, and he hadn't spoken to Dolan."

"Maybe Dolan killed three of them, and I've got us both awake for nothing. It's just a gut feeling I have that he didn't."

"Did you tell anyone at the station?"

"They weren't interested. Can't say I blame them."

"All I can do in the morning is talk to LeBaron, and the players," said Morris. "I don't deny I had a feeling something was wrong when Dolan was arrested. But I never had a friend arrested for murder before. It's all unreal to me. I couldn't believe in any of the twelve suspects. Especially since I was one of them. I do thank you for calling."

Morris tried to think. Then he was asleep.

21 ✖

MORRIS STOPPED BEHIND THE EIGHTEENTH GREEN. THE dew was deep in the grass. His shoes were covered with it. He dragged his cane on the ground, sending up a round wall of water. The course was empty. Only the caddies were swallowed up in the fairways as they walked off the positions of the pins. The sun was not yet above the trees. Alone, Morris could feel the energy of the Open, the pressure of it rising on the cool grass with the coming heat. But he could not keep his thoughts from the clubhouse, and the three men waiting to see him, and Dolan in his cell. The course lost its relation of beauty and history. He was only standing alone. He turned back to the clubhouse.

"Tough luck for Dolan. But he can be thankful they stopped him," said Colburn. He settled his cup precisely in its saucer.

Morris swallowed his own coffee. Perhaps what he said was true. Yet Morris despised hearing him say it. What did he know about Dolan, or any of them whose lives rode the slippery contours of the greens? Colburn had his tournament; the USGA had its check; he could afford to be generous. No, thought Morris, the game belongs only to those who play it; the rest of us create our own importance.

"I had a call at four A.M.," said Morris. "From Dolan's lawyer. Your man, Howard Neel." He looked at LeBaron, who made no effort to conceal his contempt for Colburn. Only LeBaron's obsession for the PGA kept him at the table.

"I know him," said Colburn. "He's a member of the club."

"He's paid to prove his client innocent," said Morris. "He doesn't have to believe it himself."

"Lucky he doesn't," said Colburn.

"Neel met with Dolan last night. Afterward, he couldn't sleep. He called me. He admitted the evidence was strong against Dolan. But, in Neel's words, he 'doesn't seem sick enough' to have done it."

LeBaron sat looking straight at Morris.

"Neel also admits a disturbed mind can fool you. That he could be wrong. But, in his judgment, after twenty-five years as a criminal lawyer, the police have the wrong man."

"Is Mr. Neel an attorney, or a jury?" said Colburn, touching his mouth with his napkin, the slightest element of humor in his voice.

"Neel's not worried about Dolan. He believes the truth will out," said Morris. "He's worried about today. If the wrong man is in jail."

"You're right about one thing," said Colburn. "Lawyers don't get paid to represent the truth. Only the client." He held up his cup for a refill of coffee.

"I'm worried," said LeBaron.

"You were last night," reminded Morris.

"Neel doesn't stand to make a large fee from Dolan. If he's paid at all. He's a member of this club. He feels a great deal of responsibility toward it. If he's concerned, I'm concerned," said LeBaron.

"In any event, it's too late for all this concern," said Colburn. "We can't call back the National Guard. And the police have made it clear. They already have their man."

"Their *suspect*," corrected Morris. "We owe it to the other eleven suspects to warn them of Neel's feelings. I've already called Travis. He and the other five golfers on Rutledge's list are waiting to talk with me."

"I saw Old Thompson just now in the caddy yard," said LeBaron. "I'll speak to him. Horton and Goodner are across the room. I might as well ruin their breakfast. I don't know where Ev Holland might be. But I'll have him paged."

"It's destructive, to stir it up again," said Colburn, "just because some lawyer has insomnia."

"And some reporter," said Morris directly to him.

"I'll have no part in it," Colburn answered, pushing back his chair. He turned without speaking and moved to join the tournament committee at a long table across the room.

"What do you think, Morris?" asked LeBaron.

"The same as you. Dolan may be a triple murderer. But I can't believe it. Maybe I couldn't believe it, no matter whom they arrested."

"We're all crazy, following a game all of our lives," said LeBaron. "I know what it is that bothers me. Dolan's too hard, too selfish to be insane."

"Maybe so. I'll see you in half an hour."

Morris showed his pass to the guard at the door. He stopped inside, listening to the sounds of the locker room, all of them hushed. The thick carpet absorbed the action of doors closing, water running in the distance, the passing steps of jacketed attendants, pockets of conversation. Against one wall was a platoon of shoes, newly cleaned, in the colors of all the flags of the world.

Morris stopped again, beside Travis Walker.

Travis and Kirkland stood up and touched him, as if he had been captive in a hostile country.

"Morris," said Kirkland.

"How's Dolan?"

"I don't know if he's insane, but he's mad. He's going to sue." Morris meant to say it solemnly, but they couldn't help laughing.

"Yeah, and if he didn't like the layout, he's probably gonna withdraw." Al Morgan came around the row of lockers, holding, for him, a rare cup of coffee.

"We better remember the people he's accused of killing," said Lee Washburn, who sat up from tying his shoes.

The carpet deadened all the sound in the room.

"Can they prove it?" Art Howard stood in the aisle, cleaning his dark prescription glasses, blinking his pale eyes under the fluorescent light. With his short arms and round stomach, he might have been a teacher of algebra.

"I don't know anything more than I wrote," said Morris. "The police say they have all the evidence they need."

"What do you *think?*" asked Kirkland, his tenor voice higher with tension.

"I want to tell you what his lawyer thinks. He's a member of this club. Name is Howard Neel. You might have met him."

"I met him," said Morgan. "You wouldn't forget his wife." He gave an obscene gesture. Nobody laughed.

"Neel called me," said Morris, "about four A.M. Said he couldn't sleep, that he had a gut feeling they had arrested the wrong man."

"Lawyers are worse than damn agents," said Morgan. "They get their share if you hang. All they have to do is *say* you're innocent. They don't have to prove it."

The word *hang* was too real in the room.

"Neel thinks the truth will clear him, eventually," said Morris. "He's worried about today. If the wrong man is locked up."

"You mean we're still IT!" said Morgan. "Some lawyer."

"What do the police say?" Howard was back behind his dark glasses, his eyes safely out of the light.

"Lieutenant Rutledge called off the hunt. He has his man."

"Your buddy," said Morgan.

"Some buddy. I should have recognized him," said Morris. "He's all cop. Believe me. He didn't care whose name turned out to be IT. Mine or anybody's in this room."

195

"I buy Dolan's name," said Washburn. "You all sound as if he's being persecuted. I believe the term is *pro*secuted. But what's three murders between old friends."

"I knew you had perfected the choke two-iron," said Morgan. "I didn't know you had taken up the judiciary."

"Somebody pour Morgan a drink. It's seven A.M.," said Washburn.

"Be careful," said Morris, "of what you eat, and what you drink. Trust nobody." He could not see any of them as suspects, only as victims.

"Let's play golf," said Travis, "and to hell with it." He dropped his shoes in front of him on the dark carpet.

The burden of his share of the lead did not seem to weigh on him, thought Morris; but the reality of the first tee was an hour away. Nine players were within two shots of Walker and Washburn and the kid from Alabama. Morris waited to feel his own blood rise at the challenge. But he only stood confused as the five players turned back to their separate lockers. Other players who had gathered in groups around them also turned away.

"You guys look out!" Morgan shouted at them. "Get it going too good and one of us five will drown you." His lone laugh ran through the room and down into the carpet.

LeBaron sat at a long table by the bar, with Ev Holland and Edward Horton. Facing them were Joe Goodner, and Old Thompson, who was out of place in his broken jacket and same ruined shirt he had worn for six days.

"Sorry, I've got a meeting," Horton said. The Players' Commissioner was careful not to be rude to the millions of Associated Press readers.

Morris sat beside Holland. All the health seemed to have gone out of his face.

"I'm sorry, Ev." He did not have to say Tommy's name. Holland swallowed, but did not speak. Tommy Fryer was the son he never had.

Goodner sat with his face closed tight. He kept looking around the room, as if afraid to be seen at the table. "Lawyer or no lawyer. It doesn't sound promising for Dolan," he said.

"No," agreed Morris. Something about Goodner's tight composure made him add, "You two were rookies together, weren't you?"

Goodner gave a semblance of a nod.

"I believe you traveled together one year. In an old Buick."

Goodner looked up defiantly, as if Morris were accusing him of complicity.

"Dolan could stay mad across five states over one three-putt," said Goodner. "I never dreamed he would kill three people. Sorry, I've got a meeting, too." He pushed away from the table without looking back.

"Nobody could caddy for Dolan three days in a row," said Old Thompson. He paused. "He never cheated the rules." The scratchy sound of his own voice made him pull back into his chair.

"Do you have a ride to Chicago?" asked Morris.

"Got a bag, too," said Thompson, his teeth as ruined as his voice.

"Stay with somebody you know today. As much as you can," said Morris. "For your own protection."

Old Thompson moved his still powerful head up and down. "Dolan never cheated the rules," he repeated, pushing himself up with his long arms. "Thanks for the breakfast." He walked for the door as if he had his life back.

"Sorry. I cain't talk, Morris." Ev followed Thompson, a round ball of a man moving through the room without purpose.

"So, we've all been warned," said LeBaron.

"How did they take it?" asked Morris.

"You saw them. What could they say? Who wants to be Dolan?"

"Not Goodner, or Horton."

"Or me," said LeBaron. "How are the players taking it?"

"Morgan's the clown. Washburn has his hate on for the world. None of us knows what to think."

"You'll see a security man with you. With each of us," said LeBaron. "It's the best I could do."

"Travis said, 'Let's play golf.'" Morris stood, looking through the glass wall as if the course had just materialized.

Morris leaned against his portable seat, propped there securely with his cane. The sun flooded down on him. The sight of a ball in the air, climbing, reaching for the green, spinning into it, and the hot sun, released him from his thoughts. He was not taking any notes. He had avoided the press tent after giving one long interview to the other reporters. Dolan was the only news. The last holes of the Open were being played out almost soundlessly, the great, sprawling gallery itself numb with the week's consequences. Still, the sun helped. And the quick, familiar gestures of the players. For the first time, Morris looked across the eighteenth green at the scoreboard.

Most of the players had completed the third round, and teed off again on the front side. Old Alfred, his face stretched almost white under the bag he carried, had willed Al Morgan to a seventy. They were a two-eleven and at least in the money chase, with eighteen holes to play.

Kirkland would not win his fourth Open. Not even his grim mouth and unmatched game could overcome his third round seventy-five.

Lee Washburn, paired with Kirkland, feeding his own anger, had birdied seven holes, and survived water once for a sixty-six.

Travis Walker stood across the lake, his hands gripping his hips. He had lost a shot at seventeen, and still he was tied with Washburn, and now two others, for the lead.

Morris found his binoculars. Art Howard's drive was fifty yards behind Walker's, but precisely in the fairway. Howard walked directly to his ball and struck it almost without stopping, or looking to see it appear as if up out of the ground on the green. He was one of three players one shot from the lead. He took short, abrupt steps, his head down, his stubby arms thrashing beside his round stomach.

Travis could not seem to get his club back. Morris felt his own hands freezing on the shaft. The people layered in the wooden bleachers, and standing along the fairway, did not move or breathe. Travis turned away, and back down again with a blur of steel, the ball shrieking into the air, burning too low over the water, hooking, now skidding with reverse spin until it rolled exhausted to the far back of the green. The crowds thundered its relief at the long sight of the ball low over the water, ignoring the massive putt the shot had left him.

Morris did not speak, even when Travis walked directly to him. Always a player's concentration was inviolate, unless he spoke first.

Travis tapped Morris's cane with his putter. "Let me hit it with that," he said.

"Knock it home," said Morris, pleased that Travis had spoken, the sun shining between them.

Travis stood, one hand stabbing to remove the glove from the other. The putt waited for him, paralyzingly long and slick with speed. Morris felt Travis's panic in his own hands. "They're waiting to stand up for you," Morris said.

Travis popped him with his glove. He turned and walked onto the green into a round explosion of noise, as if their voices alone were standing in his honor.

Morris stood, balancing himself on his stiff knee and hitting his cane against the steel rod of his seat.

Travis raised both arms like weapons. He might have been twenty-eight.

But all the time the putt waited in front of him. Finally he bent over the ball. Morris could feel the shock of the blade as Travis jabbed the ball ten feet past the cup, and missed it badly coming back. The groan from the people was for their own youth. Art Howard tapped in his second putt for a par, and the only sixty-eight he had ever scored in the U.S. Open. He seemed not to hear the quiet shower of applause.

People were standing to see Travis walk from the green to the first tee, trying with their eyes to lift him back into the lead. Howard trailed after him through the sound in his dark glasses. Their scores of two-eleven were identical, but they might have been playing in separate countries.

Morris watched them disappear into the crowd. A generation of players had been lost from public sight as accessories to the action of Travis Walker. Well, thought Morris, they owe him half of what they've made. Before Travis, the great purses were petty cash. God help Dolan, Morris thought suddenly; he might never have to miss another Friday cut, when the high scorers were exiled further inside themselves to the next city, carrying their failure among strangers.

Morris nearly lost his balance. He held onto his cane, steadying his portable seat. *What did Dolan shoot in Los Angeles?* Morris was sure he had ruined both opening rounds on the savage eighteenth hole, and missed the Friday cut. *What did Doctor Perry Moore say, exactly?*

Something bothered him, escaped him. Morris rapped both

shoes with his cane, but it wouldn't come to him, the doctor's *exact* words. Morris began swinging his bad leg, wheeling his large frame between the people pressing to follow after Travis. Morris headed in the opposite direction. His briefcase and notepad were in the press room.

Morris was thankful for the chaotic movement of the writers. They were only aware of their own typing. Untended phones rang unanswered. Other reporters drank around the raised television set, following the actions of the players, taking notes painfully, as if they were suffering the June heat on the long fairways.

Morris waved aside a question from the local AP bureau chief. Then he was lost in his notes. The words, the fragments of phrases, brought back entire sentences. He could remember the inflections in the doctor's voice. And in the Lieutenant's; the viciousness of his questions came up out of the pages. Where was it? Oh, yes:

"Ted Dolan." The doctor repeated his name, to give the impression it might have slipped his mind. *"Has anything happened to Mr. Dolan?"*

Then Rutledge's voice.

Then the doctor: *"I don't prescribe medicine, except to my own patients. Amphetamines can be dangerous."*

And who mentioned amphetamines, remembered Morris. It was when Rutledge had called him back. And accused him of lying, hinted he might be an accomplice in murder. Here we go, thought Morris.

Rutledge speaking: *"You're the only one talking about amphetamines. We're talking about triiodothyronine."* The way he pronounced the word was an indictment.

Doctor: *"Oh, God. He got them."* A pause. *"He used them to kill someone? I can't believe it. I only brought ten tablets. Ten fifty-microgram tablets."* The doctor kept talking.

Then Rutledge.

Morris himself had asked: *"Who suggested the T-3?"*

Doctor: *"He did. Mr. Dolan seemed to know a great deal about it. Frankly, I . . ."* He started to say *rarely.* *"I never prescribe it for weight loss. It can be risky."*

Rutledge: *"But you weren't afraid to risk Dolan's life?"*

Doctor: *"He asked me for it. I didn't have it with me. It's not the kind of drug you carry with you."*

200

Rutledge: *"But you got it for him?"*

Doctor: *"Yes."* A pause. *"I brought it Sunday."*

Morris read his notes again. He was certain he hadn't misquoted him. *"I brought it Sunday."* And the doctor had already said, *"Oh, God. He got them."*

Morris read further down his notepad. Then the next page of notes. The last thing the doctor said, he asked: *"I . . . Has Mr. Dolan also been killed?"*

With his own tablets? Morris asked himself. If he had them in his possession, why would the doctor imagine he might have been killed with them?

I'm an idiot, thought Morris, a gimpy-legged, overweight idiot. Moore *brought* the tablets *Sunday.* He gave them to someone. To *take* to Dolan. Someone who *did* make Friday's cut. But who?

Morris could not stay seated in his chair. The doctor's telephone numbers were in his notes. He propped himself erect with his cane, and dialed the operator with his other hand. It was possible Dolan had stayed over until Sunday. The hell it was. Dolan never stayed over at a tournament in his life when he missed the cut. Not at the Masters. Not at the Open. Certainly not in Los Angeles. Morris looked at his watch, ten A.M. in Atlanta, seven A.M. in California.

The maid answered the telephone. Morris nearly strangled the receiver. He could not tell her Spanish from her English. She did not remember him. She finally understood. The doctor was not at home. Morris cursed himself. He thought he understood the doctor also was not at his office. Morris cursed aloud. The maid was frightened. Morris apologized. He apologized again. *"Don't hang up, please."* He managed to calm her. Yes, she did have the hospital number. She gave him *four different* hospital numbers.

Morris sweated in the air conditioning. He struggled to decipher the four numbers from three thousand miles and another language away. He hung up, exhausted. He had forgotten to leave the press room number. He called back. Yes, she was sure she understood it. Morris dropped the phone and sat down again. Just to be sure, he dialed Moore's office. No one answered.

Morris suppressed his impatience. So they were back to "eleven good men and true." Not quite. The one man who didn't kill Tommy Fryer was Dolan. He never got the tablets from Dr. Moore.

What if he did get them? What if someone brought the tablets to him from Los Angeles? thought Morris. He had others in his golf bag. He needed twenty tablets to kill Fryer. And how could he know old Doctor William Moseley was going to live forever, and run a radio-immunoassay on Fryer, not because of physiological evidence, but because a young athlete was dead who should be alive. And then Dolan left the extra tablets in his own bag? No. Dolan never got them. He never knew what happened.

The first murder was not logical, thought Morris. No disputing that. It was luck, sick luck, that no one saw it. The other two murders were all preparation. Sick? Yes. But luck was not involved. Someone on the tour accepted the tablets from Dr. Moore. Maybe he meant to use them all along, after the doctor had warned him how dangerous they could be. Maybe he meant to steal ten more tablets from Dolan, and take them all himself, and end whatever nightmare he was living. Maybe.

On the eighteenth floor of the Peachtree Towers Hotel, something broke loose in his mind. Nothing dreamed of. He threw Jim Rossi to his death. Why? God knows. Having killed the greatest teacher, he turned to the players, the leaders of the Open. Simple as that. And as irrational as that, thought Morris. John Whitlow could not swim, a failure of technique that cost him his life.

There was no end to the army of blond young players. Tommy Fryer took the lead. It was simplicity itself to match the doctor's tablets with ten more from Dolan's bag for a lethal dose. Opportunity was everywhere to dissolve them in orange juice. Give them to Fryer in the locker room. Four to six hours later came the maximum effect from the drug, T-3, accelerated by the steam bath. And then, "follow the leader," said Morris to himself, but it was not a game anymore.

Lucky Dolan, he thought. Safe in his cell. But out on the course, or in the clubhouse, was another mind. Somebody who *was* there on Sunday in Los Angeles.

Morris could only sit. Dr. Percy Moore would show up at one of his four hospitals, or at his office, or at his home, in Spanish or in English, and call. He's too frightened not to call, Morris thought. He hoped. And what if my notes are confused? If I misheard him? The hell I did.

Call Rutledge? Morris asked himself. He tapped the shoe on his outstretched leg with his cane. He picked up the telephone. Why was he always surprised when Dr. William Moseley answered his own calls?

"You're still living forever," said Morris. He did not have to identify himself.

"Oh, yes." Moseley's voice was shockingly young.

"I need your help."

"You have it. You could not have gotten it any later. I'm retiring. Leaving the papers in my desk. I'll not see another body in this world. Not even my own." His laugh was so old. It was a joke on his young voice.

"Did you find any drugs, any substance to be concerned about, in the things the police took from the twelve suspects? *Us* twelve suspects," said Morris.

"I can't say. That information doesn't belong to me. That was my other life. Before I retired." He laughed, even older.

"The wrong man is in the Fulton County jail," said Morris. "The Los Angeles doctor said he *brought* the tablets on *Sunday*. Dolan didn't make the cut in Los Angeles. He wasn't there on Sunday. Somebody took the tablets from him, and kept them."

"Or Dolan's a fool and a murderer, a likely combination," said Moseley, his voice tiring with the effort.

"We have a murderer loose. The fool works for the police," said Morris.

"Call him. Call Rutledge." There was no belief in the old man's voice.

"Rutledge wanted Dolan. Who'll he want next? Your AP reporter?"

Moseley was all fatigue. "Rutledge knows. Not about Dolan missing the cut. He knows I found cyanide in a paste. A hellish paste. In a chapstick."

The old man was now coughing. He had a deep fit of coughing. Then he was laughing. "It like to knocked me down. I touched it with my tongue. Just touched it."

"Whose chapstick?" Morris was standing up. He held his cane like a reprimand.

203

"Oh, Kirkland's." The old man's voice was empty. "Rutledge knows. He's holding it, digging into Dolan's past."

"The fool." Morris's own voice went up an octave. "Did he tell Kirkland?"

"Why would he?"

"Would it have killed him?"

"Could've. If his lips were cracked and split enough. And he smeared it on deep enough. Whoever made the paste knew what he was doing."

"Would it take a chemist?"

"Nearly," said Moseley, his voice hardly to sustain one word. "A pharmacist, maybe . . ."

"Why would a man collect lethal tablets," asked Morris, "compound a deadly paste, *before* he committed an *unpremeditated* murder? Can a man prepare himself to go mad?"

"I told you once," said Moseley, "you can't do a biopsy of what's in a man's mind. Morris, call the California doctor." The old man said it like a stroke of invention.

"I'm trying. It may be hours. He's making rounds in one of four hospitals. His office doesn't answer. I'm afraid." Rutledge knew THAT! thought Morris. And would risk the life of Kirkland, the world's finest golfer, a decent man, while he played detective.

"You've known for a long time what Rutledge would risk," said Morris.

"I tried to warn you once."

"I know. 'Never get between him and what he needs,' " Morris quoted.

"He's not wrong often." Moseley did not say it as an apology.

"What's *often* in a man's life?"

The old man did not answer.

"I'll buy a beer tomorrow, on your retirement," said Morris.

"I'll drink to that."

They might have been old friends from a lost war.

Morris put the phone on the hook. He looked up almost in surprise at the sounds being typed in the press room. The television cameras were on Travis Walker taking a double bogey on the fourth hole. That should put Pete Kirkland on number eight or number nine, Morris thought. He went off four holes ahead of Travis and Art Howard. But Kirkland played so deliberately, with such glacierlike precision, he might be anywhere on the front side. The camera was suddenly on him. His square, powerful face filled the screen with concentration. The camera fell away, trailing the putt across the green into the cup. Morris saw enough terrain to know it was the eighth green. Kirkland was "savaging" the course. But too late to make a run for the title. But a round to remember, and a life to remember it in. What other chapstick did Kirkland have? In his plane? In his hotel? Even possibly in another bag? Morris could catch him at the turn. He tapped the AP operator on the shoulder.

"I'm expecting a call. From California, a doctor. Don't let him hang up. No matter what he says. I'll be back in ten minutes."

Morris spun his weight on the left heel of his stiff leg, and swung wildly past the main clubhouse, scattering hostility behind him. He forced himself into the deep half-circle of people around the ninth green, his cane moving before and after him. He stopped against the roped-off exit from the green to the tenth tee.

Kirkland was putting directly toward him, the ball passing six feet beyond the hole, as if caught up in Morris's sense of urgency. Lee Washburn circled the hole without mercy, seeking the invisible line of his own putt. He backed away from the ball twice. Morris checked his watch. Washburn took his stance and pushed the makeable putt just above the hole. He jammed home the par, and turned his back, leaving his caddy to lift the ball from the hole.

Kirkland took even longer, poised over the six-foot putt as if waiting for fate to assert itself, then deliberately stroked the ball into the heart of the cup. He stopped at the edge of the green to mark down Washburn's score, and flinched at the touch of Morris's hand on his arm.

"Damn sorry," said Morris. "I have to tell you something." The urgency of the information was in his eyes.

Kirkland did not question it. He stepped on the rope barrier so that Morris could swing his leg over it.

"Last night, the police found cyanide in your chapstick," said Morris.

Kirkland touched his cracked lips.

205

"It could have been bad. Maybe lethal."

"Lucky it rained Saturday," said Kirkland, still testing his lips with his finger.

"Did you keep it in your bag?"

"No, in my locker."

"Don't trust any drugs you have. In your room. Your plane. At home. Dolan didn't kill anybody. But whoever did has access to your locker."

"I used the chapstick Friday," said Kirkland. "Saturday, I tried to talk the police out of taking it. Thank God there was no sun. And that I don't have the gift of persuasion, like Travis."

"What do you mean?" asked Morris.

"Don't you remember? Travis talked them out of taking his nose drops. They never had a chance. Morris, how do you *know* Dolan didn't kill anybody?"

Morris gripped his forearm. "You're sure Travis kept his nose drops?"

"You know Travis. He was laughing at me, afterward."

Both of them jumped as an approach shot landed nearly between them.

Kirkland looked at the scoreboard. "Travis must be okay. He's on the sixth hole. You know how he uses those drops. How do you *know* it wasn't Dolan?" he asked again.

"Dolan never got the tablets. He missed the cut in Los Angeles. Somebody picked them up for him Sunday. I'll know who before the day's over."

Morris released him. "You better catch up. Keep it going."

Kirkland disappeared into the tunnel of faces around the green. Morris looked at the scoreboard. Travis had birdied the sixth hole. He had to be all right. I'll come back here and catch him at the turn, he thought. The damn phone might be ringing. Sweat ran off his palm onto his cane. His shirt was stuck against him. He wheeled himself toward the press room.

"How about a ride." It was LeBaron.

"I owe you," said Morris, climbing into the golf cart.

"Press room?"

He nodded.

"What were you doing, giving Kirkland a free drop?" LeBaron laughed.

"Too complicated to explain. Dolan didn't kill anybody. I'm waiting on a call." Morris hated being evasive.

"The police?"

Morris shook his head. What the hell, if LeBaron was the killer, what was the use? "No. From the doctor in California. I'm sure Dolan never got the tablets."

"What does that have to do with Kirkland?"

"Somebody tried to kill him, Saturday. Put cyanide in his chapstick. Can you hold the cart here a minute? I've got to go back and catch Travis on the ninth green. If I can reach the idiot doctor."

LeBaron nodded.

Morris rolled out of the cart. The guard, like an old servant, opened the press room door. Morris steered himself through the writers, too frantic with deadlines to notice. The AP operator was feeding the computer, ignoring the telephone behind him. It was off the hook. Morris jammed himself against the table and picked up the receiver.

"John Morris," he answered.

There was no answer.

"John Morris, in Atlanta."

"Oh," someone said.

"Dr. Percy Moore?"

"Yes." His voice was uncertain.

Morris did not mention the Associated Press. The doctor might imagine he was with the police. "The T-3 tablets," said Morris. "I must know the man you *physically handed* them to."

"I've talked with my lawyer. He advised me to say nothing, except in his presence." The doctor's voice took on confidence.

Morris held his own voice dead level, as if he were controlling it with his gripped fists. "You said yesterday you *brought* the tablets on *Sunday*. You couldn't have handed them to Ted Dolan. He didn't make Friday's cut. He wasn't in Los Angeles that Sunday."

"I'm sorry. My lawyer . . ."

"Your lawyer will send you a bill, whether you're practicing medicine, or being extradited as an accessory to murder. Dolan is in jail, without bond. Charged with first-degree murder, using *your* tablets. I don't think he ever got them. Other men's lives may be in jeopardy. Think about it before you refuse to answer. Who did you *hand* the tablets to?" The ruthlessness of Morris's own voice disgusted him.

"A friend. A golfer . . ." The doctor's voice was all capitulation. "He offered to take them. He had a drink with us, our foursome, on Tuesday. He heard Dolan asking me. I was going to tell you yesterday. Howard. Art Howard . . ."

Morris lowered the receiver without speaking. His wet shirt made him shiver in the air conditioning. Art, with his loopy swing. Always down the middle, a threat on the tight courses. Not enough distance to win the major championships. Always blinking behind his dark glasses. Quiet. Never married. Tough. Not afraid to win. My God, he'd won three-quarters of a million dollars. And never made a commercial. Not with his short arms, and round stomach. Dr. Zero, they kidded him. What snapped? What happened? With Rossi, and the others? No one would ever kid him again. Morris looked at the scoreboard in the press room.

It struck him. Art was paired with Travis. They'd finished the short, par-three seventh hole. Travis had bogeyed again. Morris poled himself between bodies, his cane working the slick gymnasium floor, sweat running under his shirt.

LeBaron sat listening to his walkie-talkie. Morris lurched into the cart, which dipped and swayed under his weight.

"The eighth hole," Morris said. "Fast!" He couldn't get enough air in his lungs.

LeBaron hit the accelerator. The cart jerked forward, despite their weight.

"Who can you reach on the radio?"

"Anybody."

"Break in," said Morris. "We need help on the eighth hole."

"What kind of help? We've got security on every hole."

"I'm afraid for Travis. His life. His damn nose drops." Morris did not make sense.

LeBaron dodged between the restless, shifting gallery. "His nose drops? You're serious?"

"Damn serious. They might kill him. Raise the marshal on the eighth tee."

LeBaron kept saying the code word: "Red." He seemed to have somebody's attention. Now he had the eighth tee.

"Tell him Travis's nose drops have been poisoned. But if Travis reaches for anything in his pocket—ANYTHING—stop him!"

LeBaron repeated the instructions.

"Where exactly is he?" asked Morris.

"Starting down the eighth fairway."

"He has a routine for using the drops," said Morris. "Tell them to watch him if he kneels by his bag."

LeBaron repeated the warning to the marshal. Questions must have been flying on the radio frequency. LeBaron cut them off with his voice. And the code word, "Red."

"We need cops," said Morris.

LeBaron called again. "We'll have four when we get there."

They made an agony of progress until they broke clean from the crowd at the ninth green. Now they were picking up speed near the seventh tee. The eighth hole doglegged toward them around a small lake. A great gallery was pouring along the fairway. From this distance they could hear rolling shouts, urging Travis Walker to attack the hole.

"If Dolan's not the killer," said LeBaron. "Who is?"

"Our friend Art," said Morris, no inflection in his voice.

LeBaron nearly ran over a large woman in a yellow blouse. She fell into her husband, who pitched backward on the grass.

"Art's paired with Travis." LeBaron turned his head toward the trees rolling at them over the uneven ground.

Morris held to the cart as they bounced over the tree roots, his two hundred eighteen pounds lifting and dropping in the moving seat.

"Can we arrest him?" shouted LeBaron, as if over the noise of engines.

"To hell with him. Get to Travis."

"We can stop play," said LeBaron. "By God, we *will* stop it."

"Get me to Travis," said Morris.

A boy hollered. The gallery, in a panic, piled together in front of the cart. LeBaron stood on the brakes, the balloon tires sliding on the pine needles, turning them backward. Two men plunged over the rear of the cart. A scream ran down the crowd, a woman's. Morris released his grip and lifted forward with the momentum of the cart onto the ground, his cane magically in his hand. He pushed, swinging over a fallen boy, who was crying. Feet broke into a run along the fairway. Travis moved in slow motion in the fairway, bending toward his bag.

A cop was running desperately toward him.

"Stop him!" yelled Morris, pitching forward, his stiff knee failing him. He was amazed in midair at the fear in his own voice.

Travis had the drops in his ungloved hand. The last thing Morris saw before his face hit the ground was Travis Walker inhaling the drops.

22 ▚

T HE RISING GROUND DROVE THE BREATH FROM MORRIS'S LUNGS. Grass was in his eyes. His cane was still in his hand. His breath seemed impossibly gone. His lungs sucked dryly, and then there was air. All he could breathe. He raised his head and forced himself to look. Travis Walker squatted amazingly alive by his bag. He was looking at Morris, and did not see the cop diving on him. The two of them sprawled on the grass. Travis pulled himself to his knees, and drove the cop terrifically backward with his fist.

"Wait!" Morris pushed himself upright. The cop lay motionless. His hat rolled on end in a circle. Travis turned toward Morris, who waved his cane over his head. "Wait!" he shouted again. Travis, shaking his head in disbelief, moved quickly toward him.

"Morris, what the hell's going on?" There was a ridiculous smile on Travis's face. His shirttail hung out of his trousers. He hitched up his belt in his famous gesture.

"Your nose drops," said Morris. "They may be poison." He was out of air with the words.

"You're crazy," said Travis. "I've used them all day." He held them up. "We've both used them." He turned from Morris toward Art Howard, who stopped only two steps from them.

"My nose drops," said Travis to Art.

Morris saw Art's face drop, his mouth come open. It was as if Morris saw through his dark glasses into the pupils of his eyes. His mouth opened rounder. Then he was running. Truly running, low to the ground, his stubby arms beating the air, an iron club shining in his right hand, his short legs pumping into the ground. Morris leaped ahead of his cane, his breath safely in his lungs.

"You're all crazy!" yelled Travis to his back. He was laughing.

Morris was close enough to hear the first scream coming from the low figure while Howard ran swinging the club wildly over his head. The great gallery broke, thousands among them now running, stripping the needles from the young trees, falling into them, breaking them down, not knowing what they were running from or toward, dodging great piles of people tangled together, all of them now an amazing scream in the air. Into the edge of the lake ahead of them people ran, terrified with the water suddenly up over their legs, falling, scrambling into the large trees to the left of the green, hitting the trunks, crying to be away from the water, stumbling into traps, falling with sand in their mouths, tearing over the green itself.

Morris swung ahead to keep the low, heavy figure of Art Howard in sight in the fairway. All the screams in the air were this one man's bearing down on a huge cloverleaf trap, its sand ravaged, a lone black man bracing behind a rake to protect himself as the people parted in front of him. The club swung terrifyingly over Howard's head, driving the black man out of the trap. Howard stopped, his round stomach rising and falling as his lungs sucked desperately at the air. He dropped the iron in the sand covering his shoes, and reached carefully into his pocket. His hand and an object came steadily up— never hurrying—to his nose.

"Wait!" screamed Morris, wheeling himself nearly to the trap.

Art Howard's arm and hand fell away from his nose as he dropped to his knees. "Gaaaaa!" a sound only of terror, came out of his mouth, and his face pitched into a scar of dry sand.

The air was suddenly stiller, the people standing among the

211

trees exhausted. Low cries could be heard separately. Morris stood with his shoes in the trap, his own cane sunk in the sand. Art Howard lay at his feet, his dark glasses pitched unbroken in front of him. The left half of his face was turned inside his thick arm, the eye open. Morris lifted the bottle of nose drops out of the sand.

23 ▦

MORRIS CIRCLED THE DRINK IN HIS GLASS. HE DRANK UNTIL HE felt the ice against his teeth.

"One more," he said to Julia Sullivan. All of his chest hurt when he breathed. He was sore in places he couldn't remember.

"Old Morris, wobbling down the fairway like a broken-legged duck." Travis stood up and imitated the action with an invisible cane. For the first time, laughter cracked into the room.

"Know what Dolan said when I got to him?" LeBaron looked around the room. " 'Somebody owes me a shave and five grand.' " He caught just the ragged edge in Dolan's voice.

"He knows about Art," said Morris.

"I told him. He never answered."

The black gloom rolled back into the hotel room.

"I lead the Open for sixty-three holes, and what do I get? An asterisk by my name." Lee Washburn rang down his glass on the table and stood up. Nobody laughed.

"You get three-fourths of fifty thousand dollars. That's not bad punctuation," said LeBaron. There was no fun in his voice.

"We should have stopped it sooner," said Morris. "We risked too much. *I* risked too much."

"How could anybody know?" said Sullivan, touching him. "How could Art have stopped himself? No matter what town you were in."

"Why did he do it?" asked Travis. "Why?"

"He was broke," said Morris. "I talked with his banker an hour ago. Investments gone to hell. His game faltering. He must have asked Rossi to help him with his swing."

"How can you help a terminal disease?" said Washburn, heading for the door.

"I can hear Rossi now," said Morris. "No phony encouragement. All honesty. All cruelty. Telling him to forget the tour. That he'd had a good ride. That he would help him find a teaching job. Something in Art must have broken."

"But he had saved up tablets and cyanide," said LeBaron. "How do you explain that?"

"Maybe he meant to kill himself all along," said Morris. He hoped that it was so. "Why didn't we read your own promotional stuff," he said to LeBaron. "You wrote twenty years ago that he was a mate to a pharmacist, on a destroyer."

"Good Lord, I remember that. He used to hit golf balls into the Indian Ocean."

"Why did he take back my poisoned drops, Morris?" asked Travis, standing, too tense to sit down.

Morris swallowed his vodka, to give him time so he could speak. "Maybe seeing you. Maybe being with you reached him in some way." Morris took another pull of vodka.

"Was he able to say anything?"

"No," said Morris. He did not describe the desperation of his scream.

Travis tugged the end of his cane. "Thanks for coming after me."

Morris raised his glass.

"Everybody out," said Sullivan. "I've got an exhausted writer on my hands."

"We'll see you at the funeral services," said Travis.

There would be no tournament in Chicago. Golf was burying its dead.

LeBaron stopped in the door. "We didn't finish the Open, Morris. But the game goes on. That's worth something." He closed the door.

Sullivan mixed a fourth vodka. Morris stretched out on the bed. His good leg seemed as stiff as the other.

"Mind if I ask about it?"

"No." The fourth drink is like starting over, he thought.

"When did you know it was Art?"

"When I heard the word *Howard*. I almost expected Dr. Moore to say my own name. How do you explain that?"

She drank from his glass, and stretched out beside him. "Art was two strokes off the lead. What if he had finished? What if he had won the Open?"

"A man can't kill his competition and count it. Except in war. It would have been an even more unholy mess."

"Could he have gotten away with it?"

"Only if Doc Moseley had not lived forever. And proved what killed Tommy Fryer. I could have condemned an innocent man, misreading my notes from Dr. Moore."

"You thought of the doctors in the pro-ams," said Sullivan. "We might have lost Travis. Why didn't he kill Travis? Why did he switch the drops again, Morris?"

"He started on the tour when Travis was great. Maybe he ̣ ̣mbered those days. Maybe he realized what he had done. ̣

"How did Art play so well? Under such pressure?"

"I don't know. Maybe insanity released him in some way we can't understand. The last ball he hit was twelve feet from the flag. Sink it and he's one shot from leading the Open. With ten holes to play."

"I wonder what happened to the ball."

"You would, Sullivan."

The telephone rang beside her. "Shall I let it ring?"

"No," said Morris.

"It's your Lieutenant," she said. "Want to speak to him?"

Morris had given his statement to Chief of Police, a thin, ineffectual man who kept clearing his throat as if he were giving the evidence he was taping.

Morris took the phone. "Yes." He could hear the button on the ballpoint pen clicking in Rutledge's hand.

"I told you we had an opening in Homicide." There was no apology in his voice.

"You also have an opening in jail cells."

"True."

"Would Dolan have been convicted?"

"Damn right." There was no doubt in his voice.

"That bothers you?" asked Morris.

"It would bother me more if there hadn't been enough evidence to convict him."

"Do you need me?"

"No. We can't try him, can we?"

"No," said Morris. "You can't."

He handed the phone to Sullivan. She hung it up.

"I've got a place in Colorado. You can see for seventy-five miles. Nothing but mountains. Nowhere you could build a golf course."

"How did you get stuck with a place like that?" said Morris.

She took a long drink out of his glass.

(VG-EXC)
10/23/84

I probably would
have enjoyed the
book more if I
knew more about
golf. Still, well-
written, a good
mystery.

215

About the Author

John Logue, a former wire-service reporter and sports writer, is presently Editor-in-Chief of Oxmoor House Publisher and Creative Director of *Southern Living Magazine*. He has written about golf at its highest level for twenty years, and lives in Birmingham, Alabama.